the
dark
trench
shadow
series

FRAYED

KERRY NIETZ

FREEHEADS

FRAYED by Kerry Nietz
Published by Freeheads
www.kerrynietz.com

Cover Designer: Kirk DouPonce
Creative Team: Nadine Brandes, Dawn Shelton, Jill Domschot
eBook Conversion and Design: Kerry Nietz

ISBN 978-0-9971658-2-1

Library of Congress Cataloging-in-Publication Data
An application to register this book for cataloging has been filed with the Library of Congress.

To all my Realm Makers friends
And my faithful readers
Back to where it started.

OTHER WRITINGS
BY KERRY NIETZ

FICTION

Dark Trench Saga:

A Star Curiously Singing
The Superlative Stream
Freeheads

Peril in Plain Space:

Amish Vampires in Space
Amish Zombies from Space

"Graxin" (short story) appearing in *Ether Ore*

But Who Would Be ~~Brave~~ Dumb Enough To Even Try It?
(contributor)

Mask

NONFICTION

Fox Tales: Behind the Scenes at Fox Software

ACKNOWLEGDEMENTS

First, I'd like to thank editor Nadine Brandes for taking up this challenge. Despite your trepidations, you identified exactly what was missing, and where to find it.

A big thank you to fearless reader Lisa Godfrees. Your efforts made this a better book. You rock.

Thanks to proofreader Dawn Shelton. This might be the first book where the timestamps are right!

A green-handed slap on the back to designer extraordinaire Kirk DouPonce. You always have time for me, despite your ever-busy schedule. Also for the shove in naming this book. Can't thank you enough.

I'd also like to thank Jeff Gerke. Even now, you always make yourself available for my random questions. And for the book title! Genius!

Thanks to Leah for riding the waves in the maelstrom of our home, and for being a consistent book promoter.

And as always, thanks to the Lord for purpose, and ideas.

I'M LOWLEVEL. I'M NOBODY.

I'm also jittery, but I can't help that. I'm in a graveyard. A techno-logical wasteland. The sky is dark, as it would be in any scary tale. There is no rain, but there are flashes along the horizon. I don't know if they are moving toward me, or away. The stream, the information current that flows through the implant in my head, says the trouble is over. The storm has passed. But I don't think it ever does. Not in the today. Not in the Imam's world.

"Thread?"

The message itches my implant, but I ignore it. Bull is trying to start again. Happens every time he's near. The competition. The quest for significance.

I simply keep moving forward. Try to focus on the problem. To find one particular problem, I mean, and fix that. I'm surrounded by them. I'm in an expansive stockyard. Behind me is the Great River—if I listen close, I can hear its billowing torrent.

Ahead and around me are the shells of dead machines. Most of them are driftbarges. Barges are heavy, lumbering conveyances. There's nothing pretty about them. They have triangular control sections in front and back, and a self-loading bay in the middle. They take product all over the country, all on their own. Oh, and they hover.

Except none of these do. They're dead, dead, dead. I've counted at least a dozen so far. I'm searching for the beginning of this mess. For something that is moving aside from me.

"Come on, BareBare, I know you're out there. I can feel your slippery implant from here. Speak up. What do you say? Are we competing or not?"

"I'm busy, Bull," I send back.

Hazers, why do I attract them? No matter where I go. No matter what I am.

I touch the side of the barge to my right. It is smooth, wet, and ice cold. Sickly even. I pull my hand back and try to rub the moisture away. Feels like there's some oil on it too. Sticks. Doesn't want to leave. I move ahead.

I smell the next barge before I see it. Something about its refrigeration unit has to be bad. That would be in the bay section somewhere, I think. I rarely work on barges. The storm brought all of us out. All the debuggers. Masters' orders!

Usually I work on the nasty stuff—the stuff that kills people. They're big and heavy too, of course. This disaster is an opportunity for me. To do something different. Maybe get noticed.

Thankfully, the barge's specifications are in the stream where I can reach them. As I approach the rear section, I use the teardrop in my head to search. The barge is an X-34 model. Really recent. It should be working. They're supposed to be foolproof. I'm young, but I learned early that almost nothing is foolproof, no matter what they say.

The specs light up my vision center, filling my mind. I bring up a map of the barge, and standing about two meters from it, rotate the map so it outlines my machine. I search for the fridge unit. Map says it is in the exact center, about halfway up.

That means a bit of a climb—*if* I can get the thing to extend handholds for me. I sing out to the barge. It gives me a soft, almost wounded, reply. There's more than one system gone in this thing. I have an unsettled feeling. It won't be quick. I wish it was quick. I need quick.

I ask for the handholds. There is some hesitation, but then they pop free of the barge's side. Nice, except they don't extend all the way.

I ask again. There is a grating sound and the handholds ease out a little more. I can barely get my fingertips around them, but it will have to do. I climb a couple steps up, and balance there. It isn't comfortable.

"Place is a zoo," Bull streams me. "You do all this?"

Again, I ignore. Frowning, I ease the supply bag off my back. I lean into the machine for leverage and feel around in the bag for a roll of sheets. There should be a whole cylinder of them in there somewhere. Rails, balancing is awkward. I swear and heave the bag back on. I'll try code riding first. It would be better to focus that way, anyway. Get my mind off the spooky.

"Still," Bull streams. "Isn't so bad. Can probably handle it myself. Four fixes to win. What do you say?"

I shut my eyes and query the stream for the proper X-34 instructions. The machine says it is made by TransGrit, so I head to their domain. They're upfront and transparent. Code is easy to find...

Except they didn't make the refrigeration unit, and my nose is reminding me of where the problem is. Another search, another domain jump. Like islands in the ocean, really. New domain has a simple name: FrigidEx. Their structure is haphazard, though. Can barely find the unit's specs, much less the code.

Now I *really* need a sheet. I have to physically see inside to the refrigeration unit to find its code. I shift, and pulling the bag around to my gut, start to root through it again.

Maybe I can get the model number from the mind of the barge itself? I have a link to it open. I'm still balancing, still rummaging.

"Hey!"

A female voice. It tears me, because frankly, that half of humanity makes things strange for me. I don't know why. Can't spec it, can't debug it. But over the last year or so—they blur things. Even though they're not supposed to.

The voice must be in my head. A domain trying to shill me or something. I close all my open connections. Clear everything out.

"You mute?" The voice again.

There is so much wrong with that. I'm in a stockyard with dead machines, remember. Should be only male debuggers like me out here.

I pry open an eye and look around. To my right at ground level is the silhouette of someone. Looks like another debugger. Bald head, green jumpsuit. Attitude evident in the posture. Lots of that. Arms cross and the hip shifts. Okay, the shift seems out-of-spec somehow. Angles are wrong, or something.

"Mute or rude?" the debugger asks.

I shake my head, partially because the debugger *is* female. Not simply young, but female.

"HardCandy," she says. "And yes, I'm a girl. Move over it."

"Sorry," I say. "I have this thing with girls lately."

Her posture changes again, growing more solid.

"I mean—" I feel my connection to the barge start to fade. I sing to it, telling it to hold on. I mindlessly start paging through its command structure. It is something I do when I'm nervous. Plus, it keeps the link active.

"You handle old bots?" she asks.

"Old?"

"Yeah, flexmetal-encased. Can you debug them?"

Not at all. I've never once worked on a bot that old. I'm not even sure what flexmetal is. I think it is the skin of the thing. But I bet no one else out here knows either. Even Bull. *Especially* Bull.

"Sure," I say. "No problem."

"Good," she says. "Because there's one up ahead. In the middle of everything."

Something slides—my bag, or my foothold, or something. I get the sense of falling, then feel air moving past me. Panicked, I stream something at the barge. Try to get it to help.

I hit the ground hard. Then there are noises. Growly, grinding noises. HardCandy yelps and I know I should be doing something. That something went wrong.

It is difficult to breathe. My sides are all locked up. I suck in air through the pain, but it doesn't seem to help. I'm still out of oxygen. Like I might die.

"Knocked the wind out of yourself," she says. "And nearly hit me."

Hit her...?

I roll onto my side. That seems to help a little. Still really hurts.

"Come on," she says. "You didn't break anything. Didn't fall far enough."

Coupled with the pain now, is anger. I pry open my eyes and look her direction. She's leaned against one of the barge's four loading arms. It wasn't extended before. That must've been the grinding noise. Did I do that?

Her arms are still crossed. "See what you did?" she says. "Dropped them all. Rails, lowlevel."

The pain is subsiding. I move my hands along my ribs to be sure. I don't think they're broken. I'm not sure I'd know, but I don't think they are. I force a couple deep breaths and try to sit up. "Lost my connection for a second."

She shakes her head. "Noob panicked. Had a headburst. Dropped the arms on me."

"Stow it." I want to ask her all sorts of questions. Get her to maybe share something with me, but I doubt that's going to happen. Hers might be the most interesting story I've mixed yet. It would have to be. I groan and slowly climb to my feet.

She stares at me a full second before pointing a thumb over her shoulder. "So, can you handle the bot or not? I don't mind digging into it, but it has the Imam's crest, so it must be his. You're his too, right?"

I nod. That's me, another of the Imam's servants. One of the forgottens.

"I'll handle it," a voice says from behind me. Bull's voice.

He found me. I can't hide my annoyance.

Hard looks between me and my slightly-larger shadow. She pauses to study him.

"BullHammer," he says.

"Heard of you." She nods, glances at me again. "Between the two of you, maybe." She steps around the loading arm then, and disappears.

I feel emptier for her going. I test my ribs again. They're a little sore to the touch, but not blindingly so. I'm probably okay.

Bull paces to stand in front of me. Gives the barge a once over. "You reek, Thread. Reek bad."

"Stitches, Bull," I say. "Lots of them. Funny as a—" I wanted to say "cartoon of the founder" but my implant stops me. It gives me this warning buzz that causes me to bite my tongue. Literally. A small bite, but rails—hurts! The buzz keeps all debuggers in line.

Bull grins. "Lack of control, Thread. That's why you lose. Why you're always forgotten."

"You are too!" I move as if he isn't there, touching the barge's distended loading arm, then taking a few steps forward to glance back. The thing looks like a frightened arachnid now. Arms all drooped and touching the ground. Plus, the refrigeration is still busted.

I shake my head. If there's more Imam property ahead, that should be my priority. The exit is that way, after all. Need to work from the front. That's a Tanzer rule. Have to follow Tanzer. He created debugging, after all. I shrug my bag higher on my shoulder and jog ahead.

"Don't leave me!" Bull says.

I have no problem with that. "Bot's mine," I say. "Go fix something."

THE BOT IS THE COLOR of rust and roughly humanoid. I mean it has a head and arms, but no one would mistake it for a man. There are heavy wheels where the legs should be.

It does have the Imam's yellow ellipsis stamped on its forehead, though. I can hardly believe it. Can't imagine why our ruler would have such an archaic model in service, but I've been surprised before. I'm surprised a lot, actually. That's why they generally keep me hidden in a garage.

I sing out to the thing but get no response. That means it is worse off than the barge I just attempted. Going to be a tough night.

I try to pattern match the bot using the stream. I pass through thousands of models looking. Many are close, matching in all aspects except one or two. Head and shoulders match here, but not the torso. Same upper body, but legs instead of wheels. Almost, almost, almost. It is frustrating!

Finally, I find the model—and yeah, it is like a decade ago.

Specs say the eyes should be "glowing with life." I'm not seeing that here. Not seeing any glow. Has to mean a burnt motivator or fried headchip or something. The specs are poorly written, like they were written by someone who doesn't speak the language. Except everyone does. They talk about *resets* and *access*. Rails, it is old.

Time to use a little hands-on. To get right into it. I slide my bag to the ground, and start to rummage. Need another sheet.

"Ain't done yet?" Bull asks from close behind me.

I jump, which I'm sure he sees, because he laughs.

"I can handle it," I say. "Shift off," I stream.

"Can you?" he streams back. "Like that smelly barge back there?" His barge is almost fixed, he says, but to finish would be pointless since my new chore is in the way. "I'll foul the hovergears running it over."

I bury my head in the bag. Sheets have to be here somewhere. Finally, I find the cylinder, open it, and shake a rolled sheet into my hand. I tear off the stickum that holds the thing together and unroll it, making it taut. I pivot toward the bot, and frowning, size it up. Should I start at the head or the chest?

I consult the specs again. The flexmetal shell is throwing me. Normally I would start at the chest since it's the largest area. See as much as I can. But there isn't an obvious place to put the sheet. There are lots of bumps and edges. Will it go over all of that?

"You want me to do it?" Bull asks. "Face it. I'm better. Bolder."

Chest it is. I set my teeth and push ahead.

I get a "Stop" in the stream from another debugger. I hesitate, glance at Bull, then try again.

A shadow blocks out the yard lights. I see the standard bald head, but the face is unfamiliar. Generally handsome, as far as debuggers go. We don't think about such things—but if we did, I'd start hating him.

"TreArc DR," Bull streams me. "Level twelve, moniker Sandfly. TreArcs are trouble. Let me handle this." He points toward the front of the line. "Your drifts are up front, twelve." He smiles. "Tres get preferential treatment."

A smile crosses Sandfly's face too, then he snorts. "Rails, right. Only the Imam's own before ours." He looks at the bot. "What's wrong with it?"

"I'm fixing it," I say. "Just trying to get a read on what's wrong."

Sandfly shakes his head. "That a new sheet?"

"Yeah," I say. "Got it at Grim's. Yesterday."

He says my sheet won't work. That it will break the bot more. Like I don't know what I'm doing. Like I don't know anything.

Next Bull starts in, throwing slams my way. But he's a forgotten too. He isn't much more than nothing. I want to strike him. Want to wipe that sneer right off his face. I raise my fist. "Bull, you blinking—"

And whammo, I get hit. A blinding shock to the brain. So intense my vision fails. I have to say something to try to dispel it. To drive the buzz away. "Peace be to you," I grit out. "...brother."

Bull smiles cheekily and returns the blessing. I hate him too.

Sandfly shakes his head, frowning. "Do you want me to try?" he says. "Give it a pitch for you?"

I stumble toward the bot, vision still a little blurred. "Rails," I say. "I've got it." I brace myself on its chest and slide the other hand down its midsection. I have no idea what to do, but I can't give up. I lean closer and squint at the ridges in the skin. They have holes...maybe I can see inside?

"What are you doing?" Bull asks.

"Trying to see what's wrong!" I can't see anything. I step back and shake my head. "Rails," I say. "I give." I don't look at the other two. I can't.

Sandfly steps in with a small tool of some kind. Soon the bot's innards are staring us in the face. Those look old too. Almost foreign. Sand calls for a light. I attempt to pull one from my bag, but Bull beats me to it. He lights up the bot and Sand keeps working. He touches a few places inside, and the bot's eyes start to glow. "It needs time to check itself," he says.

"Hip work there, twelve," Bull says. Probably thinks he has a new friend. A new hero.

Sand shakes his head. "Twelve is only a level." Then, like some legend, he turns and sprints away.

I try to think of something quippy. Something to make me feel not so low and useless. Instead I think about the girl. "HardCandy is up there somewhere," I stream at Sandfly. "Be careful."

He acknowledges, but sends no reply. Typical.

"That was rich, Thread," Bull says, chuckling. "Now, go find something else to mess up. I'm already up one."

AN HOUR LATER I'M still working on the smelly, broken barge. I have the refrigeration fixed, I think. The smell hasn't lessened, but I can hear the coolant moving and feel the soft vibration of it through the barge's skin.

The barge itself is still immobile. You'd think it would be a quick job—only a component or two. But no, I think the thing was actually struck by lightning. There are whole sections fused together. Most barges are self-healing if you can get the nanos headed the right direction. But this one? Don't know. I have limited replacement parts with me. Might need to downride out and come back.

I glance at the sky. There is more lightning on the eastern horizon. A new storm. A different storm. I frown. I don't want to come back.

"On my third barge now," Bull streams. "Things are cake."

"Yeah, cake," I mutter.

I'm atop the front section of the barge. I have a nanoprobe installed and I'm taking a microscopic survey of everything. I find a place where the nanos are stalled, spinning in circles. Their normal pathway appears to be blocked—could be the thunderstorm, or could be overuse. Either way they're pooling up and it won't be long until they break out and start free ranging the entire system. Like a burst artery in a human. Not pretty.

The stream chatter has diminished. Many of the debuggers have finished or been recalled. I estimate less than a dozen out now. The main stoppages are free and the reactivated barges are drifting into the night. Delivering their wares. It figures that I'm one of the last ones. Stuck out here.

Need to—

Something hits me in the shoulder. At first I think the barge's now-retracted arms are fritzing again and dropped near me. A quick check shows that not to be case. I raise my head and look around.

About ten meters to the right is the next closest barge. Swarming around it are a group of men—four or five of them. Freeheads all. Not debuggers, but real free men. Older than I am, but still move young. Heads wrapped in blue, except eyes and chin. They resemble antitex goons, aside from their shirt and pants. Those make me think they're antitex-wannabes. Or maybe initiates. Either way, they're trouble. Antitex don't like us.

One of them is looking my direction. I can feel his malice from here. He doesn't say anything, simply raises a hand holding a rock and waves. Those with him are smiling too, many of them talking and laughing.

I notice movement at the top of the barge they're near. Another debugger. Isn't Bull. Maybe FrontLot? Difficult to tell from this distance.

One of the men takes a few running steps and pitches a bottle into the air. It spins end over end until it hits one of the moving barges ahead. The whole group laughs. "Debug that, debugger!" he yells.

How did these Abbys get in here? This kind of attention I don't need. I sink into a dip in the barge's canopy. Then, remembering the handgrips I used to get up here, I tell the machine to retract those. It does.

"We have company in the yard," FrontLot streams, messaging everyone in range. "I almost got hit."

"*I* got hit," I message back. "Look like antitex, but maybe not official. Faces covered. They knew we'd be here."

One of the intruders yells something and the whole group runs forward. I wish they were leaving, but I don't think they are. I keep my head low. Try to return to my work. I want out of here. Seconds go by. Things seem to quiet.

Suddenly the chatter begins again. Lots of messages, so many that it is hard to keep track.

"They've got me!"

"HardCandy?"

"Where's security?"

The messages are coming in all forms, including FI—Full Impact—which means they're filled with emotion. That messes with my brain too. Puts me all over the map: Anger, fear, pain.

"Makes no difference. Bluecoats will never make it in time…"

I focus on the messages. Try to sort them out. Get to the heart of what's happening. The antitex wannabes have grabbed one of us. HardCandy! She's struggling, but overwhelmed. She isn't sharing anything now. Probably too busy fighting.

I feel bad for her, because there's nothing we can do. Nothing I can do. I'm a nobody. We all are. We're restricted. It shouldn't bother me, but it does.

"I called security," Bull sends.

Okay, so there's one thing we can do, but that won't help. Won't be quick enough. Especially in this weather. I lift my head and look at the barges ahead of mine. She's up there somewhere. Is anyone else? Sandfly, maybe? I message him, but get back only a clipped "I'm working!"

The stream goes silent again. We're useless in this. All prisoners within our own skin. Our own heads. I feel an urge to be violent, but even that tweaks me a little.

More seconds go by. I should refocus on my chore. There is a blockage to correct. Via the probe I can see it in my head. It seems unsolvable. How do I get the nanos to move around the—

I hear shouts. More yelling from the freeheads. I try to mentally distance myself like I always do. But I can't. I hate them, whatever they are.

Focus, I need to focus. Work the problem.

My problem is meaningless. Minimal compared to what's happening up there. To HardCandy.

I hear lots of footsteps. I peer over the barge edge as the goons rush by. What is this? Why are they running?

"I'm okay," Hard streams out. "They left. The arms of my drift dropped and they…got scared."

"Security is here," someone says.

The arms of her drift dropped? How did that happen? I wasn't near them. I'm not even sure where she is.

Plus, if they dropped on purpose, if one of us did it, then that debugger endured a lot of pain. Endangering a freehead? Heaps of pain. Could HardCandy do that while fighting off antitexes? I don't think so.

"Who dropped the arms?" Bull asks.

I have a theory, but it doesn't make sense. Doesn't seem possible with the stops and all.

"It wasn't anything," Sandfly streams out. "Nothing to talk about. Go back to work everyone. More storms are coming."

Sandfly dropped the arms somehow. Sandfly saved her! How did he save her?

"Finished my fourth," Bull streams, full of pride. "I'm done, Thread. I won. Again!"

ONE HOUR, FORTY-THREE minutes, and seven seconds later, I'm back home.

My whole world is this green-painted garage. Heavy grease lines the walls, the paint is chipped in multiple places. There are stacks of tools and bot parts lying around. Mounds of them, actually. Greasy, grimy mounds. I'm as much afraid of falling as I am of infection.

That's how life is for a forgotten. Unlike most DRs, we don't have our own apartment outside of work. We live our job, and for me that's the BHSG, the Boundary Heavybot Service Garage. The Imam owns seventy debuggers, scattered across his domain. I'm one of them, and in the stack ranking, I'm nearer the bottom than the top. Stuck in the lowlevels.

I'm lucky, though. I'm within shouting distance of the border. A little place called "The Delusion" lies on the other side of the wall. It has been skirmish-ville for as long as I remember. A mixture of anti-tex and wrong thinkers fighting the Imam's rule. It's a lost cause because this Imam has been ruling for decades. And before him, *some* Imam was always in power. Centuries of Imams.

Regardless, the conflict means there's a never ending stream of heavies headed across the border. My garage is shielded and heavily insulated, but I frequently hear the attacks. Like I said—lucky.

Right now, I'm tired. I worked a full day even before the stockyard. Before the humiliation and getting hit by a stone. Things are quiet in Delusion, thankfully.

I take another look around the garage.

There's a broken heavybot filling most of the space. Painted tan and brown, in real desert fashion. Hardly a nick on it. The head is large and solid, slightly conical. It blends into the shoulders with little in the way of a neck. Powerful arms, able to extend, full of armaments. Bone-crushing treads. Perfect for defending against the Imam's enemies.

But inside, the bot is a mess. Heavies are temperamental. Strong in battle, but dumb. They break a lot. That's where I come in. I'm waiting on parts with that one.

Frowning, I walk around to the garage's southwest corner and a rusting metal stairway. I scale it to the loft overhead. The loft has what a debugger needs to survive. A food conditioner, running water, and a cinder chute for sleeping.

My chute is the nicest thing in the place, but it isn't that nice. Secondhand when I got it. A little smelly. Rectangular, with a rounded see-through canopy—in case someone ever wanted to check on me, I guess. Like sleeping in an aquarium. The chute doesn't have a proper support pedestal. It rests atop a metal table. I keep waiting for it to give way while I'm asleep. Send me tumbling and screaming.

None of that matters now. I run through my usual nighttime ritual of lavatory, eye drops, and a mouthful of water, then stream the chute canopy open. I lay down, and as the canopy descends, try to get comfortable in the too-matted interior. I hear the ventilation fan kick on and feel the breeze over my face. At least that's relaxing.

I receive a chime in my head, a connection offer from a friend. The unopened connection swirls inside my inner eye. I will it away and try to clear my thoughts. The chute is supposed to help with that. As soon as I engage it, it will block all the outside chatter. Plus, it is supposed to stir my mind—help me solve sticky problems. The only problem I have right now is how to not be here. How to change my level and better myself. Chute can't help with that.

The offer is from FrontLot. He's a good guy. A level twelve, but a bit of a mix pusher. He doesn't see it that way. He sees it as life sharing. Through the wonders of the implant, debuggers can swap memories. Live portions of each other's lives. Typically, I'm an easy mark for mixes. Anyone's life is better than mine, even if it is another DR. But tonight I'm not sure. I should sleep. Stir my own memories.

I open my eyes and look through the distortion of the canopy.

The ceiling is this kaleidoscope of greens. The same old greens. I contemplate FrontLot for a moment. Should I answer?

I shut my eyes again and bring up the offer. Open it. Soon Front and I are live messaging, Standard Impact—meaning voice, image, and text—flows between us. I can't go beyond that. I'm too tired for feelings.

Front is a year or two older than me, with darker skin. He's dressed in his blue jumper still, which means he's probably on a job somewhere. There's a blue wall behind him. "Did I catch you napping?" he asks, smiling.

"Almost," I say. "What is it?"

His smile broadens. "You said you wanted dibs on new mixes. I traded for some."

I feel a prickle of anticipation. A curiosity surge. "Something cheery?" I say. "Something warm?"

"You really *are* tired."

I send him the image of an eyebrow going up and down. "You were out there."

He shrugs. "I only had two barges. Spent most of the time waiting."

"Team player, Front."

He chuckles. "Masters are territorial with their toys. Don't want outsiders messing with them." He raises a shoulder. "Plus, you were handling it."

I yawn in my head. Seriously. Yawn. "Handling nothing," I say. "Bull did all the handling. Beat me four to one." I send Front a blue frown. "So what do you have?"

"Got one from DataSheer. A bit of his childhood at the cattle farm. It is nice. A little mellow, but nice."

I shake my head. "No thanks. The air, the pollens...something always leaks in. I get a rash."

"Okay...what about one from Skythistle? He was in the civilian corp before he got picked. Lots of action. Lots of—"

"Do you know where I live?" I say. "No munitions."

"Right. Let me search..."

My mind wanders to the night's events. The debuggers I met. The strangeness. "You have anything from HardCandy?" I ask.

He startles. "That would be a hot commodity, wouldn't it?" He shakes his head. "We're on good terms, she and I, but she doesn't share much, even verbally. Mixing is...way too personal for her. Even in small slices."

"That's too bad. She was—" I feel the tingle of a stop and pause to redirect. "Interesting, I guess." I yawn again. "I'm tired, Front. Maybe not tonight. Maybe tomorrow."

"Got one with Sandfly in it. The hero of the night! Will that work?"

"Sandfly?" I want to hate that guy, but I have to admit, he did something unusual at the stockyard. Rails real. Not sure how he pulled it off. Endangering freeheads to save Hard? "Shouldn't have been able." There's something uncommon there.

"Shouldn't what?" Front says. "You mean, Sand? Yeah, he's a mystery. So you want the mix, or not?"

"I sort of hate him."

"But you're interested?"

"Maybe. If it helps me understand what he did."

Front shrugs. "It might. That would take introspection, though. I never watch to introspect. Only to be entertained."

I stifle a yawn. "It'll take what, ten minutes?"

"The mix, yeah, like dreaming. Lot happens in little time."

"And the charge?"

"A couple credits, Thread. You know I don't do it for that."

"Right, it is about the sharing. The community." I shuffle my shoulders and try to relax. "Fine. Credits sent."

He nods. "Got 'em. Are you ready?"

Another anticipation surge. "Blind me."

"Sending..."

WE'RE IN ZIMIT'S TECH shop, one of the upscale clang and clicks. Zimit keeps everything in order, makes it easy for a debugger to find what he needs. I doubt I'd ever be that in line, were the roles reversed. Place smells of hydrogen peroxide. Zimit likes to scrub.

There's a rack of blue, cone-shaped bot motivators in front of me. My master doesn't really need any, but some of his bots are on the old side. These motivators are shiny and lean. I want to install one, I really do. If I could break a bot on purpose...

My protégé Sandfly is with me. He's a row over, looking at hats. The hats must be Zimit's idea of a joke, because no debugger would wear them. We're not allowed to. Skinscreen on the bald head or nothing. Showy dress will get you zapped.

Sandfly is a bit of a rogue, though. Never know what he'll try.

I receive a blaring job request and push it along to Sand via the stream. A couple milliseconds later he comes around the corner wearing an oversized red cap. It drapes over his ears, and severely clashes with his blue jumpsuit.

"Eloquent," I say.

He smirks and readjusts the cap. "I like it."

"And it suits you. Not sure what your master will say, but—"

"He doesn't have to know, Grim. I'll only wear it at night. Around my place."

I frown. "We have work."

He nods, and slips the hat over the top of one of the bot motivators. I shake my head, and he shrugs. "It'd interfere with my implant, anyway."

I get another message, this time with a spike of pain attached. They're in a hurry. Sand must notice the strike in my eyes, because his eyebrows rise. We quickstep it out of the shop to the nearest down-rider cone. We climb into a circular downer, reorient it, and we're on our way. Riding the strings over the city.

We're packed in side by side. Cozy, but Sand is generally clean for a lowlevel. Rarely smells.

Buildings begin to flip by. "You know this master...um...Waali?" he asks.

I shake my head. It is odd that we are being sent. Debugger loans rarely happen. Usually we stay within our masters' domain and fix their machines only. Sand and I have separate masters and cross-pollinate, but that's because he's a novice.

"And this job?" Sand says. "A chute break? DRs fix their own chutes. That's like class two. Right after the rules."

Again I shake my head. There is unease in this, but little of life is easy.

Fifteen minutes later, we reach the cone nearest our destination. The weather has changed so there's a touch of mist in the air. Makes our descent from the cone to the sidewalk interesting, but we manage. I don't like the mist on my head, though. Makes me wish for one of those Zimit hats.

Sandfly snorts when we reach the pavement. "Rails, the smell of this place," he streams me. "Lowdowns are close."

"Keep your attitude pure." Even with built in stops, it is always a wrestle for the lowlevels to be obedient and calm. To avoid the pain they'll get should their implant decide they've overstepped.

The area known as the lowdowns *is* near. Maybe one stop over. It's where the worst off live. Those the masters feed only enough to be placated, but never enough to be happy.

Our address is a palace, however, with stone walls and ten meters of space on all sides. There's a metal gate with two armed guards. Typical for masters. The guards notice our heads, glance at our idents, and wave us through. We walk fancy stone pavement to an equally fancy wooden door. A humanoid servbot opens it for us.

In case you wondered, yes, masters have normal human servants too—lots of potentials in the lowdowns, after all—but most desire servbots like this one. It is akin to all the fancy land vehicles they like to own. Status and power. Toys. The stream tells me that Waali has thirty servbots in his house alone. That's why masters need debuggers. Not sure how Waali's debugger managed though. That's a lot of bots.

The bot at the door is clothed in a green robe, and is slightly feminine. Its head is wrapped in green too, even though bots are generally as hairless as debuggers are. It bows to us both. All I can see is its silver blue eyes.

I'm a little confused by our locale. "We were called about a malfunctioning chute."

"That is correct, DR."

I glance at Sand. "This is a masters' residence," I say. "A Master Waali?" Most DRs live on their own. It is one of the few freedoms we're allowed. Chutes are usually at the debugger's apartment.

The bot bows again. "Yes. This is the Waali residence."

"And the chute is *here*," I say.

"Yes." It backs up, bringing us into a marble entranceway. The walls are red and gilded. There is a grand winding staircase to the second floor. A golden chandelier above. "The chute is upstairs. It is used by DR 103."

"And 103 resides here," I say. "He sleeps here?"

"Yes. He is upstairs, as well."

I can see Sand's eyes taking it all in. "This place is rails nice," Sand messages. "Maybe 103 gets breakfast in bed? No reason to leave?"

"Or with all the bots has no time to leave," I message, then send a frown. "It doesn't seem right. All master houses are impressive. Why is his chute here?"

I try to contact 103 on the stream. I get nothing but static back. That isn't right either. I manage to find 103's name, however: Liquid-Forest.

The bot is on the stairway now. "Please come," it says, sounding urgent. "You will see."

I frown, but follow.

The second story has wooden floors with a thick red runner. I sink into it as I walk. Feels real good. The ceilings are about four meters high. There's more intricate gilding on the walls. Waali has credits.

We walk two long halls, make two left turns, then the bot pauses at a door.

"Maybe this DR is above chute work?" Sand messages. "Soaked in wealth, and now can't even steam his own clothes."

I shake my head. "Where is 103?" I ask the bot. "Why is he unable to service his own chute?"

The bot swings open the door. The room has a blue color scheme. Dark blue walls with light wood paneling. Matching blue carpet. Fine cabinetry. A large private bath.

The chute is the focus of the room. It is shiny, black, rectangular, and positioned so that the foot end is nearest the door. Some would call chutes casket-like, but debuggers generally hate that analogy. This one has golden embroidered letters around the edge of its lid—a verse from the Scriptures. Beneath the bed portion, the matching pedestal flares gently outward for a meter before it reaches the floor.

It might be the prettiest chute I've ever seen. The lid is down and the side lights indicate it is on. I move toward it and Sand follows.

Is this the problem? The thing staying on somehow? That's an annoyance, generates lots of wasteful draw, but for a master like Waali, I doubt the cost matters. He doesn't strike me as frugal.

"103," I say. "LiquidForest, where is he?"

"He is within," the bot says, indicating the chute. "He has been there for over twenty hours."

I feel like I ate a wilted salad. "Twenty hours?" I walk to the right of the chute, and lay a hand on the lid above where Liquid's head should be. It feels warm. I squint at the bot. "Is he ill?"

The bot approximates a shrug. "We do not know. We cannot wake him."

Typically, a debugger can wake himself whenever he wants—we have virtual alarm clocks in our heads, after all. Failing that, a master's controller signal should do it.

"Is the chute keeping him asleep?" Sand asks. "Can they do that?"

"Not that I know of." Chutes are a required appliance for debuggers for two reasons: To insulate our implant from stream interference, and to augment problem solving through dream stirring. It interacts with our implants to influence the dreams we see. It is a fusion of art and science. I turn toward the bot. "Is this an experimental chamber? A prototype?"

"I do not know, DR."

"Is your master available?"

"Unfortunately, he is not. He has an afternoon errand."

"I see." I glance at Sand again. He has his tool bag off his shoulder and his eyes fixed on the lower portion of the chute, where the controlling mechanisms should be. I smile. I like that about him. Always ready to fix. "We will take over now, RS-124."

The robot bows and backs its way out of the room. I contemplate having him wait nearby, but dismiss the thought. We can find him again if we need to. He doubtless has chores.

I remove my own tool bag and circle around to the opposite side of the chute. I place my bag on the floor, and crouching in close to the machine, begin to scan the lower surface. Sand is doing something similar on his side. "See anything?" I ask after a few moments. "It reminds me of an Aerodel model, but..."

"You tried querying the machine itself?"

"Soon as the bot left," I say. "The ident is masked."

Sand chuckles. "Good, I thought it was just me. Thought my implant was fritzing. Why would it be masked?"

I have my suspicions, but say nothing. Usually masks mean either black market parts or spurious dealers. I hope for neither and keep looking. Finally, I find something at the very bottom of the pedestal. An external marker plate. I lay down close and make use of a hand light. "Yeah, it's an Aerodel. Still can't see the model number, though."

"Got their domain live in my head," Sand says.

I hear him moving around again, then hear the floor creak. "What are you doing?"

"Standing back to get a good visual of the whole thing. Going to do a pattern match."

I smile again. "Good thinking."

Sand sends me respectful feelings, and a written word of thanks. "We can't just open it, right? I mean, I know what I've been told, but—"

"It will fry his implant, and hurt *your* head. Don't even think it."

"You sure? Because I've never actually—"

"You want to explain it to his master? He paid a bundle times two for an implanted debugger. Not as much as this house, maybe, but close."

"But his debugger is stuck inside."

I don't answer that comment, because if Sand can't figure it all out, he will soon. It is what's in our head that makes us special, and little else. "You find the specs?" I ask.

I hear him moving again, doubtless shifting closer to the chute pedestal. "I got it. Sending your way."

Soon I see the schematics for the chute in my mind. Rotating on my inner eye. I shut my human eyes so I can concentrate. I get a good overview of what connects where inside. How it all fits together. Then I push the image away and open my eyes again.

I access my tool bag, and taking out a rolled sheet, spread it over the side of the chute nearest me. It presents a private window into the inner workings. Nanopaths, conduits, filaments—you name it, I can see it all in vivid color. I compare what I see to what the specs show. The placement and the rhythm all look right. I send my thoughts to Sand.

"There's a nanopump here with some wear on it," he says. "But it is functioning. We could replace it and see if that helps."

I shake my head. "Longshot," I say. "Maybe later."

"Other than that..." Another floor creak. "The flow timing is a little slow. Adjust?"

"Sure. Bring it to spec."

I hear his bag of tools slide, then the clinks and clanks of him rummaging through it.

"Remember to go a size smaller than the access port, and—"

"Got it," he says. "Sending the timer in." There's a few soft grunts followed by silence.

I give a last visual inspection to my current sheet view, then lay another sheet a dozen centimeters back and up. Start to check there. All looks right.

"Flow is at spec now," Sand says.

"Good, check the lights."

Sand grunts, then sighs. "Lid says he's still out."

I figured that. Good to check, though. *Code*, problems are almost always in the machine's code. "I'll check the shield layer," I say. "You handle the dream sequencing."

"Crichton, you're giving me the hardest part."

"You're a debugger, aren't you?"

Using my implant, I begin to communicate straight to the chute's mind. I find its code lair, and grabbing ahold of the bit beast, wrench it out. I don't bother to ask Sand about "Crichton." He seems to have an affinity for using archaic words as profanities. Not sure where that came from. Wish it would go back.

You shouldn't train out creativity, though, no matter what form it takes.

I start at the upper level code bundle, try to feel my way for how it all comes together. I suspect the errant code, whatever is locking 103 up inside, is in the code Sand is looking at, but it doesn't hurt to check it all. Thoroughness is paramount.

Ten minutes pass, an eternity for us. Finally, I see something that looks strange. I jog out to the Aerodel domain again, and search for their code maps. Compare the standard to what I'm seeing here. I frown. "Anything in your code?" I ask.

"None so far," Sand says. "You?"

"I'm seeing mods from standard." I slice out the incriminating portion and send it his way. "What do you think?"

"Yeah, looks like a block alter. Nothing getting through this chute shield. Nothing rousing him. Still don't see how...wait, I've got mods in dream sequencing too. Take a look."

He sends me a segment of code back. I frown because it is a large chunk and the problem isn't immediately evident.

"I put a comment on it," he says. "Look for an 'S*'."

"Could've used color, Sand. I...oh, now I see it. Yeah, that isn't right. At least, it isn't what the manufacturer says it should be." I study the code a full minute longer. "This stuff is complicated. I'd forgotten so much since training. All the bits that go to the brain. The different areas. What section governs sleep?"

"Man, I don't know organics."

"You're an organic."

"Yeah, but the brain isn't my place. Not human brains."

"Well, could you look it up?" I lay a hand on the chute's pedestal. It is warm too.

"Looking...several areas in the brainstem and hypothalamus are involved. Seems they send signals to the cerebral cortex. Some signals arouse it, others inhibit arousal. It is crazy complicated. Not a simple Boolean operation like you'd think." He is quiet for a few moments. "Yeah, it is messy. Can I go back to chute code now?"

"Never mind," I say. "I see some of those areas mentioned in the comments here. Curiously, the additional lines are comment-less. They aren't giving anything away."

"Looks tough to remove," Sand says. "I think I see a trap or two here. Crichton, where did this mod come from? I mean, chutes are heavily isolated, right? They shouldn't be getting stray mods from the stream."

"You mean a hack?" I say. "Only God hacks now."

"Somebody might try."

"And avoid the implant storm in their head? The rules—there would be lots of tweaks. I doubt anyone could work through the pain."

"But someone?"

"Someone real desperate. Maybe someone already in pain."

My back starts aching, so I climb to my feet. Sand grunts and does the same. We look at each other over the top of the chute. "Clarke, what do we do now?" he says. "Is this a universal problem? Are we all in danger of eternal sleep?"

I bite my bottom lip, and do a full stream search, looking for any record of this sort of thing. I can't find any. Of course, there are black areas in my search. Places outside of the Imam's domain.

"Enemies?" Sand says, reading my mind.

"It would be a strange way to attack," I say. "Going after random debugger chutes." I frown. "Possibly it is an Aerodel problem. Something that got sent out accidentally. Not ready for general consumption."

"And it happened to wind up here? On this DR's chute?" Sand shook his head. "103 is one unlucky debugger."

I get a strange thought then. I touch the bot via the stream, asking him to bring me something.

Sand notices the look on my face. "What are you thinking, Grim?"

I shake my head.

A few minutes later the bot returns. He is carrying an ornate silver box in his hands. "I am not permitted to give you a controller," the bot says.

"That's fine," I say. "I'm not permitted to take one either. I only ask that you show it to me."

He opens the box to reveal a red interior and a silver crescent-shaped device resting inside. It has a small matrix of buttons on one end. "Master has more than one," the bot says. "But this is his favorite."

I study the controller for a long moment. The fact that Master Waali has numerous controllers suggests something, but I don't want to jump to any conclusions. I check over the buttons, paying special attention to one in particular. Finally, I nod. "That's all."

The bot closes the box and bows. "Is there anything else?"

I look at the chute again. "No. Not now." I feel a hollowness in my chest, enough that I stream some of it Sandfly's way.

"Rails, Grim, what is it?" he says. "What are you thinking?"

"I think we don't have to worry about a global outbreak."

He streams a feeling of relief back. It doesn't help.

"So it isn't a hack?"

"It is, but not by an enemy."

"Then who?"

I place my hand on the top of the chute. It seems warmer now.

He looks at my hand and finds the conclusion. "Oh...*103*. You think 103 hacked his chute? Who hacks his own chute?"

"Review my statement about who might do such a thing."

I wait as he traces through the messages we've exchanged. "Hmm...someone desperate. Someone already in pain." He frowns and shakes his head. "I think I'm still missing something. Why did you want the controller? I thought you were going to try to wake him with it, before I remembered we can't do that. Nor could the bot unless his master willed it."

"The tweak," I say, meaning the head pain we debuggers get.

"Whose tweak?" he asks. "Did you get tweaked?"

I shake my head. Lowlevels.

Sandfly squints. "Rails, you mean 103 is getting tweaked? Now? While he sleeps?"

"Not now, no," I say, "but frequently."

Sand studies the lid of the chute, then glances at the still-open room door. "You mean Master Waali is tweaking him," he messages me privately. "Like he's a heavy tweaker? Someone who likes to lean on it?"

"That is why I asked to see the controller," I message back. "The tweak button shows heavy wear. The label was nearly missing, in fact."

"Maybe it is old?"

"It is last year's model," I say aloud. "I checked that too."

"And the bot said Waali has more than one..." Sand sends me the audio of a soft whistle. "Which suggests they *all* get lots of use...lots and lots of use." He looks me in the eyes. "So 103 rigged it to keep sleeping, because that's the only peace he gets."

"I believe so," I say. "His way of escaping his master, without physically running away."

"But he'll die in there."

"It may be preferable to what he has out here," I say. "At least, to him."

Sandfly seems to ponder what I've said, then disappears behind the chute. I hear the sounds of movement and the clank of tools. Then he pops back up, tool bag thrown over his right shoulder.

"What are you doing?" I ask.

He shrugs. "That's it then, right? We send our End of Task report and go our way." He raises an eyebrow. "Maybe back to Zimit's?"

Technically, he's right. We've solved the mystery, but it isn't a solution. I hesitate, still staring at the chute. I focus on the writing. Translated, it means "We made your sleep for rest, and the night a covering, and the day for seeking livelihood." A paraphrase, and a nearly poetic one.

"Listen GrimJack, I just got another job request. We have things to do."

"If we revert the code—"

"He has it trapped. Changing it will harm him."

I look at Sand. Say nothing.

"Rails, I'm not lying. Can't lie. I saw the traps and they're bad. Want me to show you?"

I shake my head.

He walks to the foot of the chute, partially blocking my view of the door. "I don't want to change it anyway. You can report me if you want, but I don't."

I raise an eyebrow. "That is a dangerous thought, debugger. Fighting against the rules, the stops—"

"I know. It hurts me to think it. But I still don't. Rails, I don't."

I frown and glance at the chute. "That is what we *should* do, however. Attempt to back out the code."

He gives a halfhearted smile. "Yeah, my head tweaks thinking about not doing it," Sand says. "My heart tweaks if we do."

I return the smile. There is still much boy in him. I'm glad for that. Hope it lasts.

I shrug. "Then there's only one thing we can do."

"What? What can we do?"

I indicate his bag. "You have a pry bar?"

"A small plastisteel one, yeah, why?"

I feel the tingle of a warning, but divert my mind. Think of something uncontroversial—like flying a kite. Whatever that is. "Quick," I say. "Get it."

He pulls off his bag and lays it on top of the chute. Time seems to slow as he rummages through it. Finally, he holds the bar in his hands. His looks at me, face serious. "You want to pry it open?"

I don't want to affirm in any way, because that'll certainly bring on the pain wave. I only back up and find the lid seam. Trace it with my eyes.

"You won't have the strength," he says. He is wincing now too. "But maybe...maybe if we do it together?"

I'll blame him, he'll blame me. It could work.

I put out my hands. He takes the lower end of the bar, me the upper. We wedge it under the lid, and lift.

The pain is present, but bearable. I just keep focusing on Sand, on what *he's* doing. Lifting the lid and frying Liquid's implant, but freeing him too. Making him normal. It is a shame, really. Someone who did what Liquid did—that's a quick brain, a fast worker. If it wasn't for his master's tendency...

The lid pops free with a hiss. A light on the front begins to flash, then all the lights go out. The smell is a little acidic. Not sure if that's the machine or Liquid. Sand and I drop the bar. It slides off the chute and hits the ground.

Sand's eyes look bloodshot, and his forehead is wrinkled with lingering pain. "Now what?"

"We call the bot and have him get Liquid to the medicals," I say.

"But what we did..."

I shake my head. "We found a hacked chute. We had no choice. The hack could spread."

"But his master—"

"*Our* masters will understand. We stopped a risk. Terminated a potential problem. That's all that will matter to them."

Sand is bent over, with his hands on his knees. He nods his understanding, though.

I give myself another moment to recover, then I summon the bot.

Sleep for rest, and the night a covering. That's about right.

That's all we have.

I WAKE UP WITH questions, which is good when you've viewed someone else's memories. It shows you got what you paid for—that you've been challenged. Will it make me a better debugger? Probably not. But it was entertaining, and possibly I learned something. So there's that.

I stream the chute's canopy open and sit up. My internal clock tells me it is just after eight in the morning. That's good too. Usually the emergencies don't happen until later. Even warriors take the night off.

I look to my right, toward the food conditioner. It is an old model, from when the technology was new. Doubtless a military grade castaway. It is generally rectangular and twice my width, though starting at just below my chin. The notable exception to its otherwise box-like shape is the inverted bell that is the dispensing platform. It is already making my morning meal. Typically, that means something light with lots of fish protein. Have to keep the brain moving. Keep it fed.

I message Front. He answers right away, Standard Impact, meaning still text, sound and video. He could've gone Full Impact and sent emotions too. I'm feeling generally good today. But I leave things as they are. His choice.

"Did you like it?" he asks.

"Made me hate him less," I say.

He chuckles. "Sorry, I missed the goal."

"That wasn't Sandfly's mix, though."

"I told you it wasn't."

"Came from someone named Grim."

"Yeah, he runs a shop now, I think. GrimJack's."

That jogs me out of my stupor. "I know that place. No debugger runs a shop." Our masters wouldn't let us. They pay a lot for us. We're too valuable for commerce. Plus, we're always on the clock.

Front sends me the image of a cartoon bear tapping his head. It is ancient and a little fuzzy, but I get the idea. "He got it removed," I say. "Ouch." Implant removal never happens willingly. Those that lose their teardrop are never the same.

Front nods.

"Not hard to see why," I say. "A bit of a rebel. Was it because of the incident in the mix? The timestamp is old. Years back."

Front shakes his head. "I don't know what happened. But I've been to Grim's and I'm not sure he knows now either. Nice shop, though. If you can't find it there, it can't be found."

I climb out of the chute and drift toward the food conditioner. There's a plate of something there, but I can't see it because of the transparent-yet-steam-filled cover. I push a button on the side of the machine. It groans a little, makes a coughing sound, then the cover lifts. I'm still not sure what the meal is exactly, but it looks like eggs. Smells okay too. I pick it up and try it. Not bad.

By the way, I've checked the machine's groan and cough before. Those are all per spec. Can't fix 'em. I'm forgotten, but not incompetent.

"You eating?" Front says.

"Mmm-hmm," I stream.

"Streaming with your mouth open?" Front says, smiling. "Rude. Rails rude."

I snort. "Says the guy who bothers me when I'm sleeping."

He laughs. I feel some of his mirth, and laugh too.

"You never told me if you liked it," he says.

I take another bite, and raise a shoulder. "Explains Sand some. Where he got his tendency to fight the buzz. To deviate." I frown. "And Grim shows where that ends. Never good."

"Sand is a twelve," Front says. "Single master and a place of his own. Maybe a little rebellion helps?"

"I doubt—" I feel a tingle, the beginning of my master's call.

Front notices, probably feels a bit of it too. He ends the message with a knowing nod.

Twice in a week? I don't get sent outside that often. Usually my work finds me here. The garage door opens, a heavy gimps in, and I start to work. Not lately, though. Lately it is "Bother Thread. Drag him out."

There's a small vidscreen on the wall near the chute. It is unnecessary—I could easily see and hear everything my master has to offer in my head. But masters cling to screens. Maybe as a reminder to us, to debuggers, that they don't have an implant. That their job doesn't live in them. That their heads are free.

The screen flickers on as I approach. The image that appears is of an elderly man with a short, white beard and a matching white cap. He is slightly stooped with age. This really isn't my master. The Imam doesn't have time for technical dross.

"ThreadBare!" he says.

"Submaster Badr," I say. "Peace be unto you."

He circles a hand in the air. "And peace...eh, you know the rest."

I try not to smile. "I do. Thank you."

He claps his hands. "No need to be cordial. You are required. I am sending you the address."

I gasp as the information trickles into my head. It is an odd location. A bit off the beaten path. Nowhere near Delusion. Or the conflict. I don't mention any of that to Badr, because I know from experience he doesn't care. "I have it now, Submaster. Thank you."

He signs off with a grunt and a nod.

Ten minutes later I have my bag on my shoulder and I'm leaving the garage. I hesitate a bit when I open the door. I always do. I have this fear that a misdirected explosive will hit me as I leave. A shell or a missile or something. It is juvenile—the battlefront is kilometers away—but there it is. As I mentioned, sometimes heavies are dumb. And the enemy is determined. Occasionally they get something over the wall.

Usually a ten count is enough for me to overcome my dread. I focus on the sidewalk outside my home. There is a deep crack down the middle that lasts for many meters, and the permacrete on both sides of the crack slope inward. Narrowing the path. That's pretty much my life. A crack in the middle of a gully.

I take a deep breath, and head out, walking quickly. The buildings in this area are utilitarian, shades of grey, yellow, and white. Most aren't higher than a couple stories. Generally, it is low cost housing with an occasional tired-looking shop thrown in. The only bursts of color are from the occasional four-color flag of the caliphate or a mural of the Imam.

There are few people out now, though I do pass a building where a watchful girl is sitting on a step. I can see only her eyes for her clothing, but that is enough. They speak of hopelessness. Of a future where she'll be the third wife of an old man, and be lucky if she finds a good one. One that will not beat her.

After three blocks of following the crack, I reach a downrider pylon. I stream to it, and a ladder lowers to ground level. The ladder is narrow, and the loading platform is two stories up. A difficult climb, but I'm young. All debuggers are young. At the one story mark I'm able to see into the larger city. I glimpse the dark towers and the colored rooms of the temples. Dozens of temples. The nearest one is twenty kilometers away. Not that I'm required to go. Debuggers can't go. We're a distraction. And our destinies are fixed.

At the midpoint of my climb, I hear the familiar scream of an approaching downrider. I look up at the cable, the "string" above the platform and think I see a bit of movement. The drop caused by the downrider's weight. The scream intensifies, causing me to want to block my ears, then the wheel-shaped craft arrives. When I reach it, the downer detects my proximity and the door opens. I climb inside, feed it my destination, and I'm soon speeding over the city. Feels like flying.

Two-story buildings give way to three story. Cracked pavement gives way to parks and schools. I reach an interchange, an intersection of strings, and the downrider stops. The interchange mechanism frees my downer and carries it to a string heading east and locks it into place. Then I'm off again, screaming and flying. I spot a handful of kids standing at a bus stop below. They are looking my direction. Nobody waves, though some point. Downriders are fun to look at, I'll give them that. Sleek and fast. Might be the best part of the job.

Fourteen minutes later I make another exchange, which points me southeast. Ten minutes after that, I arrive at the closest pylon to my destination. As I climb out I take a quick look around. The neighborhood is relatively new. The paint on the buildings is clean. No cracks anywhere—it's probably safe.

I descend to street level. There are many pedestrians here, which makes me a little nervous. Some of them glance at me, but I don't see any disdain. Mostly curiosity. I ignore them and bring up the map grid in my head. It says go south, so I turn to my left and start walking. I pass a market followed by a series of shops. There are small crowds, all are polite. No one stares. I walk in peace, marveling at how quiet everything is, how structured and warm feeling. It seems like a place where nothing could go wrong. What brings me here?

Something hard strikes my shoulder. I cry out, and then see the antagonist as it bounces down the sidewalk in front of me. A large, blue ball.

"Sorry," someone says. A female voice.

I look to my left. There's a young woman there, maybe four years younger than me. Her face and figure are completely covered, but her eyes seem apologetic. Hard to know, really. She's with a younger boy, possibly a sibling. I'm not sure which of them threw the ball. The boy runs ahead of me to get it. I look at her a long moment, expressionless. I feel a glimmer of something. A strange hopefulness that starts in my chest. But then my head tingles and the feeling goes away. I look ahead. Toward my goal.

Eventually my surroundings change. The houses and buildings go from looking new, to looking unfinished. Many are only skeletons, with no outside covering. No siding. There are strange, somewhat unpleasant, smells in the air. Acidic odors. I hear the sounds of engines in motion. Construction noises. Men yelling and cursing. The sidewalk becomes loose stone. None of the ground is green. It is all barren—unplanted. Cleared.

Seven minutes later, I arrive. There is active demolition going on. Large machinery. There's a group of men standing around, many in hard construction hats. They look at me, but no one says anything. There is a three-story white building ahead. It is a simple, four-sided design. There are broken sections on the face and corners—places where the underlying bricks are exposed or missing. Lots of chipped paint. I assume they are taking it down.

I glance at the men again. Someone should be telling me something. "Someone wanted a debugger?" I say. "I was sent to this address."

One of the men nods, and indicates the structure. There is an entranceway in the exact center. A doorway missing a door.

Freeheads. Since speech is their primary form of communication, you'd think they'd be better at it.

"Inside?" I say.

"Yes," one of them says. Finally.

I shift my pack from one shoulder to the other, frown, and walk toward the door. I'm a little worried for what I might encounter. I don't like vermin. I'm okay with the grease and smells in my home, but there are no animals. A place like this seems like it might have animals.

I enter a wide yet shallow room. There is refuse strewn around the floor, but generally it is empty. I notice a couple small tables on one side, against the wall. The other side has a large quantity of chairs all heaped together. There is a strange smell, but it isn't unpleasant. Sweet and also old. There are a pair of doors, one to the left and one to the right. There's no one here to help me, though. I frown and contemplate going outside again.

Then the door on the left opens. A middle-aged man comes out, grins, and waves at me. He has a blue hardhat on, and yellow overalls. "Come, come," he says.

I follow him through the door to a much larger room. Light filters in from above somewhere, I want to think through breaks in the ceiling, but that doesn't seem right either. There is a skylight, or something.

There are lots of colors here. An indescribable amount. The walls on both sides have some sort of built in glass. Large panes of mixed hues that form images. I identify people and animals. The people's clothing...is strange. Not of our time. I quickly run a pattern match to try to identify what era. It gives me a number that can't be right. Close to a thousand years ago? From an era the stream calls "medieval."

There are angels and demons in the glasswork too. Many of the depicted scenes are familiar—the story of Noah's Ark, for instance—but also subtly different. I'm not a student of either history or religion. There is little need today. We are drowned by both.

I see silver crosses, and greying statues. Some have portions falling off. Slices of faces or missing appendages. Still, there is a beauty here despite the decay. A suggestion of what it might have been.

I notice stacks of framed yellowing objects leaned against the wall to my right. I drift that direction, and putting a hand out, draw one of the objects back. The other side is painted in vibrant colors. It is a scene of a man standing outside a door. He has one hand raised to the door's surface. About to knock.

"Over here, debugger," the middle-aged man says. "Quickly." He is to the left of the entrance, near the center of the wall. A square meter-by-meter machine is next to him.

I walk closer. The device is unknown to me, though it is stream aware. There is no vidscreen or other output interface. There are a few blinking lights and some buttons. I check its ident in the stream. It is cryptic. It identifies as 'KB-63G. The latest and the best!'"

"It does not work." The man wears a badge that I squint at. "Kadeer" is his first name. He places a hand atop the machine and pushes the black button there. "This is to arm it, but nothing happens. I keep pushing and pushing. Nothing."

"Arm it?"

"Yes," he says. "It is a safe K-Boom. We are to demolish this building."

My first instinct is to run. Especially with the way Kadeer keeps whacking on that button. I hold it together, though. If it hasn't blown yet, another whack shouldn't make the difference.

I glance back at the glasswork, the broken statues. They are as beautiful as anything I've ever seen. "Demolish?"

Kadeer nods, and pushes the button again. "We are putting up new houses. Certainly you saw on the way."

"Yes, I saw." Something about it doesn't seem right, though. This place... I ignore my feelings, and streaming out to the machine, make it run a full diagnostic. I also start consulting its manual. "You haven't used one of these before?"

"Yes, of course," he says. "Many times."

I frown and, having found the K-Boom manual, start to internally leaf through it. It isn't that long. Thankfully, the black button isn't as important as Kadeer thinks it is. He is inadvertently resetting the thing's timer over and over. "Arming" requires him to hold a safety switch, as well.

I look at him. "What is this place?" I ask. "What *was* it?"

He shakes his head vigorously. "I do not know. It is a building of heresy. It needs to come down."

"Are you taking those outside?" I ask, indicating the paintings. "They are—"

He doesn't look back. "They are idols. Wretched things of the past."

I look at the images in the glass. One is of a bearded man in a green park. He is praying. There is a crowd of men with swords depicted behind him. "Idols to who?" I say. "Not A?" I point at the one depicting the Flood. "Is that not our forefather Noah?"

Kadeer's face grows red. "They are incorrect representations, debugger. Deviant and heretical. Our law forbids such things. Surely you know this."

"Incorrect?" I say. "Deviant?" I feel a warning in my head, a "buzz" of confirmation for what Kadeer has said. The Law requires destruction. It seems like an unnecessary waste, though. "Certainly, a museum—"

"No museum would have this." His hands make fists and he trembles with emotion. "You must fix this machine. The Imam wants it fixed."

I consider walking away, but the consideration brings another shock, another stop. I avoid wincing at the intensity, which is more severe this time. I think of the datamix I saw. How brave Grim and Sandfly's actions actually were. Fighting the implant.

I am not brave, though. I sometimes question, but I always comply. I get another reminder shock and shake my head. "You aren't doing it correctly," I say. "The machine. I shouldn't have to show you this."

"What have I done wrong? Show me quickly!"

On the side opposite the K-Boom's black button is a smaller red one. "This is the safety," I say. "It needs to be held down while you triple-press the other."

He raises both hands. "Ah-yee, so simple." He begins pressing both buttons.

"Simple," I say. "Right." I frown. "Don't blow yourself up." Though I sort of wish he would.

I can't help but glance at the glass images again. They must've taken someone many months to create, years even. Especially these medieval people. Who knows what tech they had?

What would Sand do here? Or Grim? Even together they couldn't make a difference. And is art even worth it? It is only glass and paint.

Kadeer raises his hands. "I think that worked." He stares at the machine for a moment, then looks at me. "Did that work?"

There is a red light that screams "Armed!" That should be enough for him, shouldn't it? "Yes," I say.

"Then come along, debugger," he says. "We need to be outside."

Again, I hesitate. Why does this bother me?

The headbuzz comes in the form of a migraine this time. Hemisphere splitting. I follow him to the next room, and then outside. There is a semicircle of men waiting there. They read the look on Kadeer's face and his waving of both hands and so turn and start jogging away.

I jog to the nearest heavy machine, a bulldozer, intent on making my way back. On getting away. I move past more machines, stepping over large chunks of rock. My feet scuff on the uneven ground.

Kadeer grabs my elbow. "You should see this," he says. "It is quite fun."

I shake my head. "I'm not much for destroying things." I stare at his hand until he removes it.

There is a loud "thump" and a "boom" followed by a waterfall of crunching noises. The building falling in on itself.

"Rails," I mutter. "They were paintings and statues. Bits of pretty glass." I feel them, though. It is like a part of me exploded. Or got crushed.

Kadeer is turned away, looking at the destruction. He is breathing heavy. "What was that?" he says. "What did you say?"

I shake my head. "No matter. I'll send my End of Task Report."

My pack seems especially heavy as I walk away.

WHEN I GET BACK to the garage, the parts for the heavy have been delivered. It takes me thirty minutes to introduce them into its system. I do a quick check of its matrix, have it perform a diagnostic, and give it a final voice check.

"Are you ready?" I ask.

"MS-77 is ready." It talks loud. Voice rattles my eardrums. "What do you require, DR 23?"

"Recognition," I say, frowning. "And to be loved."

The bot's head rotates to look at me. I expect it to say something. I almost hope it will say something relevant. Give advice from somewhere deep within its matrix, or share insight that its creator left around for such a moment. But ole MS-77 simply stares.

I hope I didn't foul his head, somehow break him again...

"Get back out there," I say. "Go kill something." I take a couple steps away so I don't get inadvertently crushed. Heavies aren't particularly careful. I wouldn't be the first debugger who became a bump in a heavy's path.

MS-77 approximates a nod, then its body rotates so that it is facing the door. The bot rolls forward. The door notices its closeness and begins to ratchet upward. Clank, clank, clank.

A hot breeze blows in, along with the distant sounds of gunfire. I notice small piles of sand near the doorway's edge. The cleaning bot must need attention.

MS-77 rolls into the street. I watch it for a few moments and then look past it to the one-story building on the other side. I suspect it is used for prostitution. Men show up there at all hours of the day and night. I've glimpsed the women too.

To be honest, I don't simply suspect, I know. I stream searched once and found the shill ads for that particular address. The tendrils of their crime. The scriptures forbid such behavior. Stoning is often the punishment for those caught.

Yet here it is, in the Imam's domain.

The door of the prostitution building opens, and a man and woman come out. The man is in tan clothing. The woman is covered in black. She looks my direction, and I nervously step back into the shadows. The man takes her elbow and leads her to the right, toward town.

I wonder if the Imam knows? Certainly he would do something if he did. He and his sons.

I consider covertly sending a message, but as the couple moves up the sidewalk, I think better of it. If punishment comes, it won't be on the man.

I stream the garage door closed again. I walk toward the nearest pile of sand and push it over with my foot, smoothing and stamping it into the permacrete floor. I glance toward the stairway. Maybe I should take a nap. I rarely get those, but I feel like I could use one.

A message finds my implant. I almost groan when I see who it is from.

BullHammer...

I cross the floor to the stairway, placing my foot on the lowest rung.

Bull sends another message, and then another. I sigh, and closing my eyes, focus on his first attempt. It is a Full Impact request. I adjust the settings to Standard Impact, and connect with him. I see an image of him, dressed in debugger blues, sitting on a sea of grass somewhere. Behind him is a lake and some trees. Looks nice.

"ThreadBare," he says, smiling brightly.

"Yes?"

"Can you see where I am? See all this?"

"Looks nice." I sigh. "What is this about? Because you're taking my time—"

"I'm in!" he says. "I'm moved up!"

"To what?"

"I'm leveled and I'm up here..." He stands and partially spins, arms wide. "The Imam's north palace."

What? How? It is a large step. A rails big step. It means Bull is somewhere notable now. He's no longer forgotten. "That's bliss, Bull."

He appears to lean in close. "Are you jealous? You're jealous, right?"

It is hard not to be. He's up—he's a twelve. I look at the stairway, then back at the garage. *And I'm here.* "I need to go..."

"But I've got more to share!" he says. "I have my own private suite on the premises. It is twice the size of the apartment I had before. Twice the size!"

"Uh-huh..." I make my way up the stairs. My little loft comes into view. My ancient chute.

"I spend half the day dangling my feet. I'm in the entertainment hub, this little room on the second floor. I make sure that the family, the younger children mostly, can find all the entertainment options they want. They have a dozen nanny-bots too. I keep them working. But Thread, this equipment is so new, even the bots, they never break down. It is a flipping dream. I wish you could see it."

I stream open the chute and take a seat on the edge. "Yeah, me too. Sounds amazing."

"And you know what? A lot of this was because of that storm op we were in. Because I got things fixed so quickly. That's what my submaster told me."

"Is that so?"

"Yeah, rails so. I'm calling everyone I know. Picasso, this is great."

"Picasso?"

Bull lifts a shoulder. "I'm experimenting. Trying to develop my own segment lingo. I'm thinking of using artists. I think Picasso was one."

Names as lingo? That's flipped. Bull is flipped.

I do a quick stream check. I find "Picasso" on a banned art list. So yeah, he was an artist. And you couldn't find anything he painted anywhere. Not even on the stream. I'm told there are places where that's not the case. Spots where you can browse information that has been lost for centuries. I sort of doubt it, though.

Those pictures I saw...were any of those Picasso works? Now blown to the sky?

The Law has a way of removing distractions. Of winnowing out anything that is not of A. It has worked for centuries. Who am I to question? I'm nobody.

I think I know why the K-Boom experience bothers me, though. The lost art. The winnowing process homogenizes, forcing everything and everyone to a sameness. But I don't want to be the same. I don't want to be another lowlevel debugger.

"Did you hear me?"

I return my focus to Bull, still smiling and sitting in the grass. "Yes, sorry. What?"

"I said it is the least I could do."

"What was?"

"For all the hard time. To get you up here."

I squint. "Me? In the north palace? Is that what you mean?"

"Why not? I'll recommend you."

I don't trust anything BullHammer does. Nothing. "Why would you do that?"

"Because we're friends. You don't want to stay with the heavies forever, do you?"

We're friends? Bull has an uncommon definition, I think. "I'm sure they have plenty of debuggers there," I say. "Highlevels even."

He gives me an annoyed look. I notice the trees moving behind him. "They do, of course they do. But they don't last forever. A cluster went offline over the past few years." A frown. "We don't last long , Thread. Need to enjoy what we can."

"Offline?" I say. "Who went offline?" I know it happens. Especially among those of a certain age. But I want to know what he knows. This offline cluster.

"You're playing with me now. The weekly offline lists? The inactive DR numbers?"

I nod slowly. "I know the lists. But those are routine. People die, Bull. Go to their reward."

He raises an eyebrow. "Never any explanation on those lists, you notice? Only the numbers we should no longer access. The numbers to forget."

"I don't pay attention to lists," I say. "Afraid I might turn up on one."

"Especially where you live, huh?" There's a ripping sound, then Bull brings up a handful of grass. He releases it to the wind. It swirls around and away.

I scowl. "Never been anyone I know," I say. "Usually highlevels. Oldsters."

"Yeah, like late twenties," he says. "Old, old."

I yawn and lay down in the chute. It feels real good. Not green grass good, but good.

"I'm tiring you out, huh?"

"I got up early." I haven't eaten in a while either. Maybe I should do that first? One of the construction guys had something with ginger in it. I could smell it on the air. Ginger might feel good. Especially before a nap. I sit up and look at the food conditioner. Can it do ginger?

"Okay, I'm going," Bull said. "But I meant it. I'll give them your number. Never know."

"Right," I say. "Never know."

Bull drops off. I feel a small amount of relief. The guy bugs me.

I'm still in the chute. It feels right. I'm torn between it and the food. I'm also contemplating messaging Front again to see if he has anything new. Let's face it, mixes are my life.

I climb out and walk toward the conditioner. Ginger first, mix next, then sleep.

I think about the statues and paintings. That wasn't only someone's work. It could've been their specialty. Their legacy.

The large door downstairs begins to open. *Rails*. I hurry to the stairway and make my way down. The door is about halfway up now. I don't see the treads of a heavy. Nor do I see any of the other appendages that bots use to travel—spider legs, rollers, hoppers. I glimpse only a human form. I catch my foot and almost trip down the stairs. I decide to focus on my feet until I reach the bottom.

Need to be careful here.

THE MAN AT THE DOOR is army—black helmet, sand swept fatigues, wrinkled features. There is a gun in his hands, held loosely. I'm a little concerned.

"Peace be unto you," I say. It is a bit ironic, but I'm following the rules here.

The soldier is squinting and his eyes are darting. Then I realize he is attempting to search the room behind me, instinctively looking for the enemy. The darkness undoubtedly makes that difficult.

"You are DR 23?"

I nod. "Yes, ThreadBare."

He lurches forward, grabbing my arm at the elbow. "You need to come with me."

Now I'm scared. I pattern grab his face and search the "Debugger Abuser" list with it. At the same time, I prepare to activate an emergency beacon. It won't help if he shoots me, but maybe they'll get here before he strikes again. I find no match on the list, but that isn't much comfort.

I pull my messages, scan them, then shake my head. "I've received nothing from my master," I say. "No new task. And my master is the Imam."

He gives my arm another tug. "The Imam, huh?" He chuckles. "I have a convex outside. Let's go."

I plant my feet. "Go where?" I glance beyond him. There *is* a vehicle out there. Something small that his body almost obscures. I let my eyes drift toward the Delusion wall. It is made of grey brick, and stands ten meters high.

"I was sent for the skin at heavy repair," he says. "That's you, correct?"

"Yes, but this isn't how it's done." His grip is starting to hurt my arm. I attempt to pull away.

He eases up, but doesn't let go. "You are required. A machine needs attention."

"Where?" I ask again.

He flips his head right, toward the wall. "Out there. Only a short distance."

I shake my head. "Machines come to me." I lift my free arm to indicate my grease pit garage. "Here. Not out there. That's for soldiers. For heavies."

He releases my arm, but the gun lowers. "You're a servant of the Imam," he says. "As am I."

Surprisingly, the headbuzz is silent on the matter. My heart is thumping like a hopper with a bad motivator, though. A few hops more and it might slip the string completely. Fall to the ground.

Plus, there's the gun. Not a nanopounder, but a lethal. I look at the wall again. The thought of going through it...I feel ill. I should contact the submaster. See what he thinks. I tell that to the soldier.

"There is no time," he says. "We are the Imam's guard. The hand of A. No permission is needed."

This has never happened before. That might seem strange with me being so close to the conflict, but it hasn't. The war stays over there where it should, and I stay in my garage.

I attempt to contact Submaster Badr. He's the one I get most of my chores from. There is no response.

The soldier grabs me again and pulls. "Come now. We will go."

I find myself thinking about BullHammer and his plush landscape. How nice that would feel. To just lay there and stare at the sky. I wonder if there are many females near him? Perhaps dancing or singing?

"I need my bag," I say. "My debugging bag." I point toward the workbench where I always leave it. "It is right over there."

He releases me and I walk toward the bench. The garage's smells seem to infuse me now. A mixture of petrochemicals that the vent system can't keep dissipated, despite my having upgraded it five times. I try the submaster again and again. No response. Where is he?

I dip into the implant's message store, looking for previous work requests, other submasters. The first one I find is from two years ago—Submaster Adi. But I'm fairly certain he was transferred to the sacred city. Across the sea. Little help.

I grab the bag and sling it over my shoulder. I always keep it ready, unfortunately. Can't beg off for a supply run.

I check another submaster—I get a message saying his account has been deleted. Everywhere I turn: no response, no response, no response.

I feign a smile as I approach the soldier. "I'm ready now."

THE CONVEX IS A THREE-SEATED vehicle, two wheels in front and one in back. It is tight configuration. The seats are essentially placed where the wheels are not. The vehicle's color matches the soldier's uniform—desert camouflage.

The soldier orders me into the lone front seat and claims one of the back seats for himself. Doubtless so he can watch me.

The third and final seat is filled with his pack. It appears to weigh at least 70 kilos, or as much as I do in winter with my bulkier chill suit on. The vehicle's controls are in back with him and are composed of the sorts of knobs and buttons that freeheads require.

There are no stream-sensitive controls in case I change my mind. Figures. The convex is a big ole taker. No give. A transparent canopy closes overhead as we start to move, though, so that's something.

Passing through the wall is a non-event. We roll up to where the street ends and the door disappears. We drive through and it appears again behind us, solid as ever. No one even waves goodbye.

I'm shocked by the landscape. The buildings are similar in construction to my garage and the buildings around it. Rectangular, in shades of grey and yellow. But none of them are complete. All have portions missing. They have been unused and unattended for a very long time. The road is broken too.

The canopy is little comfort. The surroundings feel more oppressive, more dangerous. Like the temperature has increased a dozen degrees. It hasn't, but the feeling is real. Omnipresent. I'm itching and sweating.

My captor does a fair job of maneuvering. We miss most of the potholes, despite our increasing speed. After only a short time the buildings dwindle and we begin to travel through broken prairie. I can feel the tall grass against the convex's underside. The engine drags with the effort. I hope it has had all its maintenance. I'm not sure I can fix it if it breaks.

On the horizon I see grey sky and flashes of light. I hear low thumps, but it is not thunder.

My fear increases. "Take me back," I say. "I'm not for this."

The soldier laughs. I am beginning to hate him.

More buildings appear ahead. A forgotten settlement nearly two kilometers wide. I search the stream for what it was, for the type of people that might have once lived there. It was a heretical sect, a band of wrong-thinkers. But they are distant memories now. Long since conquered or converted.

"Is that where we're going?" I ask, but get only a head shake followed by more laughter. The vehicle turns sharply, taking us straight for a stepped section composed of stone or flattened concrete. We bounce down the first step, then the next. It is all I can do to keep my forehead from hitting the canopy. My insides are shaken. I yelp with pain.

Again, he laughs.

We pass one demolished settlement after another. I glimpse images of past lives—blackened vehicles or burnt-out homes. Occasionally I see abandoned military encampments or machinery. It has been a long conflict. Endless.

The ground flattens out again and the long grass becomes less frequent. I see a series of large green tents ahead, along with more buildings. There is a heavy bot close by too. I can sense its presence in the stream. It is reporting lots of wear, and some disabilities. War always breaks things.

We arrive at the tent encampment, the convex stops, and the canopy opens. There is an acidic taste to the air, along with the hint of smoke. A group of black-helmeted soldiers stand nearby, some with grey smokesticks in their hands. Such vices are illegal now, but I doubt that news is important here. All the rules.

The soldiers look at me as I exit the convex, but none of them moves. They are large men, older men, and I feel very small. I grab my bag and pull it over my chest. It brings me some comfort.

My captor motions for me to follow. We wind our way into the settlement. Through the tent openings I notice men sleeping or eating. I try not to look very long. I only follow. At one tent I hear what sounds like a woman's shriek, and I pause. My captor grabs my elbow again, and hastens me on. I'm unsettled.

I'm brought to the entrance of a large, brown shelter. There is a spirited conversation going on inside. "Wait here," the soldier says, and disappears within. The conversation changes, then quiets completely. The soldier returns and bids me enter.

There are six men inside. Judging by their uniforms and information from the stream, they are all officers—*mulazims* and *naqeebs*. The one in the center of the room is a *fareeq*, a general, and has the highest rank of them all. He has greying blond hair, and is clean-shaven.

"Debugger," he says. "I am Fareeq Uday Abbas. How good of you to come."

I had little choice, but I don't mention that. "Peace be unto you," I say with a bow.

"I apologize for the methods, but we have a disabled bot and are on a tight schedule."

"We have a demonstration to stream," one of the mulazims says. He is a thin man who seems to swim in his uniform. I think he might be gravely ill. I can sense a device controlling his heart. Keeping its rhythm steady.

"A demonstration?"

The thin man glowers. "For the stations, for the people. A vid."

I'm aware of the nightly updates from the front. They are one of the longest running shows on the stream.

"The proper clearance will be given," the general says. "The proper channels for you to be here. Our enforcer is immobile and I knew you were close by. I sent Saaiq to find you."

I nod. "Saaiq" means "he who drives the right path." More irony. I resist smiling.

"There will be no trouble in this," the general continues. "We all work for the Imam. And he and I are family." He points at ole

RightPath. "We should waste no more time. Take the debugger to the machine."

Saaiq nods and touches my elbow again.

"I can follow you fine," I say. "Just lead." I move my bag onto my shoulder and shake it into the proper position. There is comfort in that.

We exit the tent and I follow. I really don't need his help at all, because the heavy is the one thing in this camp that I could easily find. It is twenty-two meters from our current position.

When we reach the heavybot I have to swallow hard. It has seen lots of combat. There are long, dark streaks across the length of its body. One of the tread protectors is missing and the head, normally smooth and cone-shaped, is dented to the point of having lost all symmetry. If it were human it would have no teeth. This could take days.

The bot is positioned at the north edge of the tents. Ahead of it is an opening between tents large enough for it to drive through. There are two trees here that partially shade us. A bonus.

"It responds to commands," Saaiq says. "But it will not move forward."

I feel for the mechanical. All its plastisteel and galvanic components, neural networks and nano stores—such a collection of technology—yet it is stalled in place. Might as well be parts in a box. Or a child's climbing toy.

I scowl. "They require maintenance, you know? Regular maintenance." I shake my head. "They shouldn't get like this."

Saaiq laughs. "You've never been in battle."

"Not physical battle, no. But I've had lots of pain." Freeheads have no idea.

I frown and circle the bot. Despite the missing protector, the treads themselves look fine, as do the wheels they ride on. I think back to the electrical storm, the barges I worked on. There's been a lot of stopped vehicles lately. This one isn't surge related, though. It has been used until destruction.

I touch the bot through the stream. There are lots of red and orange messages. System errors. Lots of synthetic pain. The primary trauma is less ancillary, though. Something code related?

"You are communing with it," Saaiq says. "Speaking to it with—" He points to his temple. "The device in your head."

"Yes," I say, glancing at him. "And no, it does not hurt." I focus on the bot again. "I apologize. That question always comes next."

"I was not going to ask," he says. "I do not care if it hurts. I was shot in the leg last year. It still hurts. I do not care."

I nod and focus on the bot's error reporting. I drift toward the side nearest the tree, away from Saaiq. I hope it will be enough to get him to leave. I don't need an audience. I'm insecure enough as it is. "You've had a difficult time," I stream to the bot.

"MS-45 is incomplete," it says aloud.

I glance across at Saaiq, and walk nearer the bot. "You can stream me directly," I say. "No need to talk out loud."

"I cannot," it says. "It pains to do so."

Well, that's interesting. Is that a symptom related to the lack of motion? Or a separate problem?

I toss my pack up onto the bot's treads and start to rummage through it. My hand finds my roll of sheets first, so I pull them out. I stream to the bot, telling it to extend its handholds. Nothing happens. Another attempt still gets me nothing. Again I'm reminded of the barge. What is it with bots and their handholds lately?

I set the roll of sheets down and try to hoist myself up onto the treads. Can't quite do it the first time. Or the second, or the third.

Before I know it, Saaiq is standing right next to me.

"One more time!" he says, smiling. He stoops and grabs me around the legs. He lifts me up enough that my knees touch the tread's top surface. The experience is uncomfortable—I don't like being touched, and I especially don't like being squeezed. But I'm where I need to be. I grab on and scramble up to crouch next to the bot's head. I nod at Saaiq.

"It was no problem," he says. "You are light. Like a palm leaf."

I turn to the bot's head and spread a sheet on the nearest side. It makes for an uneven image. Rippled and wavy due to the head's many dents. Still, I see nanopaths and conduits. A rainbow of color. One would think that models like this would have simple designs: *See enemy, kill enemy!* But in actuality, they're the most complicated. Especially their decision matrices. Like counting bees in a honeycomb.

I've stared inside these models so often that I don't need to consult the specs anymore. Despite the dips and valleys everything appears to be in the proper spot here. It is a miracle.

I climb around to the front of the head and apply another sheet. The insides look fine there too. Some of the pathways are a little worn, but otherwise things are good. I spend another forty-six minutes working my way around the head, covering every angle. Nothing strange anywhere.

I reposition myself to take the pressure off my knees. I feel a trickle of sweat on my forehead and wipe it away. I start chewing over the bot's inability to stream messages to me. It couldn't bring the handholds out either. Typically, those two together would indicate a problem in its stream center, except it can accept stream messages just fine. It answers me when I stream to it, after all. It simply can't respond that way.

"Did you recognize me trying to extend the handholds?" I stream the bot.

"Yes!" it says, a little too loud.

"But you didn't obey the command."

"The handhold activator does not respond. Diagnostics suggest a broken linkage."

"And how long has that been a problem?"

He gives me the robot equivalent of a shrug. Citing a date range that is too large to be meaningful.

"How about your inability to move? How recent is that?"

"This morning," it says. "ED seven point five."

Yes, morning. Early morning. I look down the bot's side. I'm tempted to address the handhold problem first, since that's doubtless an easy fix. Sometimes it feels good to get an easy one out of the way.

But the soldiers don't care about that. They want movement! I start paging through the bot's error messages again. Rails, it has problems. Saaiq is still standing near the treads. "This may be awhile." I say.

He shrugs, backs up to the nearest tree, and leans against it. My audience isn't leaving.

I notice that there are other soldiers in the vicinity. Some are outside the tents ahead and right of the bot. Others are grouped on the left. They are marking the edge of the large corridor between the tents. Dozens of meters ahead, near the middle of that same corridor, is a larger group, fully armed. They seem to be clustered around something or someone. I recognize the skinny mulazim there with them. He's looking my direction.

Don't they have a war to fight? I shake my head. I hate expectations. It hasn't been that long, Abbys, and this bot is a mess.

There are many things that could be broken between the bot's cranium and its treads, of course—gears and circuits and large components. I'm not seeing many errors from those areas, though. The sort of things that any freehead mechanic could fix.

I feel a little lost here. Afraid that I can't get it done. That they might need a higher level DR than me. I also feel for the bot. Like I'm going to let it down. And I've been doing so well lately.

I need to focus. Find out where I am.

Where I am?

I look at the bot's head again, all dimpled and scarred. "What is your position, MS-45?"

The bot responds with utter garbage. Instead of numbers, I get two characters—an "X" and a "T".

"Well...that's not good..." Via the implant, I have the bot run a diagnostic on its positioning system. There are layers of interfaces between its decision matrix and that system, lots of winding pathways and tributaries. I peel off each one, testing as I go. Every step of the way it is garbage. All the way to the core.

Pos units have been unchanged for decades—centuries even. They never fail. But this one apparently did.

I glance at my bag. There's nothing like a pos unit in there. They're small, but I can't carry everything. I could manufacture one, of course. Get the specs and let my forming device squeeze one out. It is more fun to improvise, though.

I look at Saaiq. "You have a communicator around? Something you use to talk to base, or whatever?"

He holds up his helmet. "We talk through here," he says.

Of course they would. "Can I see it?"

He hands me up the helmet. It is heavily insulated. I could take out a sheet and look at it, minimize the damage, but then I remember our ride here and Saaiq's incessant laughter. I start tearing away the insulation.

True to form, Saaiq laughs.

I throw tuffs of black and white material away. On the helmet's right side I feel a bump. That's the bundle, the good stuff. I pry it away and strip off the dark outer cover. To most people what's inside would look like an uneven tangle of string. Or a hairball.

I roll the ball between my fingers, looking for the pos. I find it—an oblong piece, brown in color. I leave it within the ball, set it aside, and reach for my bag again. There's no breeze today, thankfully. Inside the bag I find my micro-cutter. I use it to cut a small opening just behind the bot's head, right where the main nanopath ascends. When I'm certain I've found the path, when I can see the blue of it, I find some tweezers and introduce the helmet's pos unit to the system. Then I alert the heavy's nanos to its presence. Seconds later the pos is taken inside and the hole resealed.

Through the sheets I can watch the unit's journey down the pathway. I sing to the nanos again, making sure their code is right. Ensuring they know what to do.

Five minutes later the pos unit is installed.

"Are you ready?" I ask the bot. It is a standard diagnostic inquiry.

"MS 45 is ready," it says.

I almost hold my breath. "And what is your position?"

It tells me its coordinates. Our coordinates. I feel joy in that.

"And can you move?"

There's a low rumble and the bot's treads engage. It shifts forward a full meter.

I smile and collect my bag. Saaiq comes close and puts up a hand for me to hold onto. I wave it away, climb down onto the tread, and jump off. The ground is hard, it hurts a little, but I'm okay with that. At least I wasn't held again.

"So it is fixed?" Saaiq asks.

"It moves," I say. "I can't say it is fixed. There are lots of things wrong. I could spend days on the wrong. I'm guessing your boss doesn't want me here for days, though, does he?"

Saaiq smiles and shrugs.

I hear a small commotion coming from inside the camp, past the heavy to where the larger group of soldiers are positioned.

I really don't want to be around this group any longer. They are noisy and smelly. "They can bring the bot in if they want the other errors fixed," I say, frowning. "You know where I am."

"Yes, of course. Do you want to stay for the demonstration?"

Job requests have come in while I've been here. Small things, most of them I could safely ignore, but they give me an excuse. "I have things to do," I say. "Can someone take me back?"

The bot begins to move forward, toward the road between the tents. My curiosity tweaks me enough that I follow it while peering beyond it to where it is headed. More men are coming out of the tents. Those who were sleeping or eating before.

"I will get the convex." Saaiq moves behind me and then jogs into the maze of tents on my left.

"Wait!" I take a few steps to follow, then realize he has purposely left me. That I wasn't quick enough. I frown and look toward the heavy again. There are men following it on both sides now. I'm certain there is going to be some sort of group photo with them huddled around the bot. Lots of flags and shooting in the air. I see the blue flag of the Imam being raised.

The group of men near the flag, near the center of the "street" coalesce and reconfigure. The skinny muzalim is waving at the bot and also talking to those around him. I find myself pulled along by what is happening. Two of the soldiers near the muzalim are holding small recording devices—I can tell because they keep bringing their hands near their eyes. One is recording the heavy, and the other is alternating between it and something on the ground. A row of things, actually. From here it looks like an ornamental presentation. The objects are arranged equidistant from each other. They are white in color and elliptical.

The bot turns, and the men shift around so that I lose my view of the objects. I keep walking forward. Curiosity drives me.

I hear the whirring sound of a convex behind me. I glance back but don't see Saaiq. I sense he is coming, though. That he'll be here soon.

I squint at the tableau ahead. What is going on? I keep drifting forward. No matter what it is, I am happy the heavy is working. Another small success. I watch as the bot shifts and turns again, positioning itself very close to the elliptical objects on the ground. What are the soldiers using it for? It is too massive to help move the objects.

I realize the elliptical objects are white because they are wrapped in cloth. I can make out the rough edges now.

The heavy's tread draws near one of the objects. The object begins to move, to shake. I hear noise coming from it. Human sounds. Muffled, but unmistakably human. Pleas, shouts.

Those are heads. Human heads. Those are people, and their bodies are buried beneath them. The heavy moves forward. I hear a terrible sound.

Then blackness.

I WAKE UP IN THE convex again. The sky is many shades darker, but I can make out the shadow of the city wall far ahead and on our left. There is the hint of lights behind it, bundled tight within it. I hear low thumps somewhere behind us, along with the clipped sound of gunfire. The never-ending war.

"Are you okay?" Saaiq says from behind me.

I groan and reposition myself. My back and neck reveal new aches. I try to stretch my neck out.

Saaiq laughs. "I knew you were all right," he says. "The meds, they were worried. Afraid they couldn't fix you if you were broken."

"They couldn't have," I whisper.

"What's that?"

I simply grunt and shake my head. I keep staring at the city, willing it to come closer. To be safely behind the wall again. Away from Delusion. Away from all I experienced.

"You didn't like the demonstration?"

I glance at the sky, noticing the first stars of the night. They are yellow and red. The view is a silent treasure. I rarely look up, and when I do, I rarely see.

Inside, I am empty. More a wasteland than what surrounds us.

He laughs again. "The people forget us if we do not show them something. They need to know that we are working. That we are winning." I hear him sip from something. I hope he is drinking only water. "I don't know that we are winning, skin. But we are necessary for the Imam."

"And those people," I say. "In the dirt?" I try not to think about *the sound*. That awful popping sound.

"Infidels," he says. "Polytheists. They found A's judgement. He is not mocked."

"There is only one A," I say, but don't feel. Will I ever feel right again? Not artworks this time. People. People smashed and wasted.

Saaiq laughs again. The city is drawing close. There is no reason to talk any longer.

"They say skins are martyrs," Saaiq says. "That you are guaranteed paradise without dying."

"And without really living," I say. "We have surrendered our lives to service."

"Yes, without living." He takes another sip. "Without believing too, I think."

I say nothing. Only stare at the wall.
"Why should you?" he asks. "If I were guaranteed the virgins for only living, I would be happy. But some of us...most of us...have to earn them. To earn our place."

* * *

I contact FrontLot as soon as I am home. Right after the garage door has closed and I hear the whine of the convex moving away. I tell him what I've experienced over the past day. The increasing sense of purposelessness I feel. The aloneness.

"A debugger is never alone," he says. "You know this. We're always, all of us, right there in your head with you. Only a message away. Remember our instruction. Remember Bamboo."

"Yes, Bamboo," I say. "Our teacher. I wonder what he thinks. How he is."

"He sends regular messages."

"I stream them. They don't say anything. They are system updates. Implant improvements."

Front chuckles. We're messaging only Extended Easy because I want simplicity now. Only voices in my head. "That means he's okay. That he is performing his assigned task. Doing what he has always done."

I walk blindly through my nightly routine. It is difficult not to recall what I've seen. The sounds, the screams. The part I played in it. I had no choice, though. None.

What Sandfly did at the stockyard was a fluke. An impossibility. And his lifting the chute lid in the mix? That time he had help. Even then it seems unlikely. Like the mix was altered to make the two debuggers seem heroic. Debuggers aren't heroes, though. We're slaves.

Before I know it, I am standing next to my chute, with the canopy moving upwards. "I don't want to repeat that," I say, knowing my words are out of context. "I don't want to go out there again."

"This is the first time it has happened," Front says. "It won't happen again."

I frown. "There are no guarantees."

"Maybe Bull will come through for you. Get you a transfer."

I don't share that hope. I'm stuck.

Moments of silence pass.

"Are you looking for a mix, Thread?"

I gaze at the bottom of my chute. At its worn out lining. "I said I don't want to go out there again," I say. "Not even in my dreams."

"Right. Sure, okay. Someone else's dream it is. Anything in particular you're after?"

Something unexpected pops into my mind. A welcome tangent. "The lost debuggers," I say. "The ones who have gone offline? Do you have anything from them?"

Front is silent for a long moment. "I don't understand, Thread. Who do you mean?"

I lay down in the chute. "Remember, when we were talking before...?" Oh wait. It wasn't Front I was talking to. "Never mind. Bull mentioned the lists. The offline debugger lists? Can you cross-reference a recent one and see if you have a mix from one of them?"

"Sure...give me a minute." A pause. "That doesn't seem very happy. Mulling dead debuggers."

"Maybe, maybe not. Somehow it feels right." The chute lid closes over me. With a thought my rest will begin. But not my dreams.

"Okay, I think I have something. How do you feel about childhood?"

I remember the stars I saw in Delusion. "Childhood is fine," I say. "Give me that."

"Queued up," he says. "Here you go."

"Bill me..."

ALL I CAN THINK about is the trip, the lift.

It is a sunny morning when we arrive at CA zone. I barely remember the flash train ride that brought us here. Only glimpses of buildings zipping by. The occasional blur of graffiti on a guard rail or cement wall. Images of dirty and broken places where no one should live, but thousands do. Plus, the spired temples, of course. Everywhere the spires.

The lift is a spire of sorts too, one that reaches all the way into the sky. It is the elusive ziggurat, the dream of Babel, now transformed, manifested within a technological marvel. It is as if the deity A, for this generation, for our century, has changed his mind, choosing not to halt our stretch into Heaven. And perhaps he has! Our motives are pure, after all. The whole world under the same banner of piety.

Religion isn't my focus today, though.

The studiopad is a donut-shaped building, built to encircle the lifting platform. It has large windows on all sides, both inside and out. It gleams of silver in the sun. On its floors are mosaics of the stars and planets, on the walls the heroes we've been given—warriors, holy men, and explorers.

Waiting is painful. The windows of the pad, those that face the lift's route, don't seem large enough. Don't seem high enough to see what I want to see. I perceive only blue sky.

There is always the ribbon to watch. It is this black, impossibly thin band that anchors the lift. It seems like jinn magic must hold it as it is, with one end attached to the ground, and the other ending at a station at the far edge of space. How could it be, this miracle?

My father allows me to take it in, saying nothing. That is how our relationship is, him speaking only when life requires. He is a good man, a rich man, my father. A has blessed his devotion, giving him many children and many wives. I am the eldest of his first, so I am special.

"Do you know how the lift works, father?" I ask. "Have you designed such things?"

He shakes his head. "Elipserv makes only robots. Nothing this large."

"But could you?"

He keeps his hands behind his back, and stands a step further from the windows than I. "Possibly," he says. "With some help." He nods once, looking up. "There now, son, it comes."

I resist pressing my face against the glass. I know that a favorite son would never do such a thing. But it is difficult to avoid. The lift starts as only a black speck at the furthest extent of the ribbon, a tiny bubble in the ribbon's distant surface. But slowly it grows and grows, falling silently with the ribbon as its focal point. Finally, it is this giant multistory structure, a towering cylinder, suspended by only that tiny little string.

I feel like I am witnessing fiction. That such a thing could never be. The ribbon will snap, the lift structure will fall, and we will be crushed beneath it. It is a modern Sword of Damocles, a hammer of A's delayed wrath. I step away from the window to stand even with my father. Again, he says nothing. He only rests a hand on my shoulder. I'm not sure if it is for comfort or to prevent me from escaping further.

Finally, slowly, the lift meets the earth. There is a groan, a *thunk*, and a heavy whoosh as all the air trapped between platform and ground goes rushing back into space. My stomach feels excitement and fear.

The doors that separate the lift from the studiopad open, and hundreds of passengers begin to pour out. All the men are dressed in a manner similar to my father and me, with long jubbas over light pants and shirt. The women wear full-length dresses and all colors of hijabs. Everyone looks so clean and happy.

I also glimpse two debuggers—distinct because of their shorn heads and blue jumpsuits. They lurk around the crowds' edges. "I did not know they went to space," I say aloud.

"Who?" my father says.

I resisted the urge to point. "The Data Relocators," I say, using their proper name.

"They go wherever they are needed." He nods toward the lift. "Even up there, things break down."

I know of the debugger's built-in inhibitions toward sin and misadventure, but I still see them as mysterious and dangerous. Children need such things—their monsters. I fear becoming one of them. The process, their choosing, is as mysterious as their motives. Certain boys are culled from our school, from all the schools. One day they are present in class, the next they are not.

All know the name of their mentor, *The Bamboo*. Whenever a child went missing from class the rumors would go out: Perhaps The Bamboo got him. Pictures were drawn too. Caricatures of this tall bald man with evil eyes and pointed teeth. The Bamboo, stealer of children.

The debarking crowd clears and a group of security guards, dressed in brown robes over otherwise beige shirt and pants, lines up near the doors to check our idents. Their robes have patches to indicate their position and also the lift they are stationed with. The letters "C" and "A" are plainly visible.

The passengers form five lines and one by one pass through detailed scanning devices. Such caution is necessary, but I feel it shouldn't be. Not if all followed A as they should. Not if all sought good. But I know enough, even about my own heart, to know that men don't always follow A. Despite their best intentions.

My father allowed me to carry my own ident, and I am proud of that fact. It means I am old enough and worthy enough. Responsible. When it comes my turn to present mine, I step forward and beam at the guard. He only stares at me expectantly. I feel for my ident in my front jubba pocket, but do not find it. My face suddenly feels flushed. I nearly scream. I can sense my father's eyes on me. The weight of them on the center of my back.

"Ident," the guard says.

I shake my head and feel for the card again. I can visualize the train ride home in my mind. The shame of what I'd lost. My arms drop to my side.

"Son?" my father's voice.

I feel the ident. I'd placed it in my pants pocket after all. I quickly draw it out and hold it up. The guard scowls at it, and at my face. Finally, he waves me through.

A few minutes later we are in the lift's circular shopping plaza. There are many sights and sounds to distract me. Unusual foods and desserts. Lift-shaped toys. Small mechanicals. Even a pet store.

The motion around the shops is all very controlled and proper, not like the bazaars in town. The air is clean and filtered. Many of the shops are tended by mechanical men—servbots dressed in robes of green and red.

On a normal day, in a normal place, I would spend hours in such a plaza with my friends. We would sample everything, observe everything, while making jokes that only we could understand. Pointing out the unusual or the distinct. Strange faces or body types. We do not think such things are harmful. We are observers, future scientists. We only observe and report. Our commentary is a bonus.

"Are you hungry?" my father asks.

I shake my head. I should be quite hungry, but excitement suppresses it. We are traveling to new places. There is no time for food. "Maybe later," I say.

Father brings two sealed nutrient bars. "Sometimes the trip brings hunger," he says. "Is there anything else you want to see here?"

"How long until we go up?"

"Soon," he says. "But we have time to look more, if you like."

Again I shake my head. "I want to look outside."

"There is only the building to see now."

"I want to be ready," I say. "To not miss anything."

He nods, and indicates an opening in the shops, beyond which were a set of doors. "We will go to one of the observation decks."

I know that the lift has private suites, and that father has the money for one of them. Why are we not going there? I leave the question unasked, though.

He instead takes me to the largest observation deck on the lift's upper floor.

The deck is a broad slice of the lift's exterior. It has a high, theater-like ceiling, and the floor is stepped from top to bottom, with rows of small tables and chairs on every step. The uppermost step is the deepest, with more tables and chairs. There are few people here yet, only a handful of other expectant children with their parents.

As father predicted, the windows reveal little. I was hoping to at least be able to see into the surrounding studiopad. But the view is only the sandy color bricks that compose the building. There isn't even graffiti to ponder.

"Do you still want to stay?" father asks.

I do, of course. For twenty minutes I watch as people trickled in. They are of all persuasions, old and young, male and female. There is even a small group of children that I assume are orphans. They are led about by three women, and while they appear clean, their clothing looks heavily used. For them, this deck is doubtless the only option. I feel shame for having thought about a private suite.

The feeling is uncommon for me. Typically, I do not think about the less fortunate. Only my dreams.

There is a collective gasp when the lift finally begins to rise. The wall of the building slowly disappears, replaced by the view of the top of the studiopad. Then we float above it. My feet tingle from the experience. It is like walking on air.

Soon the cityscape is laid out before us. Thousands of buildings divided by roads at ground level, and crisscrossed with transport strings above. Everywhere is motion. Trains, autos, and, downriders in the sky.

I do not know CA sector well, but I search for something recognizable. Most evident are the city's handful of temples, their spires colored in purple, blue, and green. Focal points of their communities.

I spot a black TreArc building and a shining silver Aerodel. I mention these to father.

"CA has an Elipserv office, as well." He points to our right, near a circular sports field.

Sure enough, there is a black ellipsoid, a symbol of robotic engineering the world over. I feel very proud of my father, to belong to such a company. Even my friends recognize that my father has the best job of all our fathers. In many ways, he is like creator A, producing machines in man's image. It may be blasphemy to think such a thing. I never say it aloud, but I often feel it.

Gradually the view encompasses more and more of the sector, then expands out to include other sectors as well. I can see the mountains that mark the east end of the sector, and the desert areas beyond that. There are lakes of all shapes and sizes, and the vast ocean on our right, to the west. I begin to see the green of farmlands and smaller cities mixed in, winding rivers, more lakes and forests. Unlike vids I have watched of ancient rocket launches, there is little spin to our motion, little movement left and right. We are only going up. I am glad for that.

It feels like only minutes have passed, but it has been hours. My stomach reminds me of its presence, as does my bladder. Thankfully, the room has a lavatory at the back. I reluctantly excuse myself. I do not want to embarrass myself here. The trip will require hours more. I cannot last that long.

When I return, my father hands me one of the nutrient bars he purchased. I thank him and tear into it. He is a wise man.

The scenery begins to get less distinct, hazy. I can only make out large land forms—the ridge of mountains, the ocean, and the snaking path of several large rivers. The line of the horizon becomes more and more apparent to me. More and more curved. The view becomes more a mix of colors. Brown here, green there, and blue over there. Also the area above the horizon begins to slowly darken. I gasp when I realize how space-like it has become. I search for stars. Space should have stars. But I can't see them yet. I frown.

I glance at my father, only to find him watching me. Has he been doing so the entire time? Is he seeing our trip into space only in my eyes? I notice some of the others in the room then too. The glow of Earth reflected in *their* eyes. I ponder that image for a moment, grappling with what it might mean, but do not find it. I am only a boy.

More time passes. The Earth continues to grow more distant. The horizon continues to curve and darken. My pulse speeds along. I want more of this. To see it all, more so, to get out and feel it. To hold it in my hand and understand. How does it all work? How does it function, yet remain so beautiful?

It is unsettling to be poised above the world. To see my home so far away, so seemingly unreachable. I feel a touch of fear, and of loneliness. I remember a verse about A holding back the sky, about his keeping it from falling on the Earth. Everything seems very fragile to me. Why would A continue to protect the Earth this way? Man is wretched and doomed. There is no guarantee of A's favor, or of his love. He loves only the good. I shake my head at the soberness of it. And the miracle. The sky has not yet fallen.

Finally, the stars become visible. They aren't as clear as I hoped, but they are there. Distant messengers watching us. Light out of nothing. I ease back into my chair, smiling. I rest.

When I awake the room is dim and the view appears static. There is much darkness and the Earth peeks up from the bottom of the window. Are we still moving? Have we arrived?

Many of the seats are empty now, including my father's. I sit up and try to act composed. I feel panicked, though. Where is he? Should I look for him, or stay? I scan the entire room. The orphans are still there, along with their chaperones. But what does that mean? Perhaps they aren't allowed on the station. Perhaps they were only given the lift ride.

Minutes go by as I wait, unsure of what to do. I keep searching the room, and the windows. Certainly there would've been an announcement if we'd arrived? They wouldn't just let a child sleep unattended then return him to Earth? I stand and start moving toward the exit. I don't know what I will do when I reach it. I fear speaking to another guard.

I feel a hand on my shoulder and turn to see my father a step above me. He squints and points at the back of the room. Ah, of course—fathers need breaks too.

The lights in the room flicker, then there is a single chime. "We will soon arrive at the top-end station," a female voice says. "Please collect your belongings and make any remaining purchases. We have fifteen minutes. Thank you."

My fear is forgotten. I feel only expectation now. We have arrived.

Soon we join the rest of the passengers on the causeway that connects the lift to the station. It is sand colored, similar to the blocks of the port below. It is an exhilarating experience. Though the gravity of both the station and the lift are controlled, adjusted through science, the gravity inside the causeway is noticeably less than Earth standard. There are bold signs to that effect, words of caution. I turn to my father. "If they can control gravity, why make it less?"

"I'm certain the designers had their reasons," he says. "Though I would guess it is a reminder."

"Of what?"

"That we are in space. That our submission to gravity has been broken by our submission to A." He points to a verse that is etched in one of the ribbed ceiling supports: *If you can pierce regions of the heavens and the earth, then pierce them! You will not pierce them save with a Power.*

I grin. Yes, we would pierce the heavens. We already have.

We reach a portion of the causeway that freezes me. There are windows in the floor! I can see the entire circle of the Earth below me. Oceans and continents. Cloud patterns. Blue, brown, green, and white. It is incredible. Reduced gravity pales in comparison to this marvel. What other reminder was needed? We are in space! I find myself on my knees, hands pressed against the floor.

My father stoops beside me. "Son, we must keep moving. There are people—"

"Look," I say, pointing. "It is all there. Everything we've known. There is our continent, and our country. Our sector—"

"Son."

"It is as if someone could hold it in their arms. So fragile."

"Yes. But we have another place to be. Something for me to show you." He sounds concerned. "Quickly, before the guards drive us away."

I force myself to stand. What could be better than this? What more is there to see?

We exit the causeway and wind through the station halls. The station itself is very plain. White halls and white floors. Perhaps that was intentional. What sketching of man could compete with what is now outside? What combination of paint, or draw of pen? And what subject could compare? Would a uniformed soldier, or a head-wrapped imam? A landscape? A posed animal? All trivial and lifeless.

"Many luxury yachts leave from this station," father says. "Most of those on the lift have other destinations. Equatorial cruises or skips across the poles."

"But not us," I say.

"No," he says. "I've brought you to this."

I see another white door with a control pad next to it. He touches the pad and the door opens. I realized it is an elevator. The interior is primarily blue. We ride to the upper floor. The door opens into another circular room, an observatory. There are windows all the way around. There is a scattering of other people in the room, but they are easy to ignore. It is like I've been handed my own universe.

"Is this the surprise?" I don't wait for a response. I only hurry into the room. The first thing I notice, the primary focus for me, is the wide expanse of Darb Al-Tabanah, the Milky Way. It stretches through multiple windows. Stars upon stars, brothers of our sun, locked together by mutual attraction. It is overwhelming, the sight.

My father trails me as I move from one window to the next, taking it all in. I search for the constellations I know, but nothing looks familiar. All the stars seem brighter, consequently no clear patterns emerge. Thankfully, there are stellar guides—semi-interactive vidscreens—near the ceilings and floors that show what celestial body is where. With their help I am able to find Al-Maisan and the small cluster Ath-Thuraya.

On one side of the observatory, the Moon is visible. It is in its crescent stage, yet still bright enough to obscure the faint stars around it. The view of the moon is excellent, it's craters and mares distinct and vivid.

I spend only a short time looking at its bleakness, though. The image of the crescent so dominated my world below, that it troubles me to look at it in this room. Especially when there are bright stars elsewhere. It is a silent and lonely distraction from everything else. I can't understand why someone would want to go there. Or live there. They would have to be desperate indeed.

From there I move on, finding Ibet al-Jauza' and the triple star system Rijl al-Jabbar, also known as Rigel. I stared at Rigel a long time, hopeful that my twelve-year-old eyes might split the solitary light into its three component stars. Alas, I cannot. It remains a single blue-white object. I drift some more.

After an hour has gone by, I feel my legs beginning to tire. There are comfortable-looking benches near the center of the room, so I find a seat there. The view from the bench, thankfully, is still very good.

My father approaches, and handing me another nutrient bar, takes a seat next to me. "You like all this?"

"I do, father," I say. "Very much. Thank you for bringing me."

He nods, and brings out a bar for himself. "It is good we have come here. That we can spend this time." He takes a bite of his bar, and chewing, looked ahead at the stars.

"Have you been here before?" I ask.

He smiles. "Many times," he said. "When I need to think about important things, I come here."

The revelation warms me. To know that father and I share this love, along with our love of mother, was important.

He gives me a serious look. "We should speak about an important thing now."

The pleasantness in my chest begins to dissipate. I sense the conversation taking a personal turn.

"I have spoken with your instructors."

Now the warmth has left completely. I bow my head. "They are good men. I am honored to have their teaching."

"Yes, you are," he says. "And they are paid well for their services."

The trip is not what it seemed. It is something else. Something unexpected.

My father remains coy. He points toward the windows. "The stars, what *are* they?"

I focus on a spot on his chest, the lowest button in his jubba. "A's messengers to us," I say. "Silent observers of his blessings."

Father frowns, and shakes his head. "No, I mean, what are they? What are they composed of?"

A test of my knowledge? I straighten, eager to show what I have learned. "They are mostly hydrogen and helium. Through fusion, hydrogen is made into helium. The process produces both light and heat."

"Yes," he says. "They contain powerful energy, the stars and our sun. Balls of heat and plasma. A danger to all around them. Like a bomb. A weapon."

"That is untrue, father."

"What is untrue, son?"

"The danger is not like a bomb."

He looks perplexed. "It is not? And why is that?"

I hold my fingers like I am clutching a ball. "Gravity. Gravity binds them together. Holds the fire in. Keeps it contained."

He raises a finger. "Ah, very good. So, the stars are energy, contained."

I realize what the trip is about. It is the play my friends and I engage in. Sometimes it is rough, reckless. There have been injuries. None too bad, though. Not unusual for boys our age. And we are the good boys, the ones everyone wanted to be like. Not followers. Leaders! "Yes, father," I say.

"I am told that you are belittling others. That you are putting yourself above them."

I almost gasp with surprise. I shake my head. "We only have fun. We do no harm."

He points at the windows. "So you are like a star then? You and your friends? Contained?"

The stars are forgotten to me. I only bow my head again. There is a long moment of silence.

Father sighed. "You recognized the debuggers below. The data relocators. They are more like stars than anyone. Everything is contained and controlled." He paused. "They are without sin, did you know? Their place in paradise guaranteed."

I get an image of The Bamboo and suck in my breath. Is this how it happens, then? How boys disappear? They get into trouble and—?

I glance around the room, trying to see if there was someone who fit The Bamboo's description. That monstrous man. Always watching for the right boys to take.

"What troubles you?" father asked. "What are you looking for?"

My throat tightens. I find it difficult to speak. "I am sorry," I whisper. "I meant no harm."

"I trust you did not," he says. "But actions have consequences."

My eyes are wide, but I say nothing.

He looks at me a long moment. "I count on you to be aware of this from now on," he says then. "Of others."

"I will," I say. "I promise." Don't send me anywhere.

He leans close. "Someday, someday soon, we will go to the stars. Would you like that?"

I glanced around us again. There is still no sign of the boy stealer. I begin to feel better. I hope he isn't waiting elsewhere. "To out there?" I ask.

"To wherever a ship can go."

I look at the stars again, finding Rigel and the other lights near it. "Of course," I say. "I would love that."

"You must be a star to reach them, son. That is the only way."

I nod, but I am still confused. "You said the debuggers are stars..."

He gives me a quizzical look. "Yes, but they are made by others. I would rather you make yourself." He balls a hand. "Strength and power, contained. Can you remember?"

I relaxed my posture, feeling relief. "Yes."

I *would* remember. I always would.

I EXIT THE CHUTE and find the breakfast the food conditoner has already made me. It smells remarkably good this morning. I feel good. Better. The datamix helped. The stars and dreams of a young boy. I eat quickly, hungrily.

Only a few years ago I had other dreams too. I wanted to build things like this boy's father. I wanted to create the unknown.

I dress and make my way downstairs to the garage.

There is another heavybot awaiting repair. I know it wasn't there last night. It must've come in while I slept.

Another already? My good feelings start to dissipate. Can I go back to the chute? The nightmare I tried to escape somehow found me anyway. I don't want a heavy today, anything but a heavy.

As I draw closer I realize that the bot is a troop transport vehicle, not the offensive weapon I repaired yesterday. There is a large rectangular back portion. It has a similar front end and robot "head" but the rest is very different. I might be able to make it through this one. As long as it doesn't need a pos unit.

I contemplate contacting Front. I usually do after a mix. He always wants a review of what I've seen.

The boy became a debugger anyway, right? Regardless of his fears and his dreams. That's a conclusion I can't escape—otherwise, Front wouldn't have the mix at all. Mixes are only for us, for debuggers. No one else could produce them.

Plus, there's the fact that the mix's owner is now offline, presumably dead.

I felt good a few minutes ago.

I sigh. The garage smells especially greasy today. I let my eyes sweep the place—the wall of tools on my right, the workbench in front of it, the large door, and then the small door and assorted piles of castaway parts on my left.

Where is the cleaning bot? It looks like a mechanical aardvark, with four, short legs and a long, tapered head. It should at least be adjusting the scent in here. Keeping it breathable so that I don't pass out. I finally find it nestled in a corner of the ceiling. It looks dead.

I stream out to it, but I get no response. Dead, dead, dead. Rails. I look over the place again. How will I reach it now? Do I even have a ladder?

I stream open the garage door. New air begins to flow in. It stinks, but at least it is new stink. The water in this part of town sometimes has an odor. I think that's what I smell.

I walk around the heavy, still not interested in starting. I try to keep my eyes from its treads. I don't want to think about those. About the crunching sounds they make as they roll along the earth. About the popping...

My face flushes and I start to feel ill. I shake my head and look toward the doorway. It seems small and far away. I force air into my lungs. Large breaths. In and out. I walk toward the opening feeling really weak. Sand is blowing in again. Lots of sand.

Finally, I reach the doorway. I grab the side and steady myself, looking at the ground. The nausea seems to be passing. I'm all right. Breathing. Feeling better now. I push my eyes away from the ground to the street. I notice the cracks in the permacrete. Same ole cracks.

I find the building across from mine. Aside from the larger garage door, it could be a twin of my building. Of course, here I fix machines of death, and in it...well, things happen that I'm not allowed to think about. Plus, there are women involved and that makes me feel strange. A different kind of unsettled.

The door of the brothel opens and a man steps out. He is dressed in a solid green suit. Very shiny. A partially covered woman follows him. Her top half is wrapped in black, completely concealed, but her legs—her *bare* legs—are exposed at the knees.

She has one arm hooked around him, grasping him lovingly. That hand lingers over him as he takes a step away. He looks back at her and nods. She releases her hold completely and returns the nod, followed by a wave. He turns his back and walks away. The woman with the legs remains at the door, watching him go.

I feel uncomfortable again. I should return to my work, to the heavy. But I don't want to. I'm here, out here, because I'm trying to breathe. To survive.

The woman notices me. I freeze, trying to blend into the doorway, into the sand, but she still sees me. She brings her legs close together, almost shyly, and looks at me: the debugger with the green face and the blue jumpsuit.

I feel more ill now. I also sense a tingle in my head. The start of a headbuzz, a mind stop, but I'm not sure why. I only know I need to go...back to work.

She is still watching me. Why doesn't she go back inside? With her legs. Someone will see her.

She raises her hand—that same grasping, loving hand—and waves at me.

My face flushes. I notice her legs again. My stop intensifies, causing me to wince and look at the ground. I slink around the corner and stream the door closed. It clanks its way to obedience. The smell of grease enfolds me.

My brain is a minefield filled with random body parts. Legs and heads, all buried in sand. I search for my implant diagnostic, find it, and think of a rainbow in reverse and pair-swapped order to get it started. A full minute goes by. I simply breathe.

The diagnostic completes. The implant is fine. Up-to-date and fully functional. I wish I could say the same about me. I look at the heavybot. It has the Imam's yellow ellipsis stamped right on the side of its head. The mark is much bigger than it should be. Almost garish, like a child painted it on.

"Why are you here?" I yell. "What do you want!"

The bot's head swivels to look at me.

Hell comes next.

FIRST I HEAR A WHISTLE.

My mind jumps to a vid I watched once. It was about goat herders near a mountain range. One of the older and more experienced herders used a long, shrill whistle to bring the herd together. After a few seconds all these brown, horned animals appeared from the crags and the rocks. They quickly made their way to him. Bleating and excited.

After the whistle comes thunder, and cracking sounds. Things breaking and falling. Pops and rumbles. The ground pitches, then the door behind me makes this awful retching sound. I find myself flying, uncontrollably, toward the heavy. My body slams into its treads, and for a moment I look right into its soulless eyes. Then I drop to the ground.

"What is this?" I say, over and over. All the lights are out, but light from the outside is getting in. Possibly the door is gone.

There are tendrils of smoke in the air now. I hear the bot's head move. I also hear something burning, though I don't think it is nearby. It is from outside, behind me somewhere. I try to sit up, but I have no strength.

"It was a Solac Bridgebreaker missile," the bot says. "Model 153-432, rev D."

"A missile?" I say. "Did it hit us? Is it here?"

I hear movement inside the garage somewhere. Not from the heavy, but somewhere in the dark recesses beyond it. An isolated clank. Something dropped.

"It did not," the heavy says. "It impacted roughly thirty meters from here. The Model 153-432, rev D has limited blast range. It is used by the insurgents because it can be built cheaply using scavenged parts. It is rarely precise."

I groan, try to move again, but can't. I might be seriously hurt. I don't think I'm bleeding, but my muscles aren't moving. I enable the emergency beacon in my head. I tell them to look for the crater. I'm hoping they'll find me. Concerned messages from other debuggers start to pour in. FrontLot is first in the queue. Good ole FrontLot.

I hear more movement in the garage. I also hear the rafters wheeze and creak. I don't like either sound. I try to roll over onto my stomach. Doesn't happen.

I shut my eyes and try to focus. I again touch the stream, looking for information. I start to see news feeds of the event. First there are concerned men talking about it, then there are shots of a city block, my block, and a cloud of smoke billowing out of it.

"Where are the sky-eyes?" I say to no one. "I want to see from above."

If I can't move for too long, will my body stop functioning? Will the unused appendages fall off? Will I be only a head when help arrives? I can't fix bots as a head. They'll take my implant. I don't want to be a scar! I don't want it out!

I hear sirens in the distance. Through my implant I track them. They are coming, but they are many blocks away.

I hear another rattle and a thump. Then a scratching sound. Are there rats in here? I would hate to be gnawed by a rat. Whatever it is, it is getting closer. Scritch, scritch, scritch, clank.

Clank? What new abomination has the explosion made?

A few seconds later the cleaning bot walks out where I can see him. One of its legs is stuck inside something—maybe a motivator shell. The bot's head swivels in a complete circle. Its eyes pan over the heavy, and then past me toward the devastation by the door. It seems to pause there for a moment, then hurries that direction. Clanking all the way.

I hear the whirring sound of its vacuum.

"Rails. *Now* it is cleaning."

I'm starting to feel pain in my extremities—an itching, burning intensity. I start to whimper. To sob.

There are sounds outside now—human voices. I slowly turn my

head and manage to position it so I can see the door. It is worse than I thought. The door is bulged like it is pregnant. There is light streaming in on both sides of it. The cleaning bot is working near the right side, sucking up the sand. There is a lot of sand. I see shadows moving past the breaks in the door. I call out to them, but it is difficult. My voice is raspy and soft. The pain is getting worse.

There is a thump on the garage door. I try to yell at the thump, to say "I'm here" but it comes out as more of a low hiss. Not loud enough.

Suddenly everything is burning. I can't speak, all I can do is breathe. And even that hurts. *Here, here, I'm in here.* There is more banging on the door. I'm hopeful.

"Someone is coming, debugger," the heavy says. "What are your orders?"

Orders? Does it think we're in a battle now?

Pain, pain, can't escape it.

The heavy's head moves again, then I think I hear one of its armaments extending.

"No!" I stream to it. "Shut down. Reset. Go back."

I hear it move again.

Then I black out.

• • •

I dream of flying heads.

They float amidst clouds of sand. They spin and turn, these human ellipses, drifting aloft before sinking again. They soar over the silver city. Sometimes they zoom low to circle the spires of the temples, but usually they simply drift on the wind currents. They are all different colors, every face. Blue, green, and red.

Dreams are strange outside the chute.

I zero in on one head that is spinning atop the largest spire in the city. A purple dome. The image grows closer and closer. The face is grey, almost deathly so. I can't figure out who it is, whether it is someone I know. Then I realize.

It is me.

MY EYES OPEN.

I'm in a white hospital room. Positioned above me is this large, silver spider-like device. It has a long central portion and lots of appendages. I let out a clipped yell before realizing I know what it is. It is an implantation device. An implanter. It has been four years since the last time I saw one. It is the villain of my first nightmare.

I notice a chirping sound, a meek siren, and I try to sit up. I feel pain, but also the tug of restraints at my wrists and ankles. What is this?

I call out, and this time I hear my voice forming whole and recognizable words. Phrases like "Help me," "Stop it," and "Let me go." There is some comfort in that. I can move, and I can speak.

Aside from my bed and the spider, the room is nearly empty. There is a rolling stool and two closed doors.

I yell again.

A thin, bald man walks in, and smiles briefly. He is often in my dreams. Today he wears a white robe.

"Bamboo...?"

He nods. "DR 23, is that correct?" He has a crescent-shaped device in one hand. An implant controller, doubtless set for my implant. He slips that into a pocket on his robe.

"Yes."

"I apologize for not remembering you." He gives me a stern look. "You are much too young to have such a low number. I know you're not first generation."

"Third," I say. "You said I was third."

He raises an eyebrow. "I told you that? During your initial procedure?" He glances at the implanter. The machine swivels and a narrow leg descends. It stops three inches from my left eye.

"Yes," I say, staring at the leg.

"Keep your eyes open, please." A beam of light exits the end of the leg. My left eye is flooded with brilliance, the light abates, then the flood returns. The same process is followed with the right eye. Finally, the leg ascends again.

"I'm just confirming, 23. Making sure there is no head trauma." Bamboo gives me a tight smile. "You'll be happy to know—at least, I'm happy to know—that the container for your implant looks free of injury. A was gracious to you."

"I hurt everywhere," I say. "Everything hurts."

He nods. "Yes, the doctors say you're badly bruised. That was quite the explosion. Your spine was pinched, but the pain means you are on the mend. You will be scrambling over machines in no time. Again, you were fortunate."

He looks directly at me and his face grows reflective. "I am sending you something…"

An active image appears in my head. Bouncing shapes in different colors: a green triangle, a blue rhombus, an orange icosahedron. I describe them aloud in full detail. Next come numbers, then whole words. He nods after every answer.

"Now send me something," he says.

I send him a portion of my dream. The spinning head.

His eyes widen. "A spinning head? Quite disturbing."

I shrug. "First thing I thought of." I'll never forget the heads.

He grabs the rolling stool and pulls it close to the bed. He sits and looks at me pensively.

A full minute of silence goes by. I know not to say anything. The one thing Bamboo taught us was absolute respect. First for him, and then for all masters.

Finally, he sighs. "I looked over your work logs, ThreadBare. They're not as impressive as I might have hoped for someone with your number of years. You should've leveled up by now. Do you sense a problem with your device? A blockage, perhaps?"

I feel shame. "No," I say.

"Is there anything that is hindering you in any way?"

I resist the urge to look at my chest. Bamboo doesn't reward meekness. Submission, yes. But not meekness. "I have completed every assignment given me." I've tried really hard.

"Yes, but the time it takes...it is difficult, personality is difficult to factor for." He sighs again. "All types have made adequate debuggers, of course. But finding the right formula, the right balance for an outstanding one..." He shakes his head. "Difficult. And you passed all the tests."

"I am...one of many," I say. "The Imam's—"

"Forgotten? Is that your excuse?" He frowns. Glances at the implanter. "I contemplated removing your device while you were here. It would be interesting to examine it microscopically. I rarely do post-implantation reviews."

I shake my head. Removal is shame. And it is dangerous. Most never return to normal.

He looks pensive. "Would you like that? You would be human again. You would age naturally. You could pursue another profession. Take a wife..."

"I don't want to be normal," I say. "Even if I'm the worst debugger, at least I'm something."

"You are lying to me, 23. I have skimmed your logs."

The shame returns. No one should have their head opened for others to see. No heart should be so displayed. It is why I never share personal mixes. One of the reasons, anyway.

"You have nothing to say for yourself? What about your neighbors? The woman with the legs?"

There is a pain-filled lump in the middle of my chest. A large and hairy lump.

Bamboo watches me for a long moment, saying nothing. Then he places a hand on my head. "Relax, ThreadBare, I know it hurt you, this temptation. The stops worked as they should." He removes his hand. "You'll have that worry no longer."

I feel more unsettled. What did he do while I was out? What else did he alter?

"You should check the news stream. Test your implant."

What does that mean? I follow his bidding, pulling all the headlines from the hours since I've been gone. Everything that has been reported since I lay beside the heavy. The missile is the big news for the city. There are hundreds of photos. Thousands of words. I see the image of the streets and the pillar of smoke. Another of people running in fear. Then I see a shot from overhead. I focus on it, zooming in my mind. It takes a few seconds to find my garage, the buildings look so similar. But then I find it. There are sear marks even on top, places where the explosion scarred. But my building is generally intact. In fact, the impact was further from me than I thought. The street, though strewn with rubble, is no more cracked than it ever was.

But the building across the street, the place of prostitution, is decimated. There is an impact crater, a small circle with incredibly smooth looking sides, and around it only rubble. I have to look hard to even see where the walls might have been. There are only piles of indiscernible refuse. Nothing I could identify. Only sticks and stone.

"Seven were killed," Bamboo says. "Five in the building across from yours."

I open my eyes. Bamboo is smiling.

"A tragedy for the victims certainly. But to quote the scriptures, 'A slew them, and those shafts were A's not thine.'"

I try to meet his eyes. "It is so written."

"And you knew no one there, so you are unaffected, yes?"

I nod again, but say nothing. Unaffected? How could I not be affected? Legs and heads.

"Good," he says. "Excellent. Because it seems your situation has changed."

I glance at the silver machine. "Changed?"

He releases the restraints on my arms and legs, and rolls away from the bed. "Yes, you will gain a level."

"A level—?" Up? I'm moving up?

He stands. "You are a twelve now. It too has been written."

I raise up in my bed. There is pain, but also satisfaction at having managed it. "Why?" I say. "For what?"

Bamboo slides a hand into the same pocket as the controller, but doesn't take the device out. I have a hard time not flinching, anyway. The controller can bring pain at any moment.

82

"Despite my reservations, it has been so ordained. By the Imam himself."

"The Imam?"

Now he brings the controller out. Cradles it lovingly in his palm. "Your efforts have been noticed." He lifts a shoulder. "I too am surprised. But often my pupils surprise me. Again, the variables. The complexity."

I don't know what to say. I am a forest of emotion, with dissimilar trees sprouting everywhere.

"You will have a new address, of course. The garage needs repair, but even if it did not, you will not be occupying it."

Did BullHammer have something to do with this? Or Front? "Where will I be?"

"In the palace of the elder prince." He feigns a smile. "Congratulations, 23. You are no longer forgotten. Let us hope you don't wish you were again." He raises the controller. "Now, we need a final test before I release you."

What follows is both pain, and pleasure.

A DAY LATER I AM fully recovered, able to walk as a young man again. Though Bamboo was direct and often harsh, his medbots, the true nurturers of his facility, restored me. They stretched, massaged, and infused me back to limberness.

I'm seated at a table in my room and have just finished my afternoon meal, when one of the medbots walks in. It is a bipedal model, dressed in a green tunic and pants. It has a pale face that approximates that of a human. It is too smooth and shiny to be mistaken as human. This is as far as the rules will let us go in robotic design. Any further, any closer to humanity, would be an affront to A.

"It is your time to leave, DR 23," the bot says.

I push my plate aside and fold my hands together on the table. "Is Master Bamboo coming?"

The bot, RS-3729, shakes its head. "You should go now."

I stand, but I'm perplexed. "Bamboo will not deliver me?" When I received my first assignment, I was escorted by Bamboo. It has always been that way.

"No. You will have instructions when you need them. I am providing a map of the building for you now. I can escort you to the door, if you like."

I touch the bot via the stream. As it says, there is a map of Bamboo's facility floating in its memory. But that is all.

What do I do when I reach the street? Find a downrider pylon and joyride? It is the only idea that brings comfort. I have no place to go aside from the garage. And I don't want to see it, or the building across from it, again.

"I will be fine," I say.

The bot watches me leave. Five minutes later I am at the front door. The door is transparent, so I can see the sidewalk and street beyond. There is an endless stream of foot traffic. The street is congested, as well.

Bamboo's facility is near the center of the sector. The princes have many palaces, but most of them are a sector west. Am I to simply pick one?

I stare at the press of people. I don't want to go out into it, even to find a downrider pylon. How was I delivered before? Did we walk the streets together, Bamboo and I? I don't remember. At least, not biologically.

I contemplate turning around and seeking Bamboo out. That would only cement his uncertainty in me, though. His doubts.

Am I really assigned to the prince? It doesn't seem possible. Was it Bull's doing?

A message tickles my brain. I grab it and scan the digital envelope. It bears a variation of the Imam's seal. A yellow ellipsis with a single blue star in the middle.

I flip the message open. It is from my new submaster, Jahm. He is in the service of the prince. His message says to wait where I am.

Ten minutes later I hear a loud whooping sound. There is a ripple in the tide of people and vehicles outside. Many swerve and start to run.

A large transport arrives. It is green, nearly three meters high, and armored to the point that I think it might withstand the blast that damaged my garage. The whooping siren repeats and the pace of pedestrian traffic increases to near panic.

Three men, all dressed in black, exit the vehicle. They are carrying lethals. They look carefully in all directions, then one of them comes to the door.

I'm afraid.

"Are you DR 23?" the man asks. He is a half meter taller than me. Goliath-like.

I nod cautiously.

He puts out a hand. "Come with me." He doesn't touch me, but he seems to be fighting the urge.

I follow his lead. Outside, the other two giants surround me. The vehicle's side door opens, and I'm hurried inside.

The interior is red and lavish. The seats are large and soft, covered in leather. There is a frail-looking, older man present. I take a seat across from him and one of the large men sits next to him. The door slams shut.

The older man smiles. "I am Jahm, the prince's servant. You are DR 23? ThreadBare?"

I nod. The fingers of Jahm's right hand are stained. A cross-reference of the image suggests the stains are from tobacco use. The servant has a forbidden habit, or at least had one at some time. Curious.

The large man pounds on the ceiling. The siren sounds again and the vehicle begins to move.

"We are going to the prince's country estate," Jahm says.

"By ground?" I ask.

"Yes, I prefer to travel this way," Jahm says. "Call me a lover of history." He smiles, then indicates the vehicle and the man sitting next to him. "I apologize for all these...precautions. Despite our Imam's benevolence, there are always some who hate. Some who would take him or his sons away from us."

I attempt to keep my eyes away from the windows. So many people.

Jahm seems transfixed by the outside view. "It is a nice estate, the country one. You will be happy."

In truth, I am happier already. I start to believe the scriptures: No person shows forbearance but A will honor him, and no one is humble for A's sake but A will raise him in status.

The way starts to clear outside and Jahm's eyes turn toward me. "The prince takes his property seriously. He did not want you misplaced or misguided."

"I'm honored by his regard," I say.

Jahm smiles subtly. "Yes, you should be. Be mindful that you always are. You are being rewarded."

My recent terrors fade. It is difficult not to be excited, not to be overwhelmed. I remember Bull's image of himself near a palace. I can imagine what that feels like, to sit freely in the grass so. It would be better than the best vid. The best datamix.

"If I may ask," I say. "How was I chosen for this reward?"

Jahm covers his mouth and coughs. "You were recommended by a member of the royal family. For your service."

I can't hide my surprise. "The royal family?"

Jahm nods, then opens a panel on the wall next to him. There is a large box of smokesticks there. He pulls a stick out and holds it to his lips. The large man lights it for him and Jahm takes a long drag before puffing out small clouds of pollution. "Yes, one of the prince's cousins is a general. Uday is his name. Uday Abbas."

I think back to my time in Delusion. The officers in the tent. Was one of them named Uday? I think so. Then I remember the heavy. The heads. I shift in my seat and try to feel settled. It is difficult.

The smoking bothers me too. I know the soldiers were given otherwise illicit privileges for their service. They live in danger.

But Jahm? Someone so close to royalty?

He *is* old. Possibly too valuable not to so oblige. Or too timeworn to retrain. He's a freehead, after all.

The smoke starts to afflict my nostrils. I try to avoid the offensive substance, to seek the air that is unaffected, but it is difficult. Tendrils reach everywhere. I catch the wrong breath and fight off a coughing attack.

Jahm notices my displeasure, and frowns. "Our young skin does not like my smoke. How foolish of me." He waves at the other man. "Saad, a window."

Saad shakes his head. "It is forbidden in the city," he says. "Security, sir."

Jahm looks irritated. "Enable the air system then."

Saad flips a switch overhead. I hear the noise of vents opening, but no new air is introduced. I attempt to touch our vehicle in the stream. There is a long list of errors in its log. Multiple entries for the air system. Figures.

"That doesn't seem to be working." Jahm looks at me. "Do you know what the problem is?" he asks, then smiles. "Oh, of course you do. Can you fix it?"

I feel the absence of my bag and scan the vehicle for it. It isn't here. It is still at the garage. "I do not have the means to fix it, Submaster. My bag is—"

Jahm fans the air. "It is no matter. You will have all you need soon. All the accessories." He stubs the smokestick on his armrest. "See, there, I will put it out." He nods. "Debuggers are my responsibility. Forgive me. Sometimes I get lazy." He brings his hands up. "It is not usually done this way, of course. Usually they come as a group." He pauses to smile. "The palace gets the first ten from every class, did you know this?"

I shake my head.

"Well, it is so." He looks outside again. We are near the edge of the city. The buildings are only single story. "Now, I would like a nap. I suggest you take one too. We have time, and you will be busy." He leans against the wall and shuts his eyes.

I watch the big man, Saad, thinking he might talk to me now. He regards me for a few seconds before turning toward the window. Minutes of silence go by.

I lean back and close my eyes. I try to contact BullHammer.

I get no response.

I feel strangely alone.

THE LAST LEG OF OUR journey is wondrous.

We pass large fields growing grain, all of them administered by robotic implements—I sense each one as we pass. Next comes kilometers of manicured grass. This is tended by a mixture of bots and human servants. I glimpse some of the latter, distinguishable by the head coverings they wear. Rarely does a bot need those.

We reach a large, octagonal lake. It is sapphire blue and appears pristine. It is clearly manmade, and after a few seconds of traveling across it, I realize it is not a lake but a moat. In the center of the expanse of water is a small island, and in the center of that is a beige building with five sides and large, triple-story arches all the way around. It is the most impressive building I've ever seen.

A bridge over the lake brings us to the front of the house. It is even grander up close. The largest of the arches is in the center, and there are two smaller but-no-less-impressive arches on either side of it. At equidistant positions around the house large shade trees grow.

There is a wide and level permacrete drive around the whole structure. Our vehicle turns right and we circle the palace for many meters that way, passing two full sides. Each side is as impressive as the last. The brickwork on each arch is intricate, with multiple levels of detail. Adjoining arches are partially demarcated by large pillars. Past the arches is a secondary exterior wall with large rectangular openings.

I glance at Jahm again. He is awake and watching me.

"Majestic, is it not?"

"Yes," I say. "Impressive."

The guard, Saad, slides forward in his seat, acting nervous. The vehicle comes to a stop and he hops out, closing the door behind him. The other two giants join him there at the side of the car. They cluster together, talking and adjusting their apparel. They look all directions and say things I cannot hear.

Saad opens the door again and waves me out. Jahm and I are escorted through one of the arches, to an ornate and gold-tinged double door. It swings open as we reach it.

"That is you," Jahm says. "It is responding to your implant. Every door you can enter will respond so."

I bow and together with Saad, we enter. The other two men remain outside.

The inside of the building is no less spectacular. We enter a circular foyer with a ceiling fully three meters over my head and a large chandelier. The floor is polished marble and there is an inlaid plaque that speaks of the heavens being A's footstool. Beyond the foyer is a double staircase, with rails accented in gold. The design of the stairway is such that the outside edges look like two W's on end and back to back. And this is not the primary entrance. What must that look like?

The stream in the building is especially vivid and responsive. It is like stepping into a waterfall. Information envelopes me. For fun I attempt to enumerate all the stream-sensitive machines in the building. There are 8423. Many of them are thinking bots, of the types that I might be called on to repair. Medbots, cleaning bots, servbots, and a handful that are either beyond my level, or marked as proprietary. I feel a little overwhelmed.

I again attempt to contact BullHammer. This time he answers Extended Easy, which means I get text, but also his voice like he is reading to me. He sounds a little creaky and worn. I might have woken him from a nap. "Give me twenty minutes," he says, then ends the conversation.

Rude.

Meanwhile, Jahm is rambling on about the palace's facilities and technology. There are lots of smiles and gesturing. I can't believe he works with debuggers on a daily basis, because if he really understood us, he would know that everything he is telling me I either already know, or could learn in a millisecond. I nod along anyway, trying my best to look attentive.

It is difficult for all the palace's wonders. There is gold and silver everywhere, and even the ceilings of the rooms are marvelous. Many are adorned with artwork, painted images from history. Battles that had been won or temples that have been built. My eyes always want to drift upward, yet Jahm continues to talk.

Eventually he brings me to a room with a green and gold arched door. The center third of the door is completely gold and at the top of that section is a raised golden circle that reminds me of an eye.

"This will be your quarters." He indicates the door, then nods and looks at me.

I wait, expecting him to open it, but he continues to look at me.

Finally, he smiles and touches his head. "It is coded to your ident. Push at it."

Blinking stupid, Thread. By focusing I can sense the door's presence in the stream. It is there waiting for me, and I missed it. I send it an open request. It immediately snaps open.

The room beyond is larger than my loft in the garage, with all the amenities a debugger, or any freehead, might need. It is arranged much like a studio apartment. There is a kitchen area to the left of the door, and a lounging area straight ahead. To the right is a sleep chute. It is sleek, black, and rails shiny. It is this year's model, constructed only a month ago. The room's floor is tiled, but with large rugs in the lounge area, and under the chute. The ceiling is painted here too. It has a scene of a large boat with many animals.

Noah's Ark again? How strange.

"Will it do?" Jahm asks.

"I'm not to be with other debuggers?" I ask. "I've heard that—"

"Just you," Jahm says. "It will be just you here."

"But there must be dozens of us on the property." I hope I'm not the only one. Over 8000 bots, remember?

"There are, but the prince requires a debugger close at hand. You will be that for him."

That doesn't seem right. "Why would I be?" I ask. "I'm only level twelve. Certainly a higher level ʺ

Jahm stops me with a wave. "You are exactly what the prince requires. The exact level for this job. Do not fear." He coughs into his hand. "Now. I should leave you to adjust. I will send requests as I get them. Unless the prince asks himself, of course. Then do exactly what he says."

"Yes," I say. "My stops would require it."

"Please don't make me use the controller."

"Of course not."

Jahm bows and makes a step toward the door. He then looks troubled, pauses, and raises a finger. "Before I forget." He leads me to a pair of doors on the wall near the entrance and swings them open. Behind them are shelves filled with debugging tools—everything from sheets to nanoscanners. There is also a durable-looking debugger bag hanging there. "This should get you started," he says.

I pull the bag out and look inside. It is already stocked. It feels lighter than the bag I'm used to and it smells clean. Grease-free. I can't help but smile. "This will do fine," I say. "Thank you."

Jahm bows again and scurries to the door. "I will leave you now."

I STARE AT MY SUPPLY cabinet for twelve full minutes. Everything is so straight and clean-looking. Canisters, boxes, and wrapped instruments all in rows and stacked nicely. Ready to go at a moment's notice.

What did I do to deserve this?

I completed the tasks I was given. Played my role despite my reservations. Now, I'm here.

I don't deserve any of it. People died. Lots of people died.

Not by my hand. By A's will! I'm a debugger. I *have* to do what I'm told. I wanted to be noticed. Now look! A's reward! I should be happy. I will be happy. I push the conflict away. The images and sounds. The Delusion. I force a smile.

I spend the next twenty minutes simply walking through the room looking for dirt. I find none. Plus, everything works as it should. I even have my food conditioner create a pancake. The process is nearly instantaneous, and the cake tastes wonderful. This foodcon is about half the width of the one I had at the garage, and it isn't boxy in any way. It has an hourglass shape. Wider at the floor and at the top. It is about chest high. The entire machine is silver except the dispensing platform which has a transparent shell. I'm sure it is the best credits can buy.

It doesn't seem real. Maybe I'm still dreaming following the explosion? Is that possible? I've heard of early implantees, those from late Tanzer days, who sometimes lost track of reality. They walked around in a trance, barely able to interact with the outside world. Eventually they became vegetative, unable to care for themselves. Trapped within their head.

They all had faulty implants that leaked fluid into their brainpan. Something like that is going to cause problems. Leaky teardrops—bad! That problem hasn't been around for decades, right? I check the stream to be certain. No implant leakages in forty years. So I should be safe there.

Bull wanted me to message him again. It's been over twenty minutes.

I try to contact him. He answers Standard Impact this time, but I wish he would've answered at a lower setting. His eyes are darkened and his clothes, his standard blue jumpsuit, is heavily wrinkled.

"What do you want, Thread?" Bull is standing somewhere, though the lighting is dim. I think I see a grey couch behind him.

"Sorry for waking you."

He snorts a laugh. "Didn't wake me. I've been up all night. I think my chute is busted."

"Sorry again," I say. "I wanted to...thank you, I guess."

"Thank me?" He squints, focusing on my image. "For what?"

"Your encouragement. I—"

"Wait..." Bull's eyes widen. "Where are you?"

I raise my hands, smiling. "At my new master's home."

"You're not working for the Imam? Voltaire, how does that happen?"

"I'm still working for him," I say. "I got transferred. After the garage got hit—"

"The garage got hit?" He frowns. "Where have I been?" His eyes close. "Oh rails, now I see the reports. That looks...bad." He opens his eyes again. "Were you hurt?"

I raise a shoulder. "A little. But I'm fine now."

He grunts. "Place might take a while to fix. Are you going back?"

"I don't think so, no." I raise my hands and turn slowly around. "I'm here now. At the prince's palace."

"The prince? Which prince?"

"The elder," I say. "Bamboo said it was the elder."

"Bamboo said?" Bull starts to move around whatever room he is in. I see another debugger lounging in a stuffed chair and another standing at a food conditioner. I'm guessing it is the shared debugger quarters. The images are composites of what he sees, I know. The implant's approximations based on retinal downloads. If Bull wanted, he could make himself look like he's walking on the ocean, or through the middle of a battlefield. "You saw Bamboo? How is he?"

"The same."

Bull's face gets serious. "You remember how he trained us?"

I can't forget how he trained us. It was strenuous and filled with pain. It made me both respect and hate him. Not that that matters.

"All of it was important," Bull says. "Even the hard stuff." He's in another room now. One with bright colors and what appears to be a lit fireplace. "You'll need it, I think. All of it."

"Why?"

His eyes avert. I think he is receiving another message. Then to confirm my assumption, he says "Listen, I have to go. Gotta debug." He is walking again. There is effort in his voice. "I've heard things about the elder, Thread."

"What?"

"Just be mindful. But otherwise, yeah, you stepped right over me. I'm jealous, I guess."

"That isn't why I—"

"Yeah, I know. You're pure as salt." He chuckles. "Later, Thread."

Then Bull is gone.

· · ·

I pass the rest of the day in peace. I even do some exploration of the palace and the surrounding grounds. My ident gets me into a large portion of the building. In fact, I have yet to find a place I cannot enter. The palace has every amenity I can imagine. There is a small museum filled with statues and paintings. There is a large entertainment center with dozens of vidscreens on the walls and hundreds of games of skill and chance. There are five pools on the premises, three of them are inside, but another—the largest of the five—is outside and near the center of the building. There is also a small arboretum near the back of the property. It is partially outside and has a wide area of grass.

I spend some time sitting there watching the trees move with the breeze. I observe something new as I watch one tree in particular—a maple, I think. As the wind blows, and it is only very little wind, all the leaves move a bit. Most shift in concert, in direct proportion to the air being moved over them.

But occasionally one of the leaves will move with a quick back-and-forth motion, completely out of sync with those around it. I wonder what makes such a thing happen. Whether it is a peculiarity in the leaf itself, or in its position, or in a combination of the two variables.

I could stream up the physics. Attempt to calculate the math and science of it.

But instead, I allow myself to wonder. And that is rails fine.

I won't let Bull's warnings ruin this for me. Despite his intent. I did my work and now I'm here. Significant.

I'M AWAKENED BY a tapping sound.

I open my eyes and look around. A few seconds go by, enough that I think that I might have imagined the noise. Then I hear the noise again and realize that someone is tapping on the outside of my chute. Through the translucent canopy I see the wavy outline of someone's hand and beyond that, a face. Then the face pushes right into the canopy and becomes this bloated and disfigured caricature. I can't help but yell.

I hear laughing.

I search for the emergency beacon but find that the standard one is disabled. It bounces right back at me. There has to be a local one—this is the prince's home, after all—but I don't seem to be interfaced with it yet. Whoever this person is, I have to deal with them on my own.

"Come out, debugger." Another laugh. "You're in no danger."

I stream open the chute and sit up. I see the dark figure of a man pacing around the room, nearly circling my chute.

"Turn up the lights now," he says. "I don't know how to do it. I'll hurt myself."

I bring the lights up. The hour is early—I have no windows, but it has to be dark outside yet.

The man is casually dressed. He is thin, almost to debugger proportions, but taller. Easily over two meters. He has dark hair, a mustache, and a slight overbite. He is smiling. "We configured this room for your kind and now humans can barely use it. Can't find the lights. I can barely open the doors."

I only look at him. Whoever he is, I want him to leave. I'm still tired.

"You are level twelve now, correct?"

"Yes," I say.

"Excellent. Come with me."

I remain in my chute. I still want him to leave.

He looks at me and grins. "Don't you know who I am, Thread-Bare?"

I shake my head.

He throws his head back and laughs. It is an overdone display. Almost flamboyant. Too much for so early in the morning. His lips get wet from the effort. "You really do not know?" He wipes his mouth. "I thought you had all the information flowing through you."

"Are you the prince?"

He snaps his fingers and points at me. "Now you have it, yes, the elder prince Aadam. Who else?"

I bow my head. "Peace be unto you, Master. I should have known."

"Because of the news stream?" he asks. "Because of the street journals?" He shakes his head. "They tell you nothing. My image is controlled. What the public sees is never really me. Only an approximation." He approaches the wall behind my chute, the top half of which is a mirror. He places his hands behind his back and appraises himself there. "If you were to see the stream image and me together you would have no clue. Our control is that precise." He looks at me, beaming and self-assured. "In the past our leaders used body doubles. People who looked like them. This way is much better. I am always free."

I climb out of the chute.

Aadam turns and squints at me.

I slept in only my undergarments last night. I feel exposed and embarrassed. I quickly move toward the cleaning hamper at the foot of my chute, grateful that I pushed my clothing into it the night before. I open it and find my blue jumper, clean, folded, and still warm from the hamper's overnight efforts. I don't know how to stand in front of a prince to dress, so I settle for being perpendicular to him. I step into the jumper and struggle to get it on.

"You are not as pasty as the others," he says. "Nor as sickly."

I close the jumper across my chest and give it a smoothing pat. I feel a little better. "Thank you, Master."

He nods quickly. "You are ready?"

"You have something for me to fix?" I finally check the time: Five thirty-one a.m.

"Of course."

I walk toward the supply closet. "I'll need my bag."

Aadam goes outside without stopping. I grab my bag and scramble after him.

I follow him down multiple hallways to an ornate metal stairway that I haven't encountered before. He climbs it, using long legs to take two stairs at a time. I don't know how he does it, since the stairs seem awkwardly narrow to me. I cling to the handrail the entire way, moving as quickly as I can.

We ascend past the second story to the third. He exits the stairs, walks down another short hall and stops before a set of painted double doors. He touches the rightmost handle, and I hear the door lock disengage. He looks at me, smiles, then swings the door open.

Inside is a circular room filled with vidscreens. Each screen has a different image being displayed on it, a distinct news item or sporting event or entertainment program. Positioned in front of the screens are two general-purpose servbots—both humanoid in design. A stream check shows them to be this year's models.

There is a third serv lying on its back on the floor. Its head is missing. I'm getting nothing from it. Whatever happened, its stream connection is ruined. Bots can get really chatty when their heads are separated—throwing errors everywhere. It is probably better this way.

"This is the selection center for my children's entertainment," Aadam says. "The bots have been told to find appropriate programming."

I reposition the bag on my shoulder. I'm here to fix the bot, obviously, but I don't want to dive in if he has more to say. Someone should've briefed me on protocol. I doubt anything I'd find on the stream would be sufficient. No one's written *The Lowlevel Guide to Debugging for Royalty*. I'm certainly not going to.

Aadam motions toward the fallen bot. "So you see the problem. One of the bots is broken."

I nod. "Do you know what happened, Master?"

A subtle smile enters his face. "I believe it fell." He brings a hand to his chin, looks reflectively at the bot, then slowly circles it, keeping the same pose. "Yes it could only be that, couldn't it? What do you think?"

I shake my head. "I don't know. I could look at its memory. Replay what it saw."

He laughs. "You are wonderful. Perfect." He snaps his fingers. "You'll need the head, won't you? The headchip storage?" He walks to the wall nearest the doors. The head is sitting on the floor there looking at us. He picks it up and tosses it.

I barely have time to catch it.

"There you are," he says, laughing. "Everything you need. Now get to work."

I glance at the other bots. Their backs are turned, staring at the screens. "You want me to fix it in here?"

He shrugs. "Yes. I promise I won't watch."

I kneel beside the fallen serv. The last time I worked on one was during the thunderstorm, and that didn't go so well. That model was ancient, though. This one should be easier, but I'll get no help from it. It isn't talking. "Do you know what specific model this—"

I hear the door close. I glance up and see that the prince is gone. "Never mind."

The bot's specs would be helpful, and that requires I have the right model. I look at the other bots in the room. They appear identical to the one I'm working on. Yeah, that should help.

I query the nearest bot for its model number and it gives it as Model 21. Really new. Next I stream up the manufacturer's domain and grab the spec. It is the prettiest bot map I've ever seen. Easy to read and color coded. I focus on the head and upper spine portion and bring out a couple sheets. These I spread over the broken bot's neck and the back of its head. Then I compare what I see to the spec. All looks similar, except the broken parts. Even the injury itself looks clean—right between the third and fourth cervical vertebra. I can fix that, I think.

I need to reattach the spinal bundle first, the flexible conduit of wires and nanopaths that serve as the bot's spinal cord. Right now that's a mess. It looks like a bundle of grass. I scowl. It will require lots of different tools to reconnect. There's no helping that.

I pull my bag closer and find my rolled collection of microtools. I lay them all out where I can see them—crimpers, binders, spanners—the works. I spend the next hour joining the spine to the base of the head. No need to give all the details. The process bores even me. It is routine enough that I stream up some Blind Rocket and let that play while I work.

Occasionally I glance at the other bots. Their eyes never leave the vidscreens. The screens are always changing. Presenting every subject imaginable. Available in multiple resolutions and dimensions.

There was a time, in the distant past, where it seemed that all imaging would be suspended. That our society would return to the simple ways of the founder. The imaging jinn is a hard one to overcome, though, even by those with antitex leanings. All is a gift of A, the leaders said. With all following him, every gift could be used for his will. His blessing.

I'm not sure A would be okay with much of what I'm seeing now. Some of it forces me to put my head down to avoid the headbuzz. I recall the house that was across the street from my garage. What is true faith? Is it another way of justifying the same forbidden behavior? Murder, lust, adultery—the things the stops forbid of me—others practice freely. I feel hollow.

I get the bundle reconnected and begin attaching the spinal column to the head. The third and fourth vertebrae have a layer of permeable padding between them. The padding here is misshapen and partially mashed away. I check my bag for replacement material. Sure enough, there it is. I scrape the old off and smooth on the new until all looks good.

Next comes the locking mechanism between spine and head. It requires proper alignment followed by a hard push and a turn. I position my knees on either side of the bot's shoulders and hold its head in my hands. I notice then that there's a small dent in the side of the bot's head, right behind the silicon ear. Doubtless that was the reason for the dislocated head. I glance around the room, looking for what the bot might've impacted. There isn't even a table in the room. Only the two standing bots and the screens.

This is a strange job for a bot to be performing, really. Making objective decisions about subject matter that is by default subjective? I have no doubt that they could do the job, that they could learn the patterns of human likes and dislikes. But there will always be an occasional misstep. A time when the bot would inadvertently misjudge the content.

Human workers would make mistakes too, of course.

I should save such speculation for the book, right? My Lowlevel Guide?

Still, even the fact that the bot fell seems suspect. They aren't generally clumsy. Their walking mechanisms have been derived over centuries of experimentation and implementation. Thousands of revisions and redesigns. Plus, the designers have a proven system to emulate—the human system. When was the last time you fell, freehead?

Power failures do happen, as do software glitches and hardware faults.

I sensed an element of jest in the prince's behavior too. Not sure I'll ever really understand freeheads. We're both human, but we're not.

"Servbots," I say to the standing bots. "Did you see this one fall?"

The bots keep their eyes focused on the screens. "I did not see that one fall," they say in unison. It's a little creepy.

I study them for a moment, then shake my head. Of course they wouldn't see anything. They spend their day staring at screens.

"Did you *hear* it fall?" I stream for the serial number of the bot standing nearest me. "7322-5882. Did you hear this one fall?"

The bot nods without looking at me. "I heard it fall, yes."

Now we're getting somewhere. "Can you duplicate the sound?" He nods, opens his mouth...and produces no sound whatsoever.

I scowl. "That was the sound of it falling?"

"Yes."

Was there no gravity in the room?

Wait. Bots can be annoyingly specific. I'd headbuzz myself to remember that if I could. Stupid debugger. "Could I have the sound of it hitting the ground?" I ask.

Another nod followed by a crunching thump.

Yeah, that's probably it. This line of investigation is a slow road. Better to simply talk to the fallen bot after I fix it.

I return to the job of connecting its head. It takes a couple tries, but I manage to push the head down and turn it until it cements in place. The bot is a whole entity now. Feels good. I've accomplished something. It's a little creepy too, of course. Like I'm sitting on a corpse.

What next?

The headchip! I should've checked that first. Should've made sure it wasn't missing or broken. I reach to the back of the head, to where the hairline would start on a human. There is a synthskin-covered slot there...

Well, in this case the slot isn't covered. The fingernail-sized head-chip is there, in the slot, but it is dislodged and forcing the flap of skin back. That could explain a lot of things. I apply firm pressure and the chip reseats itself. All seems smooth back there now.

"I can't feel my legs," the bot says aloud. The statement is followed by a torrent of error messages, both audibly and blasted directly into the stream. I wince at the onslaught.

"Quiet!" I say. "I'll get it. I probably forgot something."

The barrage continues until I mute the bot completely. Now it simply stares up at me, looking angry. Bots.

I consult the specs again. Sure enough, there are a series of resets I was supposed to do. Also I should've reseeded some of the nanopaths for good measure. Thankfully, I haven't reapplied the skin to the neck area yet. I can seed the nanos in through there.

I fish out a small pack from my bag, unseal it, and squeeze the dark contents over the spine near the break. No need to be too precise with nanos. Simply sing the right instruction set and they'll figure out where to go. I initialize them as spine replacements and start them moving. A few seconds later the glob of seed nanos is oozing out in all directions around the injury.

I next run through all the resets I missed. Then I unmute the bot. Hold my breath.

"Are you ready?" I ask.

The bot's eyes soften and it blinks twice. Then it focuses on me, still sitting on its chest. "No errors, DR 23. Peace be unto you."

"And to you." I study the position of its head. Seems right.

"Do you still require me in this position, DR 23?"

I roll off its chest and onto the floor. It immediately stands and turns to look at the screens. Its spine is still missing its skin. Ugly.

"Wait, I'm not finished with you yet."

The bot looks at me. "I beg your forgiveness. What do you re-quire?"

I sigh. "Your head was dislodged. How did that happen?"

"I was struck by a blunt instrument. Then I fell."

"A blunt instrument? What blunt instrument?"

The bot shakes his head. "I don't know, DR 23. It was outside my optical range. I was watching the vidscreens."

"Of course you were." I glance at the screens again. A patchwork of ever-changing images. "Stream me your optic feed, starting at just before you were hit."

The bot nods. Soon I feel the tickle of his feed in the stream. I pull it in and embrace it. I see the array of screens, many of them filled with cartoon images. Walking bears and flying monkeys. Then the panorama shifts suddenly and the screens become a blur of somer-saulting color. I pause due to the illness its spinning brings. Then I jump the feed ahead until the spinning stops. I see only a single floor tile.

"Rails," I say. "Okay, you got hit. But your chip is still function-ing here. I can see—" The image of the floor shifts and moves. I get a glimpse of the other bots in the room, then a person's face comes into view. The prince's face. He is laughing. He stops laughing and his lips move as he speaks. Then the image shifts and goes black.

"Is that it?" I ask. "Everything until I woke you?"

"Yes," the bot says.

"He pulled the headchip there," I say. "That's why it ends."

The bot says nothing.

"Can you send me the audial portion too?" I ask.

"Yes, DR 23. Starting at the same point?"

"No, start just before the headchip was pulled. When the prince was talking. I want to hear what he said. Couple it with the optical feed, please."

I see the new feed in the stream and grabbing it, fill my mind. The prince's face comes into focus again, and I hear the sound of his hands moving over the bot's ears as he repositions its head. Next comes his full-throated laugh. Then he pulls the bot's head closer. His lips start to move.

"Welcome to my home, ThreadBare."

. . .

I finish the bot repairs in silence, applying new synthskin to the wound and then running the bot through a series of diagnostics. When I'm satisfied, I file an End of Task Report (EOTR) with ole Jahm—even though he didn't request the repair in the first place—and return to my room.

What sort of place is this?

Physical violence is part of our culture. The founder named his weapons and made use of all of them. His writings permitted the beating of wives, and the enslavement of women and children. He taught dismemberment for thievery and lashes for adultery. Even after two thousand years, these practices persist. They are part of the rules.

But rarely are bots the focus of aggression.

And why is that?

Lots of reasons, but primarily because bots are expensive to purchase, and equally expensive to fix. Why beat on something that is going to cost you half its value to repair? It makes no sense, unless you're crazy.

Beating on bots doesn't produce any real results either. They have rudimentary pain sensors, sure, they don't remember pain the way humans do. If a bot touches a hot surface its pain sensors will register heat, make note of the type of surface and the surroundings, recognize that the situation could cause damage and then make a decision based on all known variables. The situation will be logged for later use, but at that instance there is no emotion attached to the information. No feelings. It is all just zeroes and ones. Consequently, there isn't the same level of learning. Bots don't give intrinsic value to their bodies. Cut off a bot's arm and it'll simply shrug and calculate how to make do with the remaining one. It'll throw lots of errors, but it will make do.

All of that is outside the scope of the problem here. The problem, my problem, is the fact that the episode seemed to be solely for my benefit. Was it a test? Or was it a message too?

There is a list of masters who abuse their debuggers. Those that do so may have their property, their debugger, recalled. But even if their debugger isn't recalled, they won't get another. Bamboo is aware of the list. He may maintain it, for all I know. All I know for sure is that he doesn't want any of his debuggers abused. He may hate us as people, but we're still his handiwork. His children.

By the way, I've checked already. The prince isn't on the list.

But would he be? There might be a royalty exemption, or a gold club, or something. Not sure.

I study my chute and contemplate catching a nap. It is still morning and none of my speculation matters. I'm here now. This is my lot. If nothing else, we are told to accept our place. We are nothing. Low-level even when we're not.

I receive a text message from Jahm:

The prince congratulates you on completing your first assignment. He wants to know if you discovered the reason for the bot's condition. Please respond immediately.

I should've taken a nap as soon as I returned. That would've been a great excuse for not responding. Unfortunately, it is the only excuse. If I'm awake, I can respond.

Immediately.

Fine. I'll respond like a bot. Simple and specific.

Tell the prince that I found the cause, though I am unable to prevent a repeat occurrence.

I fully expect the next message to ask me what the cause was. I even wait a few moments when Jahm's next message appears. I resist opening it. But then I do.

Very good. Well done.

FOR THE LAST DAY and a half, I've been making repairs on the prince's grounds. Most of the repairs have been legitimate—a worn out cleaning bot, or a malfunctioning serv—but occasionally there is a breakdown that I know is manufactured. For instance, in one day I had three instances where a bot mysteriously went out a three-story window. In my years of debugging I've never once seen a bot go out a window. Until now. Until here.

There is no mystery at all, of course. The prince was responsible for all of them.

Initially I suspected the sabotage was due to the children he mentioned. Throwing or coercing a bot out a window might be an interesting thing to do if you're, say, seven. None of the prince's fifteen children actually live in the summer palace, though. They're spread across all five of his "regular" palaces, presumably with their mothers. So, yeah, the three bots filtering entertainment programs is *just in case*. Or because the prince finds it amusing. Not sure which.

I miss my own mother and father. I sometimes wonder, if they passed me on the walkways, would they know me? The boy they raised is long gone. ThreadBare lives in a different world. The nanosecond world.

Were the broken bots an ongoing situation before I arrived? It would be interesting to know what the debugger before me experienced. Certainly there was one. A house like this requires at least one.

I think of the two lists again: the debugger abuser list and the offline debugger list. I suspect my stream work here is filtered and possibly observed. It would have to be for security reasons. That makes things trickier.

Look at me. Only here a day and I'm paranoid already. Bamboo said I'm fine, but what does he know? He might've sampled my experiences, but he didn't live them. Living is worse. Missiles and heads and legs. And Noah. Good ole Noah.

I should message FrontLot. See what's available. I think I'll need a mix soon, a distraction.

At least I have the arboretum. I think I might go there now. Watch the leaves. It is getting close to the evening meal. I rarely get a request then.

•••

I've found my perfect spot. It is in the bough of a large oak tree. The tree is old enough that the branches are large and easily climbable. There is a particularly wide branch about two thirds of the way up where I can sit and rest my back against the trunk.

From here I can glimpse a portion of the fields beyond the house grounds, but I can also see into the house proper. There is a dimly lit trail that leads to a small pool there. Though I don't know how to swim, I have, late at night, dipped my feet into the shallow end. It felt wondrous.

But not as wondrous as this tree. For the last twenty-nine minutes I have split my time between gazing at the fields, looking at the trees, and readjusting my seat. After ten minutes of sitting, the tree branch starts to feel hard and I have to shift.

Okay, nothing is perfect.

There is no breeze tonight, but I wish there were. I watch the fields, hoping to see at least a ripple of movement, but all is calm. Regardless, it is beautiful. Peaceful.

I hear a splash of water and my heart jumps. I pull as close to the tree as I can and try to peer in the direction of the pool. I can glimpse only a corner, but there is a ripple of movement there. I watch quietly, hoping that whoever is in the pool will simply get themselves wet and go away.

Minutes pass. The ripples seem to increase, and then decrease. Increase and decrease.

I frown and carefully shift again. Someone is swimming laps. My room is on the other side of that pool. I will not be able to slip back without being seen. I would rather not be seen.

The ripples continue for seven more minutes, then I hear another heavy splash. I'm not sure if it is because someone entered the pool, or someone exited. I hope the latter. I hope they go away. There is silence for a couple minutes. Maybe they left?

I think they left.

That's good, because my seat is hurting. Shifting my position is no longer working. I need to get down. I stand so I can start to climb. I hear someone's voice and quickly crouch again. Someone is humming, repeating a simple melancholy tune. I don't recognize the song, but it is similar to those my mother used to sing to me as a child. Sad and warm at the same time. The singer is female.

The humming gets louder and I notice someone near the corner of the pool. The woman is wrapped in a white towel and has long, dark hair. Other than that, I can see very little. It could be one of the female servants, though those I've met are older. Plus, I'm not sure servants are allowed to swim out here. I somehow doubt it.

So is it a family member? One of the prince's daughters, perhaps?

The young woman enters the trail and begins to walk my direction. I curl up as tight as I can. Though evening is coming, it is not dark yet. I might be seen by someone who looks my direction. Me in my blue jumpsuit. I'm an oversized blue bird up here.

She walks the trail slowly, almost hesitantly. Her feet are bare. I watch every step. When she draws to within four meters of my tree I can see her clearly. She's in her late teens or early twenties—only a few years older than me. Her eyes are dark to match her hair, and her face, unhidden, is symmetrical and attractive. I feel the twinge of a stop in that basic realization, a small vibration in my head. But the fact is no less valid. Anyone would call her pretty. The rules should have no problem with that.

Except I really shouldn't see her face. The fact that the rest of her is uncovered beneath the towel is unsettling too. If she were on the street, she would be chastised. Men would crowd around her and call her names, possibly abuse her if she didn't immediately cover or return home. This is not the street, however.

And I am not a freehead.

She is beneath my tree now. Her focus seems to be on what is ahead. On her path, and not on what's around her. I'm thankful for that. She walks past my tree, looking at the fields beyond the palace. As she moves on, I stand so I can continue to watch her.

I feel another gentle headbuzz. There is some unrighteousness in my watching. I curse the rules and feel the wrath of their response—a heavier buzz. I shift on the branch in discomfort. Nearly fall.

I can't avoid watching now. I can see only her head and shoulders. Her head is bent slightly downward. As if she's studying the driveway that encircles the palace. Or perhaps the sloping ground beyond it, or even the large moat that it all drains into.

I should leave. Sneak away while I can.

I make my way down the tree, using every skill I have to stay quiet. I imagine I am climbing off a large dredge and don't even look her direction. I don't need that distraction, and I certainly don't need more head pain. I feel some comfort when my feet find the path again. I look at the pool and quickly walk that way. My curiosity tugs at every step. My interest at finding another person my age, even if she's a mere human.

Why do I feel that way? I'm a debugger. I don't need that kind of companionship. I have the stream, and whatever bot I'm currently working on. I could touch a hundred other debuggers now if I wanted. A thousand machines. What more do I need?

I trip on a root and fall, striking my knee and hand. I manage to keep from yelling, but rails it hurts. I glance back and don't see the woman. That's good. I push myself up, suppressing a groan, and look myself over. There's dirt on my pants and hands. I want to slap it off, but I don't. I have to hurry away. Back to my room. I take a step.

Rails, my knee hurts. Have to move it. Get the blood circulating. I press ahead.

"Who is there?" the woman asks.

I don't speak. I'm nearly to the pool area now. Then I can turn left, get behind the edge of the foliage and disappear. I increase my pace. I can do this.

I hear footsteps behind me. I reach the pool, make the turn, and hobble the length of the short end. I reach another, straighter, path that leads back into the palace and turn left onto it. I sense the woman back there somewhere, but I can't afford to look. All debuggers look the same from behind. No way for her to know who I am.

My knee loosens enough that I can jog. I move as fast as I can. Like I have a high-priority request. Like I'm being headbuzzed the entire way.

Finally, I reach the palace door. It swings open for me. I hear her call again, but it is too late. I'm safe.

ANOTHER DAY HAS PASSED since my encounter in the arboretum. I have not been back there since. I miss it. In the meantime, I've fixed five bots. Three were simple instruction upgrades—whoever the last debugger was, he wasn't great on keeping code up to date. Of course, given the prince's tendency to break things, simple upgrades were probably far down on the list.

I need to ask Jahm about that sometime. See who debugged here last. See if I recognize him. It feels good knowing that I can complete tasks that that DR couldn't get done. Guess I'm improving. Living up to my level.

I get this feeling. A real shot to the stomach. What if that last guy is on the offline list? Maybe he's nowhere now.

Yeah, I don't like that notion. No reason to think about it either. The prince, or those around him, like to break things. But that's their business, right? All their property.

Debuggers are property, Thread. Remember that.

Can't forget. Buzz in my head won't let me. Rails.

Right now I'm eating in my room. I didn't use the room's food conditioner this time. I instead stopped by one of the building's three kitchens. One of the chefs made me a green salad with fresh vegetables from the fields outside. He looked at me funny, like I might be beyond my rights. But hey, the door opened for me, so I guess kitchens are inbounds. Grumpy or no, the food that Abby made was great. I'm content. Not missing the garage on that front. No way.

I think again of the offline list, and then of FrontLot. I haven't talked to him yet. I need to.

I close my eyes and try to connect. He answers right away. I get a visual, his personal view, of the top of a downrider switching station. He's balancing on a narrow, red piece of the station. The city fans out in every direction around him, as do about seven strings. I feel a wash of vertigo.

"How is the high life?" he asks.

"Irony, Front," I say. "Living irony."

"How's that?"

I frown. "That's a switching station, right?"

He laughs. "Yeah, right, I get you. My mind is a little over focused right now." He squints. "You sending from your new place?"

I open my eyes and move to stand near the chute. I want that as part of the message. It is a thing of beauty.

He whistles. "Sleeping like royalty. Nice." He appears to be studying me. "You look good. Healthy."

He wants to ask, I know. He wants all the inside symphony. But talking about my current employment is a minefield. Rules of secrecy. There has to be concealment for it all to work. Can't have debuggers owned by competing companies talking. Sharing owned information. Regardless of whether it would help solve more problems. Or solve them quicker.

Rules, sometimes I hate them.

"I'm fine," I say. "Eating well." This secondhand view of Front's surroundings is disconcerting. I've been in that sort of place before, but I'd rather not do it if I don't have to. "Maybe we should go Extended Easy?"

He laughs again. The view shifts to one from his apartment. It now appears that he is sitting in a blue puff chair with a cup of something steamy in one hand. It is dim too, with slowly moving lights behind him. Soothing music. That helps, except I know he is still hanging over the city somewhere. Makes my feet tingle thinking about it.

"I can't talk long," he says. "You need something specific?"

"Maybe another from the same list," I say.

His eyes narrow. "What are you up to?"

I shrug. "Patterns," I say. "Searching for...I don't know...something that connects."

"Mystery shaking? You don't get enough of that already?"

I lean against the chute, feeling its cool exterior on my back. "Can't help it," I say. "I'm curious."

He raises the cup to his lips. Steam flirts with his face as he simulates taking a drink. "Well, there's a pattern I can recognize. We're all curious." He touches his forehead. "I'll see what I can dig up."

I nod. "Be careful up there."

"You too," he says, smiling.

• • •

I hear a knock on my door followed by Jahm's voice. I stream open the door and walk toward it. He waits outside, looking irritated.

"The prince requires you," he says.

I quickly grab my bag. I follow him through the west wing of the palace, up a flight of stairs, and down a wide, richly-decorated hall. The hall has deep, purple and gold carpet and numerous paintings of the royal family.

There are depictions of both princes, but the largest is of the Imam. A shot of his chest and head. He's wearing a black turban signifying him as one of the founder's descendants. His beard is white and forms a symmetrical ring from ear to ear. He is looking down. It is a fatherly image, a variation of which is everywhere, world over. This is the most impressive one I've seen, though.

Jahm leads me to a large door that has a bodyguard standing outside. Though the guard looks relaxed, he has a dark pistol in one hand. The guard nods at Jahm and opens the door.

The room is one of the prince's offices. It has a marble desk, fully four meters long, and shelves filled with bound manuscripts—most scientific or sports-related. There is a large mosaic of the moon on one wall. The center of the floor is an ornamental green carpet.

The prince is pacing the room, and looks agitated. My eyes are drawn to the two men sitting in front of his desk. One has a bruised eye, the other has blood leaking from his nose. I try not to stare, but it is difficult.

The prince notices Jahm and me. He smiles and waves toward the side of the room that is partially obscured by the desk. I take a couple of steps that direction and see a servbot sitting on the ground there. One of its arms is missing. No, not missing. The bot is cradling the arm between its legs. One end of the arm is reddish, no longer white.

Is that how the men got their wounds? From the arm?

The bot looks at me as I approach. Though I know it is impossible—I know they don't have feelings—it seems to have a distraught look in its eyes. Like it is feeling pain. I set my bag beside it, and crouching low, gently pick up the arm.

Another clean break. How fortunate.

Jahm bends near my left ear and whispers. "You can fix it, yes?"

I nod.

He returns the nod and straightens. He looks warily at the prince.

The prince's focus is on the men now. "You've disappointed me," he says. "And you are disappointing my father."

The men stare at the floor.

"You have nothing to say for yourselves? My family has brought you out of nothing, out of wretchedness, and you have nothing to say?"

I bring out the tools I used for the earlier spinal repair. This won't require all of them, but I like everything out before me. Especially when I'm distracted.

One of the men mumbles something. I don't think that was the right response.

"Did you hear that, Jahm?" the prince says. "ThreadBare! Did you hear what he said?"

I really don't want to be involved. I shake my head.

"See there, Obaid, no one heard you. You have to speak louder. Even the debugger can't hear you."

I need to reattach the joint first. Shoulders are different than spines. They're a more complicated design. They need to be to allow for the expanded degrees of motion.

This bot is a model 21, just like most of the others I've repaired here. Consequently, the specs are right in my head where I need them. That will help.

"We...our people are trying," one of the men say. Probably Obaid. "It is unknown what we are doing. Unprecedented. The designs, the calculations...unprecedented, my prince."

The torn shoulder synthskin and other connective tissue are a little ragged. Might make attaching the joint tricky. Maybe I should fold those back? Or get Jahm to help hold them? I look in my bag for something to bind them with. Tape might work.

"You were given all the resources you need," the prince says. "The best materials and scientists. Technicians, implants, everything. But now it is all mystery?"

"It has been mystery from the beginning," the other man says. "This is what we are doing. Uncovering A's mysteries. Perhaps we ask too much. Perhaps he—"

There is the sound of motion, and a shadow falls on me. The prince rips the bot arm from my hands and storms away. I next hear a hollow thump followed by a grunt.

"A has done nothing for me," the prince says. "*A* does not pay you. Does not provide for your family. I do."

He returns the arm to my hands. There is blood on the shoulder end. I feel ill. Stuck. I can't think what to do with the arm next. It is like all my pathways are fried. It is all I can do just to hold it. I start seeing body parts again: heads, legs, arms. Popping sounds.

Jahm takes the arm, pulls out a cloth—a handkerchief—and wipes the end off. He inspects it closely, giving it an all over pass with the cloth, then lays it back in my hands. I feel a little better. I try to refocus. The shoulder, the ragged tissue...tape!

It takes a few seconds to get the arm "bone" and shoulder exposed like I need them. Then I bring the arm up to the joint. I notice that the back portion of the socket, the plastisteel wall, has snapped. I can fuse that. Fix it. Do it, debugger!

I dig into my bag for the pen-shaped fuser. I lay the arm down as I reconstruct and smooth the socket. The fuser is warm to the touch. Also light and clean. Works wonders.

"Yet your father—"

"My father wants what he wants. His stone. And I will get it for him."

"Yes, my prince. We will undertake another journey. We're working out the problems. Trying to understand what they experienced."

"So they will go again? They are able to go again?"

"Of course. Yes. We have kept them close. Still suited, in fact."

Now it is time to reconnect. I bring the arm up, holding it with both hands. I look at Jahm. He still looks nervous, agitated. I try to ignore that. I need to ignore that. I motion to get his attention.

He stoops near my ear again. "Yes, debugger?"

"Can you support the bot's other side?" I ask. "I should be able to do this on my own, but it might go smoother if you're over there holding."

He nods and sits next to the bot. He turns slightly to brace its left shoulder against his chest, then places his left arm around its back. Almost like they're best friends.

Friends. Do I have a friend, Thread?

Yes. Hundreds. Continue with your task.

I bring the arm closer. Unlike the spine, it should self-lock, but sometimes they need a little push. I align it and shove. I hear a click and a short whir. Feels right. Next I need to reconnect all the broken linkages and pathways. Seal the skin.

"Understand quicker!" the prince yells. "Or I will go there myself."

"Yes, my prince," both men say.

"You may go now," the prince says. "I don't want to see you again like this."

I hear the sounds of the men leaving. They walk heavily, with lots of foot shuffling. Then a shadow falls over me again. My back tenses.

"Is it fixed yet?" the prince asks.

"Almost, my prince," Jahm says. "We have the arm reattached—"

"I can see that."

The top of my head is touched. I wince, but I try not to pull away. It is difficult. Unsanitary and uncomfortable. Being touched. I'm not sure what to do. I'm stalled. The prince gives my head a couple pats then takes his hand away. Thankfully.

"I'm satisfied with your performance so far, ThreadBare. I read your history and there was little to suggest such competency. But you are better than they think, aren't you?"

"If you say so, my prince." I'm not sure if I should turn to look at him, or stay as I am, huddled over the bot.

"I do," he says. "So you should believe it. Your presence with me has already improved you. Rewrote your code. Of that, I am not surprised."

I look at him, but his back is already turned. He is near the door, in fact. "Let him finish now, Jahm." He touches the handle of the door, which opens. He waves at the submaster. "We have other things to deal with now. Come! I would like to see the royal football team next."

Jahm stands and scurries across the room. "At their training facility?"

"Yes, that will do nicely. Then perhaps at *my* training facility." He laughs.

The door closes and they are gone. I turn to the bot again. It is staring at me with that distressed look again.

"I can't feel my arm, debugger," it says.

I frown. "Yes, I know. I'm working on it."

I need a mix. When I get back to my room. Tonight. A mix.

MY MASTER ASKS ME to come to his office. It is an uncommon request. When I am not debugging, I am usually left alone. My master owns an orbital ship. Each day we give trips around the earth, starting and ending at the BZ lift. It is a blessed life.

My master is kind and keeps his machines up-to-date and easily serviceable. My human needs are provided for. I am happy, even privileged. My manageable chores leave me time to pursue my true calling. My private whimsy.

The door to master's office is open when I arrive. He notices me at the door and bids me enter. The room is beautiful. There is a long window in front that provides the view outside the ship. At this moment we follow the Earth's equator. The planet slowly moves below us. I see a brown coastline and the western ocean. It is difficult not to stare. The rest of the office is trimmed in golden wood. The walls are a burnt umber color. The floors are darker wood and there is a central gold rug.

"Does something need my attention?" I ask. "My apologies if it is the guidance system again. When we reach port I will find the proper parts. Sometimes those I synthesize aren't as good—"

My master is a relatively young man. His hair is sand colored and his eyes are blue. Little about his appearance is common. He motions to a seat, and studies me thoughtfully.

"Are you not content here, ArrowMast?"

I am surprised by the question. "Of course, Master. Always."

"Have I not given you free reign on this ship?"

I bow my head respectfully. "Yes, like no other, Master. I'm truly blessed."

"Have you been threatened in any way? Has the crew made you uncomfortable?"

"No." I shake my head. "They have been generous and kind. All of them."

He frowns. "Perhaps it is your state of being, your burden. What do I still not understand?"

"Sir? What are you asking?"

He touches the edge of the desk. "I am trying to understand your behavior, Arrow. Are you ill?"

I shake my head again. "I am not. No. I can send you my last physical evaluation. I am operating perfectly."

"I have seen your evaluation. Still, I am perplexed. Why do you cloister yourself so? You lock yourself in your cabin when you aren't at work. No one sees you. No sound comes out. Even your stream usage is subdued." He leans forward. "Certainly you need human contact, even if we're different than you." He smiles halfheartedly. "Even if we have just one way of talking."

I look at the floor in shame. I have inadvertently troubled those who have provided for me. "I am sorry, Master."

He shakes his head. "There's no need to apologize. Your time is your own, of course. I am concerned for you, is all. As is my family."

I bow again. "Yes, your wife and children. They are indeed caring. I am unsure how to change, however."

"It takes only a single step," he says. "Followed by another."

"Yes, but—"

"What is it?" he asks. "What do you do during all that time? If it is work-related, if you are overtaxed—"

I hold up a hand. "No, it is not that. Certainly not that."

"Then what?"

I lift my eyes and look out at the Earth. The coastline can no longer be seen. Now there is only water.

"I am prying," he says. "Forgive me—"

I again shake my head. "The scriptures say that you cannot calculate the blessings of A," I say, "but I have tried. Every blessing since birth I have counted. A happy home, parents that nurtured me, food and clothing. Always a roof over my head. Wonderful schools and teachers. Even siblings that cared about me. All these I had for twelve years."

"Would you like to see them again, Arrow? Perhaps it could be arranged..."

"No. Please let me explain."

"Sorry. Again, I was rude." He raises a hand. "Please."

I nod. "I also had the sciences. Mathematics and physics. These I embraced and filled myself with. Always I needed to know how things worked. The exactness, the methods. These things I loved. These were what A gave me. Blessings atop of blessings.

"The greatest blessing of all was the blessing of my faith. For it was all that would endure. If I persisted. If I pleased A. Forever would I be with him. The 'if' in the equation worried me, bothered my science-filled mind." I smile. "But then A brought another blessing."

I touch my head at the temple. "His Bamboo found me. Sealed me with the sign everlasting. Placed in me the key to life eternal. Removed my 'if.' Solved that equation for me."

"The implant, its wonders, complemented my interests. Now math and science flowed freely through me. The laws of physics became lifeblood, my guides."

I glance at the Earth again. "But still the blessings continued. I am brought here. I am challenged, respected, and provided for. Also, I am given time to pursue...a gift."

My master's face fills with color. "Your service is enough of a gift, Arrow. Nothing more is required of you."

"The gift is not for you, my master. At least, not you alone. You see, I am attempting to find Paradise."

"Paradise?" he says. "Jannah?"

I meet his eyes. "Is this blasphemy? I do not think so. I think it is only the last link in the chain of science. As a servant of A, and as an implant, guaranteed Paradise through my living martyrdom, it is the proper thing for me to do for mankind."

He stares at me a full second. "Again, I don't understand. What do you intend to do?"

I let my eyes wander the room. From the earth-based vista to the wall on my left. It is decorated with moving images—snapshots of my master's life. Awards being given and family events. Also space scenes he has witnessed, such as an eclipse captured from orbit. "It is all moving," I say, "All of it. Like the waves of the ocean, always in motion. The messengers of A are able to traverse this sea of blackness with a thought. Going about their master's business." I smile at him again. "What I wish to discover is how. If I can do that, I will gift humanity the wings of the angels. The pathway to Paradise."

His eyes narrow. "You are pursuing a way to step between stars? Men have sought that pearl for a very long time, Arrow. Hundreds of years. When gravity was first manipulated we thought we'd finally cracked the code. Yet here we are, marooned in our island solar system."

"It can be done," I say. "I am sure of it. I have already deduced equations in kinematic form. It is something the implant makes extraordinarily accessible. To visualize geometries beyond the natural. To work in hyperplanar space."

"This is what you do," he says, "in your free time? Attempt to solve mysteries that have defied men for ages?"

"It is the next logical step for me. I can think of little else. Is that sin?"

His eyes widen. "No, not sin. Not wrong. But unusual. Unexpected."

"It is the place my mind goes," I say. "Space can be manipulated; I am certain of it. As certain as the ancestor who discovered gravity, or the man who defined relativity." I hold up a hand. "The way is easily explained. It is as if someone were holding a card in his hand. On this side, my side, is the Earth and its system. On your side is the star we wish to reach. The ship is written on my side. Described on the card itself. Then flipped to yours."

He raises an eyebrow. "And it is that simple."

I shake my head. "I did not say it is simple. But it is attainable. I am sure of that."

My master places both hands on his desk and stares at a spot between them, thinking. "Surprises, Arrow. Many surprises."

"I am sorry if I cause you discomfort. I have little choice."

He looks at me. "No, no, you have done well. Outperformed your brethren, I'm sure. You cause me to wonder if you should be with me, is all."

I feel a twinge of regret. "I love this ship," I say. "Your family."

He nods. "Yes, but what you have discovered, should, as you say, be shared. It isn't just for us." He looks at his hands again. "You need someone who can help you. That can verify and experiment. Like minds."

"Is there such a place in the Imam's domain? I have not heard of it."

He rocks slowly, thoughtfully. "Oh yes, there are places. I have a few connections. People in research. In fact, the royal family has such an interest." His face grows somber. "But I fear for you, my friend. I fear where it might lead. Not all masters are good."

I bow my head. "I am aware of that. I have heard. My kind makes lists of such things." I smile softly. "Still, it delights me to know that I could be used for such an effort. That my dream of giving could be realized."

He still looks worried. "Are you certain? This is what you want?"

"I do," I say. "Very much."

"I do not want to lose you," he says. "I would miss you."

"And I you. Very much."

ANOTHER MORNING. The canopy of my chute lifts away. The apartment lights diffuse in such a way as to mimic the light at sunrise. It is a warm, comfortable light. Perfect for the daybreak time of reorienting yourself, for reestablishing your place in the world.

My implant reminds me of the requirements of my faith. There is a sajada, a prayer mat, provided for me in my supply closet. I make my way to it and remove it from its heavy, black tube. I then unroll it, and after determining M is the direction of my apartment door, orient the mat that direction.

Ironically, the calculation of the morning prayer time requires two astronomical measurements, one being the declination of the sun, and the other being the difference between the eccentricity of the earth's orbit, and its axis. My present coordinates are necessary, as well. It is a mathematical exercise that the implant constantly performs.

I stand on the mat, and raising my hands, begin the ritual. Surprisingly, the stops don't require me to perform the prayers. Debugger life often makes it impossible. Imagine my friend FrontLot pausing for prayer while atop the downrider junction. It simply cannot occur, nor does our destiny depend on it. Consequently, many DRs rarely practice the prayers at all. Their implant always reminds them, though.

Today the ritual feels appropriate. Almost necessary. I move to the second position, placing my hands over my navel, right hand over left. Quietly I glorify A and seek his protection. Then, reading from implant storage, I recite the first chapter of the scriptures. I bow and say "Glory to A" three times then stand erect again and begin to praise him.

ArrowMast was a level fourteen, the highest level I have ever received a mix from. The thoughts that danced through his head trouble me in ways I can't explain. My mind feels both constricted and freed at the same time. His ideas were beyond me not just because of his training and experience, or even his increased implant storage, but because his brain operated in a mode mine can never reach. It muddles everything for me.

I prostrate myself on the mat, touching with my palms, knees, toes, forehead, and nose. "Glory to A, the Most High" I repeat three times.

My mind returns to ArrowMast. I'm grieved because his implant is on the list. Does that mean he is dead? Or has his implant simply been removed? Was it affecting his process somehow? Hindering his quest for Jannah? It didn't seem that it was.

I move to a sitting position and remain silent, eyes closed. I should clear my mind, simply pause, or recite a short prayer. But I cannot. ArrowMast. His thoughts, his theories, I need to separate those somehow. Is there a pattern between his story and that of the other DR from the list? I feel like there is, but I don't know that I can find it. This isn't the sort of problem I solve.

To be honest, I'm not that great at the other problems either. I simply make do.

I kneel to the mat again. At least Arrow's mix was generally happy. He had a good life while it lasted. Better than most.

I sit up and begin a list of standard short prayers, praising A and his prophet. I raise the forefinger of my right hand and declare my faith again. Acting as a witness to heaven. I pray for A's blessing on my family, wherever they now are.

A message from Jahm appears, flashing its way through my consciousness. There is another broken bot, this time at one of the pools in the north wing. I file it away and close the ritual by whispering "peace" to the angels on both my shoulders—those said to record my works. They serve as only backups for debuggers, of course. We have our own storage. But if mine are still following me around they deserve their due.

I stand, roll the mat and take it with me to the closet. I place it in its storage tube and grab my bag. Place its weight on my shoulder.

Thankfully, the food conditioner always makes me something in the morning. I should feel energized from my rest, but I'm wrung out. Depleted from ArrowMast and all his thoughts. All that brilliance that touched madness. Now gone?

I need to reevaluate my purpose with mixes. I'm not sure they're helping.

Food, Thread. Have to get some. Then get on with the day.

• • •

The pool I'm brought to is not the one near the arboretum. This one is larger and circular. It is placed in an equally circular room that is painted deep red and is lined with golden pillars all around. There are seats circling the pool too, along with large potted plants. Overhead is a translucent ceiling that, according to the stream, also retracts. It is cloudy today, so the ceiling is closed.

The pool area is empty, but there are signs of someone's presence—a few of the chairs have towels on them. On the side of the room opposite the entrance is a hot tub area. It is partially hidden by potted foliage, but I can see steam rising from it. I hear someone talking there too. Occasional laughter.

What I don't see is the bot that needs repair. Jahm isn't here either. I skim the message he sent again. He doesn't specify the particular kind of bot, nor did he provide an ident I can search for. Not very helpful there, Jahm.

Now what?

I'm hesitant to call out. Debuggers are supposed to be as discreet as possible. We're slaves, remember? We live in the background.

Plus, whoever is in the hot tub is enjoying themselves. I'm not going over there.

I feel bot emanations in the stream, but they're muted. Difficult to pinpoint. It is almost like whatever is sending them is in another room, or maybe outside entirely. I glance at the entrance. Could the malfunctioning machine have wandered off somewhere? *Is* it in another room?

I frown and begin a deliberate search, moving clockwise. I scan the ceiling and check behind every plant and pillar I pass. Nothing obvious. I've gone about three quarters of the way around when I hear more giggling and heavy splashes from the hot tub.

Part of me wants to leave. The door isn't that far away, after all. If Jahm wants me to work here, he should be more specific. Or at least be present.

I detect movement in the pool itself. Something out near the center. It is dark and circular—probably only a meter wide. I can't get a good look at it, but I think it is generating the stream push I'm sensing. Every time the object gets near the surface, the push intensifies. Is it a pool scrubber?

I hear the sounds of wet feet. I turn and see three young women huddling near the hot tub. All of them have white towels wrapped around themselves. Two are averting their eyes and looking like they might flee. One of them, a brunette, is shielding her face with her hand.

The third woman, a blonde, is staring at me intently. "Are you here to fix the mechanical?" she asks.

I'm not sure which way to look, so I settle for the floor. "Yes," I say, nodding. "Where is it?"

"Out in the pool there," she says. "The cleaner. It won't let us into the water. It keeps attacking."

I set my bag down and look at the water again. An attacking pool-bot and women in swimsuits. This is...difficult.

"It is all right, girls," the blonde says. "He's a debugger. He cannot sin. We don't need to cover."

I feel a wave of nervousness, followed by a dose of calm. I'm not sure where the latter comes from, because this situation is really unusual. Way out of spec. I *should* be nervous.

Technically she's right, though. Debuggers aren't supposed to be distracted by the things that distract other men. It wouldn't surprise me if that was an intentional side effect of the implant. Perhaps that is where *calm* comes from.

I feel an added bit of strangeness. A tingle of loss. As if I now miss the initial nervousness. There was something good in it. Something real.

See, this is what females do to me. Confuse things.

I hear the footsteps of the women drawing closer. I glance their direction. The brunette still has her hand raised over the bottom portion of her face. "Is that true?" she asks. "Are you safe?"

"You will not affect my destination," I say, "And I will not, cannot, harm you." I feel the surge of a stop for some reason. I shake my head, then sigh as the stop begins to dissipate.

"I am Damali," the brunette says. "They are Fania and Gulru."

Damali is very pretty. They all are, but the brunette is most striking. Scientifically, I mean. Without dispute. Anyone would say so. Then it hits me. She's the young woman from the arboretum! The one I watched in secret. Another wave of nervousness followed by more calm. Stupid calm.

I look at the pool again. "I'm DR 23," I say. "Palace debugger."

Damali takes another step closer, standing parallel to me as I stare at the poolbot. "Can you fix it from here?"

I attempt to connect with the poolbot. I can sense its push, but can't get a grip on it. It remains garbled and sporadic. The stream rarely mixes well with water, though. Like me and women. "I don't think so." I look at my jumpsuit. "I'm not sure what to do exactly. This suit isn't made for water. It would get heavy."

She moves closer, so that she's addressing the side of my face. "It's easy to lure over." Her eyes scan the room, then she points to the left. "There is a pool net over there on the wall. Maybe you can catch it that way?"

I glance at the net. It has a wide mouth and a handle about two meters long. "I probably could."

The blonde, Fania, scampers over and takes the net from the wall. She brings it back and holds it out for me. "Here you are, palace debugger." She's wearing a one-piece bathing suit that leaves a lot of her uncovered. Possibly more than I've seen my entire life, including the prostitute. The leg.

I take the net and nod. "Peace be unto you."

"You have to get into the pool for it to notice," Damali says.

I frown and kick off my shoes. "Yes, the pool." I test the water with a foot and grimace. Not only is it wet, it is cold.

"Can you swim?"

"I can swim, yes. I learned when I was young."

"How old are you now?" Damali asks. "Because you look old."

"Old?" I shoot her a look. "I'm not—"

She's smiling at me. "Probably it is the head. The missing hair. Makes you seem older."

I look at the bot again. Attempt to ignore her.

"Don't take that the wrong way," she says. "You still look good."

"In an older, brain-smart way," Fania adds.

I reach the net into the pool, hoping to attract the bot. It spins, but stays out near the center. Crafty and obstinate mechanical. I'll need to go get it.

"Here," Damali says. "Be ready." She drops onto the side of the pool then slips in completely. Bobbing at the edge, she takes a breath and with eyes on the bot, ducks under.

I watch the bot. It is moving now, tracking the girl. Unfortunately, Damali is following the outside of the pool and is swimming to the right, away from me.

I drift that direction. "How does she—"

"Wait, debugger," Fania says. "She's a strong swimmer. She will bring it around."

Yes, that seems to be what she intends to do. She's halfway around the pool now. The bot has closed the distance to about two meters, and is clearly after her. What is wrong with it?

The girl swims in smooth, powerful strokes. Much better than I would do, especially while pursued. She is three quarters of the way around and will be near me soon.

I stoop down and hang the net over the water. I wait breathlessly as Damali reaches me, then passes by.

The bot approaches. I'm ready. I can sense Fania on my left watching. The third girl, Gulru, is on my right, but further away.

I make a swing for the bot. I catch one side of it, but it tips, dives...and slips away.

"You missed," Fania says.

"Keep swimming, Damali!" Gulru says. "He didn't get it."

As if I need the reminder. This isn't right. I should jump in myself. The bot is my responsibility. My job.

Damali follows the outside of the pool for about half its length, then adjusts and cuts deeper into the interior. The bot closes some of the distance, bringing itself within a meter of her feet. I'm not sure what it intends to do when it catches her. I've never seen a poolbot go into attack mode before.

I grit my teeth and try to focus.

Damali is headed my direction now. She appears to be slowing.

"Do you want me to try?" Fania asks.

"No." The angle won't be as easy this time, but I can do it. I have to.

Damali reaches the pool's edge and stops altogether. The bot is less than a meter behind, but it slows too. I bring the net down and encircle the thing. I tug, but it reorients itself and tugs back. Damali pulls herself out of the pool next to me. I set my feet and pull against the bot. It meets my tug with a stronger tug. I lurch toward the pool. Rails, I think I'm going—

Arms encircle me, preventing my fall. I feel stifled, but also really strange. I somehow find my feet again, lodge them in the lip of the pool, and tug again. The bot is moving slowly toward me now. Like dragging in a whale.

Damali still holds me. She continues to help until the netted bot is at the pool's edge. The other two women guide the net up over the lip and onto the floor. The bot is round and flat with narrow fins and a rudder used to guide it through the water. It sputters and chatters like a fish, but it is caught.

I need to focus on the bot. Not on the contact. Not on the—her! I kneel over the bot, causing Damali to release her hold on me. I'm relieved and troubled at the same time.

I can find the bot's emanations easily now. I work my way into its command structure, ferret out the stop mechanism, and switch it off. The bot falls still.

"Is it fixed?" Fania asks.

"He shut it down," Damali says. "I'll bet he's fixing it now."

I immerse myself in the problem, ignoring those around me. It is what I do best. What I'm supposed to do. Paradise, remember? Guaranteed! I stream up the bot's specs then check for the latest command set.

"Do you like what you do, 23?" Damali asks. "Do you like this place?"

Why is she talking to me? I have a job. She's disrupting my focus. I glance at her. I want to be mean, but her eyes stall that idea. Rails. What is this I feel now? Craziness. I look at the bot again. Don't say a word. I'm a coward. A nothing coward.

I find an update to the command sets. Years old. The bot should've updated on its own, but who knows around here? The security filters probably messed with it. Kept it from getting through. I wonder what the update fixes—

Warm and soft, the woman's touch. I can still feel where her arms wrapped me. Helping me.

This is not good.

I hear multiple sets of footsteps. "What is going on here?" Jahm asks. He isn't alone.

The women abandon me. I hear the soft sounds of their feet moving to the other side of the pool. Retreating to their towels. Their things.

I glance up and see Jahm with one of the bodyguards. He is walking straight toward me. I acknowledge him with a bow. He looks perturbed. He also coughs. I think that's the norm for him.

"I'm sorry they bothered you," he says when he reaches me. He looks in the women's direction. They are wrapped in towels now. The bodyguard, one I haven't seen before, stands next to them, watching. There's a slight smile on his face.

I shake my head. "They were no problem."

Jahm sighs. "I saw them here with you. Doubtless asking questions. Delaying you." He scowls. "The prince's companions. I waste too much of my time minding them."

I check on the women. Damali is looking at me, smiling. I shake my head. "This bot has old code. I have the update now. It'll take me a second to push it over."

"Yes," he says. "Very good." He pulls a golden controller from his shirt pocket and touches the center of it.

I feel fire between my ears. The sting lasts only an instant, but I can't help but groan. After my vision clears I shoot him a questioning look.

"I'm sorry, debugger," he says. "I should give you those more often. Just so you remember."

"Remember what?" I ask. "Haven't I done all you've asked, Sub-master?"

"You need to remember your place," he says. "You hesitated while performing your chore in the prince's office."

"When the bot's arm—"

He raises the controller again, but I wave and he lowers it. Thankfully.

"Never hesitate," he says. "You work for the prince. Obey without thinking. Always."

My job *demands* lots of thought, but I don't mention that. I don't think it will help. I bow my head instead. "Peace be unto you," I say.

"And to you," he says. "Together with A's mercy."

I remain bowed. I confirm the bot's update process. It is finished.

"Return to your work," Jahm says, and walks away.

I stand and use my foot to shove the bot back into the water. It moves leisurely away to the left. I run a diagnostic as it works. Everything checks out. It is filtering water correctly, and its focus appears to be on reducing contaminates. Like it should be. I hop into the water myself to be certain. My suit absorbs water like a sponge. I hate every moment of it. But the bot doesn't even turn my direction. I pull myself out of the water, collect my bag, and shrug it on.

The women are sitting, bodies covered with their towels, heads wrapped with purple head scarves. I'm not certain that they are watching me, but I feel as though they are. I walk around the pool away from them to the entrance. I don't look back.

Will they remember me? I wonder.

Why do I care? I shouldn't care.

Will *she*?

•••

One disadvantage of my new assignment is my attachment to the palace grounds. My every need is provided for—food, clothing, even my debugging needs. Consequently, there is no reason for me to ever leave. And no excuse to.

Not that I was a social animal before, but I could at least visit a tech shop—a clang and click like Grim's or Zimit's—when I needed supplies. Or go out for food when the food conditioner was updating itself. But here there is literally no need.

Plus, I'm a little afraid to ask. Something is always breaking here. Either intentionally, or through neglect. I have as much job security as a debugger could ever ask for. Big cheer for me, I'm the most needed and well-fed slave in the kingdom!

One thing I can do, though, is explore. I'm not sure that I've found all that can be found yet. I have access to a map, but I suspect it is a little old. Some of the rooms I've run across aren't represented on it, and there are many that are mislabeled.

Surprisingly, most of the doors I've found open to me. Well...maybe that's not too surprising since the place is generally a malfunction waiting to happen. Can't get your bots fixed if you lock the fixer out, right?

Still, I'm surprised. Even most of the prince's personal rooms are open to me. That seems to vary depending on whether he is in the building or not—for instance, his upstairs office will open to me today, but on the days he is around my access will be "invite only."

I've found a couple doors on the ground floor that are blocked. Those are especially strange, because they aren't marked as belonging to anyone, and if I guess, given what I know about the rooms around them, they can't be very large rooms.

Possibly they are extra stairways. I'm not sure if this place has a basement, but if it does...yeah, that's what they probably are. Stairways to the basement. Doubtless that's where they keep much of the backbone for the home. Those machines that keep the place running. Probably also where the stream filtering code lives. Yeah, don't want me going there. Don't want the skin breaking the filter and streaming free!

So, what else can I spend my time on? Well, there's the mystery of the list. So far, I've got one connection. Outer space! *Space* connects them. The first DR loved it as a kid, the other—Arrow—lived in it. I'm a real detective, right? I found a huge, meaningless, connection that took me way too long to figure out. Maybe I should go back to datamixing for pure enjoyment. Leave the sleuth work to others.

Another thing I spend cycles on is the arboretum. I need to get back there again. Also, I need to talk to Bull again. Or maybe one of the other debuggers. I need conversation, friendly or no.

I've been thinking about A some too.

What? A debugger contemplating the infinite? Yeah, I am. But only from a ten-thousand-meter level. Our whole society is constructed around performance. About keeping the good ahead of the bad. Yet the further up the food chain I go, the more brazen the bad seems. The things that happen here, in this house, make the house that was across the street from the garage seem like integrity squared. There the men at least had to make the effort to sin, they had to go find the place. Here the sin is delivered. The prince's companions. The man has a handful of wives already. What does he need pool loungers for?

Plus, his father is supposed to be the highest religious authority in the world. He has to know about his son, right?

One thing the implant gives you: perspective. You can step outside the human condition and see it for what it is. A world where everyone hides their face. The women do so by command, the men do so through habit. Through vice. But yeah, I can see it. Plain as a nanopath under sheet magnification.

Oh, and another thing! I've been testing my stops. Experimenting with them.

Why? Because it fills in some of my downtime. Takes away the tedium.

Also, my experience with the women the other day gives me a perfect memory to play in. I simply dance around the memory segments that brought me cranial displeasure. For some reason, Damali is the easiest of the three to do my tests with. So I use her encounters most. Probably has something to do with the inadvertent hug. And possibly the exposure. Not sure. I'm trying to get to the bottom of it.

Trying to keep true to my name. Lots of threads. Baring them all.

A HEADBUZZ WAKES ME. It takes me a few moments to clear my head enough to focus, but then I realize Jahm is trying to contact me. I don't bother to get out of the chute yet. I don't even open my eyes. I simply wait for his message to come through. It is rails early. Not as early as the day the prince woke me, but early enough. Often things Jahm perceives as emergencies really aren't. A little more sleep might be possible. Maybe.

The message is active, meaning Jahm is waiting to speak with me right now. Typically, that isn't the way it is with him. Usually I get a message with a time stamp showing it was composed only a few seconds before. I don't think Jahm likes active communication. I think the idea of being present inside my head disturbs him somehow. And maybe it should.

Why stoop to my level if you don't have to, right?

Regardless, there is clearly something special here. I open the message and find him sitting in his room with his hands folded neatly on the table in front of him. He has a turban around his head, and his shirt is yellow with embroidery down the middle. Fancy dress! Behind him I see a beige wall with a picture of the royal family on it. Devoted employee, that Jahm.

"Debugger," he says. "This is a very special day. Please make sure that all your priority one tasks are completed before midday."

The image I respond with will make it appear that I'm up, dressed, and standing with my bag over my shoulder. He doesn't need to know that I'm still in bed. Let him think I'm always ready. "All my priority ones were finished last night," I say. "Before I went to bed."

"That is not true." I briefly lose sight of his hands. When they become visible again he is holding the controller. He gives it a press.

More pain for me. About a grade higher than what he used to wake me. That one was annoying. This hurts my teeth.

He places the controller on the table and folds his hands again. "As I said, that is not true. I just checked the list. There are three broken mechanicals. Two on the main floor." He leans forward. "Please pay special attention to the main floor and the prince's offices."

The pain has dissipated now, thankfully. I hope my image copied the initial wince properly. It would be embarrassing if it didn't. Me simply sitting there, smiling, as Jahm pushes the button. "Yes, Submaster," I say. "The prince will be here today?"

"Yes, of course," he says. "He stayed the night here last night."

I don't think I'm getting more sleep today. I stream open the chute and initialize the food conditioner. If the prince was here last night, he probably broke all three bots. It'll be a search for parts followed by more lessons in bot anatomy. I could draw the specs by hand now if I wanted. "I'll get to the list now," I say. "Is there anything else?"

Jahm nods. "Yes, you are to report to the front door at 11:00 am."

I make my image bow. "Very good. May I ask why?"

He looks at me for a long moment, eyes narrowed.

I expect him to reach for the controller again. When he doesn't I decide to apologize. "I did not mean to offend, Submaster."

"You did not offend me. The staff isn't privy for security reasons. But it would be appropriate to tell you, of course. Your confidentiality stops will prevent you from speaking."

I bow my head. "You need pay me no favors, Submaster Jahm."

He coughs, then smiles. "Everything must be perfect today," he says. "The Imam is visiting."

I feel a spike of nervous energy. "The Imam is coming here?"

"Yes, along with his favorite wife. Everything must be perfect."

I hear the food conditioner working. There's a smell of warm blueberries in the air. My stomach rumbles. "I will endeavor to make it so," I say.

He narrows his eye. "I would expect no less." He picks up the controller, eyes it, but does not use it. "I will leave you now."

My image bows as he disconnects. I glance at the ceiling, notice the painting of Noah, and think of rain.

• • •

The first job on the list was an easy fix. It was one of the house's five medbots. Its power generator was past its expiration date. The bot was still working, but it is always a priority one when a power generator is expired. Bots sing their terror straight into the stream and medbots have the shrillest scream of all. Wouldn't want a medbot shutting down in the middle of an operation, would you?

That was a fifteen-minute fix. I have a twenty-year supply of medbot generators right in my supply cabinet. Sleep the bot, pop out the old generator, install the new, and wake the bot. Easiest thing in the universe.

The next job was another of those I think of as a "prince party." The bot had a long strip of synthskin burnt off its leg, which suggests it was the prince's doing. The burn didn't affect the bot's functionality much, but someone must've spotted it walking around like that and reported it. Wouldn't want the Imam to spot a seared bot. That would be way outside the "everything perfect" parameters. Took me almost an hour to strip the damaged skin and graft on new material. Thankfully I have sheets of skin in the closet too.

The third job was straightforward, but debatable as a priority one. Another instruction update. While the bot was technically on the bottom floor, it was in one of the children's rooms that never get used. It had a layer of dust on it, in fact.

Actually, that doesn't say much for the cleaning bots. One of them must be malfunctioning too. Need to check on that.

Now a fourth priority one has popped into my queue. I feel a twinge of regret when I see the location, since it is near the arboretum. The fix request came from the bot itself. Jahm doesn't know about it, but if he did he'd want it fixed. I have about an hour to go until the Imam's arrival. I should get it done.

The pool that precedes the arboretum is rectangular and modest in size. Twenty meters by ten meters, to be exact. The ceiling in the pool area is semitransparent. It keeps the area warm and moist. There are many large plants here, both potted and planted.

The room is completely empty. No people, and the malfunctioning bot, another pool cleaner, isn't present either. The location it is reporting is back up the path, in the arboretum itself.

I can't help but be suspicious. Did someone throw the thing in the trees for fun? Another prince party? I frown and pass around the pool to the arboretum.

A quiet breeze moves the trees. It is comforting. Relaxing. The arboretum is large enough that there are deep stretches of shade on both sides of the path. The air is damp and cool. I breathe deep. Regardless of the reason, I enjoy the chance to be here again.

I follow the bot's location signal. I reach my favorite tree and glance up at the branch I used to perch on. I contemplate reaching it again. Jahm's list is complete, after all. I could spare a few moments, right?

I push the thought away. I need to locate the bot first, at least. It shouldn't be back here. I keep walking.

I reach the point where I can glimpse the land beyond the palace. The moat looks calm and the fields look especially green today. Peaceful and inviting. Again I long for my branch. For a few moments of quiet relaxation. With nothing in particular to focus on. No mysteries, no bots.

The bot is only a few meters ahead. I press on.

Someone steps out from behind a tree. A figure all in black. I startle and take a few steps back. Is it an assassin? One of the people Jahm talked about? Those who hate the royal family?

No, it is a woman. The femininity of the eyes makes it clear. On impulse, I pattern match their shape and color with those of the people I've met in the palace. I get a clear answer.

"Damali."

"You know it's me?" she says, moving closer.

I don't step back again, but I want to. "Your eyes," I say. "They're distinctive."

Her eyebrows rise. "Did you use your implant?" she asks. "To figure it out?"

I nod. "I'm looking for a bot," I say. "Have you seen one?"

"Yes, um…" She steps behind the tree again, then returns holding a poolbot between her hands, bottom side up. The rudder and flippers are in motion, swiveling and flipping, trying to move it somewhere. It looks very much like an angry turtle. "I've had it on its back the entire time." She holds it out, presumably for me to take. "I don't think they like that."

I let her continue holding it. I stream shutdown codes and its motion ceases. I notice that the bot's rudder is half the size it should be because the trailing corner is broken off. There are dark scuffs on the portion that remains.

I look at Damali's eyes. They seem embarrassed. "Did you break its rudder?" I ask.

"It is getting heavy."

I frown, and taking the bot, ease it to the ground. "So, you broke it?"

"I had to do something," she says. "Sorry."

"This is something you do?" I say. "Break bots?"

"No. Why would you think that?" Now she really sounds embarrassed. "I only—" She begins tugging on her head covering until her face is exposed. "I wanted to see you again. I knew if I damaged a bot you would come." She pauses. "I hoped so, anyway."

Her face is still as scientifically attractive as it was before. Maybe more so. Symmetrical. Well-designed.

I look down at the bot. If all she did was break the rudder, the fix is fairly simple. I'll need to reform one using some of the supplies from my bag. Should work. I'll need a shaper.

There are questions burning my insides, of course. The first being: Why do people in this house like to break robots? It is a little deranged.

"And why did you want to see me?" I ask.

She looks surprised. "Because you're the house debugger. You can do things no one else can do."

I focus on the bot again. Her eyes are dangerous. "No. I can only do what debuggers do. Nothing else." I glance at her. "Did the prince teach you this? Damaging bots for fun?"

She squints. "Does he do that too?"

I get a medium tweak. Strong enough to silence me. "It's not something to discuss. I shouldn't have said that."

"But he does do that, doesn't he?" She nods, looking reflective. "Yes, of course he would. He's a monster."

I peel off my bag and start looking through it. I'll need some adhesive, and a shaper. Well, maybe two shapers. Two big shapers.

"Do you think that?" she asks. "That he is a monster?"

I find two shapers of different size. The larger is about the width of the rudder. I might be able to use only that one.

"Are you ignoring me?" she asks.

"I can't have opinions about masters," I say. "It rarely helps to have opinions."

She sniffs, and squats down next to me. Her eyes bore into the side of my head. "He *is* a monster, debugger. How do you think I'm here? How do you think any of the girls are here?"

I need forming fluid. I have to have some of that somewhere. I remember having some of that.

"You could at least speak. I know you can speak."

I'm a little worried about the pathway dirt getting into my forming fluid. Have to be careful. "What would you like to speak about?" I ask.

"You should be curious," she says. "You're a debugger. You solve mysteries and fix things."

"I cannot fix people. People cannot be fixed."

She shifts her position so that she is across the bot from me. Hovering over it. Blocking my light. "He took me off the street. He saw me and decided he wanted me. Then he took me. I had never been with a man, do you believe this?"

I find the fluid. It comes in a long tube. I open it and squeeze some into the shaper. Stroke the shaper's handle so it lights up. I compare the width of the rudder. It should work. The connecting point for the rudder is a metal plate with two joining holes. Simple design. I send that to the shaper.

"Gulru was to get married the week after she was taken. Fania was married already. She is an only child. Her husband is at war somewhere. He doesn't know and her parents are dead." She pauses for twenty seconds. "You're taken too, aren't you? When you become a debugger? You're taken. So you understand."

"I was given a better life," I say. "New abilities." I glance at her.

"I'm not just someone from the street." So, am I significant now? A new level and a new master—does that make me somebody?

She sniffs. "You are better than me?" She looks out into the trees, then scowls. "Who am I kidding, of course you are. You're a man."

I'm not really a man, obviously. But if she doesn't know that, I can't help her.

I start the forming process. The new rudder begins to squeeze out the end of the shaper. So far, so good. No dirt.

"What is your name?" she asks.

The rudder is about halfway out now. Still looking good.

She grabs my arm. The shaper slips out of my hands and falls straight onto the forming end. The rudder is bent, and the shaper is oozing fluid sideways.

What was the swear word that Bull made up? *Picasso?* This is whole lot of Picasso here. I look at Damali. "You ruined it," I say. "Now I have to start over."

I retrieve the shaper and pull off the half-formed rudder. I stream the design again and get it restarted. The new rudder starts to emerge. I purposely hold it tighter, and closer.

"I'm sorry," she says. "I only wanted your name."

I shake my head. "Probably you should go." I glance at her again. "Tampering with a debugger is a punishable offense, you know."

I'm trying to sound stern and detached. I think I'm doing okay with that, but it probably doesn't help that I've used memories of her to test my stops. It interferes now. Making the interaction, the feelings here, all jumbled.

Rails, ThreadBare, you can be so low bandwidth sometimes. Really counterproductive.

Thankfully, the new rudder is nearly done. The last centimeter is being formed, the section with the holes. Can't wait.

She stands. "You're right, maybe I should go. I only thought..." Her eyes follow the path to its end. To where the moat beyond is visible. She shakes her head. "It was a foolish idea." She turns and takes a step toward the pool and the house. She is going away.

The rudder completes. I snap it off and hold it up to the light. It looks perfect. "I have it!" I say aloud. For some reason.

She pauses, then takes a step back. "Have what?" she asks.

I feel the fool now. "The new rudder," I say, shrugging. "It...it's done."

"Oh..." She frowns. "I'm glad. Glad you can fix what I broke." She lightly touches my shoulder. "You do good work."

She turns away again and I feel something. The place where she touched still tingles, yes, but there is something else it feels like I should do or say. I'm not sure what, so I blurt out: "Thread-Bare...that's what they call me. DR number is 23. Thread's my name, though."

She nods and the hint of a smile appears. "Thread...I like it."

I cock my head, raise a shoulder. "Doesn't matter. I mean, it is okay if you like it, but I can't really change it now. I have a rep." I feel uncomfortable. Not tweaked, but still strange. "On the stream. ThreadBare is a little like my address. It is where I live." I look at the new rudder, then at the beached poolbot. "With the threads. All jumbled up in my head."

She's quiet for a second before nodding again. "You really are different, aren't you?"

"I'm supposed to be." I need a tool to remove the old rudder. Two medium flexgromets hold it. I have that tool somewhere. I glance in the bag, and locating a pouched tool set, bring it out. It rattles and clicks. "Sometimes I'm not sure I am so different. Or maybe I'm *too* different." I shake my head. "It's all railed up, really."

That seems to tell her something. She looks reflective, like there is a host of neurons firing in formation. Lots of conjugating. "I need to go," she says finally. "The Imam is arriving soon. We're supposed to be tucked away somewhere. Presentable, but hidden."

"Right," I say. "I don't know where I'm supposed to be. Only available. With everything fixed."

She pulls the scarf in front of her face again. Her eyes look at me. "It was nice talking with you, ThreadBare. Maybe we'll see each other again."

I feel a small tweak. Something is forbidden here, but I'm not sure what. Women, sure, but not meeting them. Seeing them. I manage only a smile and a nod.

She waves. Then leaves.

I return to the bot. Threading.

AS REQUESTED, I'M AT the entrance hall by eleven. I'm dressed like I always am—blue jumpsuit and matching shoes—but both are from the *new* end of my closet. I don't usually like new, because it is brittle and uncomfortable, but I have little choice here. Jahm said "new" so that's what I'm wearing.

There are a lot of people here already. Servants in white, chefs in brown, landscapers in green. We're our own little indoor rainbow. Maybe that's by design. I don't know.

The front doors are wide open. They are ten meters high, and each are roughly three meters across. They are the color of green marble, with intricate patterns of gold. A red carpet has been rolled out across the entrance hall and down the sidewalk outside. Nothing but the best for the Imam.

Our rainbow group occupies space on both sides of the carpet. We are positioned close enough that our presence is felt, but far enough away that we don't look like fans. Jahm and the house supervisor—a female named Unaysah—arranged us just so. We're in short lines that together form two sizable rectangles. A strong showing of work and dedication. We aren't supposed to move from our spots.

I've been here ten minutes already and feel twitchy. I'm not used to this much standing. We're not bots, people!

The entrance hall is generally circular. At the center of the room is a gigantic, ornate vase. It is white in color and large enough to sustain the palm tree that grows from its center. There are two large stairways here as well, one on either side of the room.

The prince and two of his guards come down the stairway that is to the right of the vase. The prince is in a decorative white jacket, with a shiny red shirt and white pants. His guards are both in black and look formidable. The prince looks occupied, perhaps worried.

After exiting the stairway, he brings his palms together, and swivels them nervously. He approaches Jahm and Unaysah. Unaysah is older, though I've had little contact. Today she is covered in a deep purple robe and matching head coverings. Jahm is all in beige. Beige headscarf and matching full-length thobe.

Conversation ensues. I'm too far away to hear what is said, but the prince is talking rapidly. Intensely. Jahm and Unaysah only listen and occasionally nod. The prince leaves them without a closing comment. The two subordinates look anxious now. Chastised for some affront. Something isn't quite right.

The prince's guards leave him and begin pacing the room, eagle eyes on everything. One has a small, square device that he holds up. Possibly testing the air.

A pair of service dogs are brought into the room and led past each row of employees. One of the dogs pauses especially long on me, sniffing at my feet and hands before moving on. His master gives me a stern look, but says nothing. The dogs leave fifteen minutes later.

The prince and his guards take positions near the vase, at the red carpet's end. The swirling drone of hover engines are heard outside. The prince straightens and folds his hands in front of him. His guards become more alert.

I sense new emanations in the stream. Additional servbots and stream-enabled devices. There are other things that interest me too. A debugger has arrived, doubtless a requirement for the Imam. There is something else, as well. Something different.

More guards enter through the front doors. These are dressed in beige and hold nano-enhanced weaponry. Blue rifles with long barrels and heavy stocks. Guns capable of stopping a heavy in its tracks. They scan the room before taking positions near the door.

A gold bot enters, something unlike anything I've ever seen. It stands a head taller than anyone present. Well over two meters. It is plated—armored—in back and front, but not like the heavies I used to work on. This bot is sleek and nimble in appearance. Polished. Its sections all seem to form perfect angles, giving it an overall sharpness. Like it is a walking razor. Or a praying mantis.

Its head has an otherworldly look. The face is plated, with the largest plates being over its cheeks. Sheltered between the plating are two red eyes. These eyes move and rotate, scanning the room. The head turns too, searching everywhere. Doubtless logging and checking everything and everyone.

This event is making me uncomfortable. Why did I have to come?

I get an EI message from BullHammer. "Hey, BareBare, are you here?"

Here? What does *here* mean? On Earth?

The gold bot moves to the left of the door and the human guards scramble to get out of its way. It towers over them. Their guns may stop a heavy, but I have the strange feeling that they won't stop this creature. At least, not quickly.

The Imam and his wife enter the room. He looks very much like his picture, except heavier and older. He wears his standard black turban and a light-colored robe. His wife is completely in white, with a silver design on her scarf and veil.

I don't know how many wives the Imam has. The number is closely guarded. This one, however, looks quite young. Possibly younger than Damali. She trails the Imam by a few steps.

The prince approaches the Imam. The Imam extends a hand which the prince takes and shakes. They move closer, and the prince kisses his father on both cheeks. The prince backs up and acknowledges the Imam's wife with a polite smile. It is not his mother, of course.

Another message from Bull: "Seriously, ThreadBare, are you at the prince's or not?"

A small procession now enters. I'm not sure what all these people represent, but the wardrobe colors suggest chefs and servants. White and brown. There are a half dozen servbots in the throng as well.

The debugger I sensed is Bull himself, but I don't see him. "Where are you?" I send. "Outside?"

Bull enters after the servants. His arms are behind his back and his head is bowed respectfully. He is dressed in a blue jumpsuit, exactly like mine.

"Never mind," I stream. "I see you. Are you the Imam's personal debugger now?"

He scans the room until he finds me. "Only today," he streams. "We're rotated from the pool. I got lucky."

My eyes return to the gold bot. It appears still now, but I doubt it is. I have heard of bodyguard bots before. They are shilled as being "ever vigilant." They also cost more than the average citizen makes in a lifetime. And those are the models I've heard of. This one—

"Looking at the Imam's sentinel?" Bull streams.

"Yes. It's frightening."

He sends me a chuckle. "I think that's the intent. It stopped an assassination attempt last week. That guy looked plenty frightened when it took off his arm. The Imam was pleased."

"So it is everything its designers say it is."

"Yeah, and virtually self-maintaining. None of us, none of the Imam's DRs, have ever touched it."

I look Bull's direction. "Company fix only?"

"They send someone, I guess. Or maybe just trash the old one and send another."

"Sounds wasteful..."

The prince and the Imam are leaving the room, walking between the central vase and the far stairway toward the interior of the home. Four of the human guards go with them. The Imam's wife is led off by the house supervisor, along with a large group of servants. Jahm raises his hands, and after the guests of honor are out of sight, dismisses the rest of us with a wave. The rainbow begins to dissipate.

I'm not sure what to do next. I sing out to the sentinel, but receive only a large bubble of static in return. I would like to examine it closer, but that's probably not wise. Imagine the defense systems! I'll bet even its nanos have knives. The bot remains near the door. Silently watching.

BullHammer approaches, smiling. "This place is impressive. Ranks maybe third of the palaces I've visited so far. At least, from the outside." He pauses, and I can tell he's streaming something. "From the plans it looks nice. Lots of water, lots of green, lots of stone." He whistles. "Lots of mechanicals too. No wonder you're busy."

"You can't imagine," I say.

He slaps my shoulder. "And you can't say. Confidentiality, I know."

I grimace and instinctively pull my job list. Is there anything on it now? No. Rails!

"Don't worry," he says. "I understand." He taps his head. "You wouldn't believe all the secrets I have trapped up here."

I glance at the central vase. There are animals in its design. Lions and bears. "Can't be too many," I say.

He grins, then squints. "Hey...what do you—?"

"Limited storage," I say.

"Sure, but limited in what way?"

I shake my head. I got him. For once, I got him. "Not sure how long I have, but I could show you around, if you want."

He snorts. "And let me fix whatever you've left broken? No thanks."

"Just offering, you blinking—" And again, the headbuzz. Always the headbuzz. I don't wince this time, though. My experiments help! I'm sure Bull can't even tell I'm suffering. I shake my head. "Rails, you know what you are."

He slaps my shoulder again.

Seriously, how does he get away with that?

"It might be fun to see the place, after all. We could—"

He goes distracted, and so do I. I have an urgent message from the prince. He wants me to report to a specific location in the house. I consult my history log and it isn't anywhere I've been before. Nor is there a particular machine tied to the request. I look around. Nearly everyone has left the hall, even the sentinel bot. How did I miss that?

"Gotta go, Bare." Bull begins walking toward the vase, and the rest of the house.

My location takes me that direction too, so I follow.

BULL AND I ARRIVE, together, at the same door. It is only moderately ornate—green with some silver highlights. It is also one of the few doors I'm unable to access. A place I've never been.

"So we're both invited," Bull says, frowning. "What's in there?"

I shake my head. "Don't know." But I'm imagining a closet full of bot parts. Or a torture chamber for them.

The door clicks open. The lighting beyond is dim. I'm nervous.

I motion for Bull to go first. He's the guest, after all.

"What is he into, your prince?" Bull messages. "What secrets does he keep?"

"I don't know everything," I message back. "I know very little actually."

"Got that right."

There is a short hall followed by a stairway leading down. There are strange smells in the air. Sickly sweetness, along with raw chemicals. Chlorine and Ammonia. Cleaning chemicals? Also the scents of illegal contraband substances. Like the smokestick Jahm used.

It is well lit down there, at least.

The stairway ends in a large open space. There are lots of devices around. Metal designs made for unknown purposes. There are vidscreens mounted at various spots on the wall. Games are being played on most of them—football or horseraces—though some show the events of the day. News programs.

I hear someone laughing. It is a deeper voice. The Imam, I think.

My eyes are still trying to take it all in. I see a long bar along the far wall to our right. It is lit in fluorescent colors and there is a servant behind it. There is an impressive display of contraband drink behind him. Hundreds of bottles.

There is a small stage in another corner. I see poles and other contraptions, some hovering and possibly graviton assisted. The sort of things that circus performers might use. I also notice entertainment posters, specifically those having to do with the fantastical—space travel and ancient civilizations. These are things the average person would not have access to. Forbidden things.

The view to our left is obscured by a curved nano-curtain. It is ornamental. Designs move and fluoresce on it. Another indication of the prince's excess.

"Debuggers!" The prince's voice from beyond the screen.

One of his bodyguards appears at the screen's edge and motions for us to come that direction. We walk around the screen into a small theater of sorts. There are roughly two dozen seats centered around another stage, though this one is octagonal and approximately seven meters across. Posed on it are two sleek-looking silver bots. Smaller and less refined cousins of the Imam's sentinel, yet no less dangerous looking. Above the octagon is a narrow vidscreen. On it two zeroes are being displayed.

The prince is sitting in the last row, and across a short aisle from him, is the Imam. They are both holding devices in their hands.

"Are those controllers?" Bull messages me, then a millisecond later: "Wait, no they aren't. At least, not for us."

"The design is wider," I message back. "Flatter. More like bot remotes. Probably for those on the stage."

"Right," he messages. "Looks like a contest. Are bot battles legal?"

I try not to frown. "They might be here." I get a tweak and fight that feeling too. My life—always attempting to cover up. To conceal. To hide the results.

I only now realized. Would I make a good mix? Would anything about me inspire another debugger? Like Sandfly and GrimJack?

"Ah, ThreadBare..." The prince motions us over. "This is my latest debugger," he says. "The one cousin Uday recommended."

The Imam stares at me, appraising me like an expensive horse. "The one from the missile attack?"

The prince smiles broadly. "The very one! Fortunate. The skin who survived the fire. Either jinn or angel. I'm not certain which." He laughs loudly, childishly.

The Imam is still looking at me. Feels strange to be the focus of his attention. The most important human on the planet.

"Peace be unto you, Imam," I say, bowing.

The Imam waves a hand. "And to you." He frowns. "Do you think you were a target, Data Relocator? In the missile attack?"

A target? Who would want to target me? I'm nobody.

I shake my head and bow again. "I don't know why—"

The Imam raises a finger. "The heretics certainly knew of your garage. Of your work in Delusion. This is the way of life under A. The smallest deeds can have wide-ranging effects. Unexpected results." He smiles warmly. "Thankfully, their aim was poor. Only the whores died." He looks toward the octagonal stage. "Let us see how this goes now, Aadam..."

Images of the missile strike flash through my mind—the sound, the smells, the fire. Being trapped to the floor. Could that be for me? Others dying because of me? I'm unsettled, but again, I mask it. Pull it all inside. "You have a task for me?" I say.

The prince says nothing. He only works the controller in his hand. One of the bots on the stage begins to move. It paces first to its left, then to its right, then it walks forward and strikes the other bot across the chest. The prince cackles.

The Imam begins to work his controller too. He lands a hit to the chest of the prince's bot, and then its head. He chortles softly. "Acceptable. Better than the last model."

"Are you ready then?" the prince asks, looking at his father.

The Imam nods.

The prince grins. "One round? Three minutes?"

The Imam nods again. "As always."

The next three minutes are filled with their idle and disjointed battle. Regardless of being "ready" it takes some time for the two men to orient themselves to the robots' articulations. They gain proficiency as the game progresses, but the movements never look fluid or even that effective.

The prince's tactic seems to be to land as many blows as possible. Most of his punches go wide, though, producing either curses or peals of laughter. There is some form of scoring going on, as well. The points of impact light up, and the numbers on the vidscreen above the octagon change.

The Imam follows a more nuanced plan. He concentrates on blocking and feinting, with only an occasional shot to the head or body. He says little as he plies the controller. He only studies and strategizes. Attempting to get ahead of his son, while fending off the repeated attacks. A strategy of age and wisdom.

At the two-and-a-half-minute mark, the superiority of the Imam's plan becomes apparent. He blocks a hard swing by his son's bot, and answers with one of his own to the face. The bot's cheek plating dislodges and falls to the stage's floor.

The prince yells and redoubles his attack, throwing a flurry of punches in all directions. Again, most miss or are blocked, but the law of averages dictates that some will find their mark. The plating on the Imam's bot lights up in multiple places. The scores continue to change, though the Imam remains ahead. His punches are harder and bring higher rewards. Some of his bot's plating is dislodged however. Some of the surfaces beneath take damage.

The bots report every hit to the stream. It is like standing in a rain shower.

Finally, the match ends. The Imam wins by ten points. He is smiling contentedly.

The prince is breathing as if he had been fighting himself. There is perspiration on his face. "You bested me," he says. "After all that."

The Imam nods, but says nothing.

The prince glances across the aisle. "We should have a rematch, yes? Another go?" He looks at BullHammer and me. "The debuggers will patch them up. We'll go again."

The Imam contemplates, but then nods his head. "One more time, yes."

The prince bobs his head enthusiastically. "There. Very good. We'll go again." He waves his hands toward the octagon. "You heard me, debuggers. Go repair them."

"Yes, Master." I walk toward the octagon. I don't look at Bull, but I feel the presence of one of his messages in my head.

"This how you spend your time around here?" his message asks.

"More or less," I reply.

Ten minutes later the bots are repaired. As Bull and I work, the Imam and the prince have food and drink delivered. We return and find the air around them smelling of garlic and alcohol. The Imam has finished whatever he was eating and looks content. The prince still has a plate of half-eaten meats and cheeses on the seat next to him. There is a drink in one hand and an unlit smokestick in the other.

"Yes," the prince says. "Still in their suits, can you believe it?" He shakes his head. "They must know something."

"Perhaps you should go see for yourself," the Imam says.

The prince shakes his head. "I can't stand it there. The food, the view..." He sips his drink. "Makes me ill, you know that." He scowls. "Plus they want it quarantined. For safety! But if I could..." He makes a fist. "I would understand. Everything that happened, believe me."

"Much has been spent," the Imam says. "Much in time and money. A solution must be found. There is a great need."

The prince grimaces, then sips his drink. "Our bots are ready," he says. "Let's try again."

Another three minutes are spent. The prince attempts a different strategy this time, circling the bot around its opponent. He jabs and moves, jabs and moves again. The Imam acts similarly, but connects with his swings more often.

Frustration is evident in the eyes of the prince. He gradually reverts to his old patterns. A flurry of activity on his controller, and within the octagon. By the end of the match he is beaten by nearly twice as many points. Both bots show more areas of damage, though perhaps not as severe. Plenty of squeaking in the stream from both.

"Your boss is manic," Bull sends. "I'm beginning to understand why he's not next in line."

"Next in line?" I stream back. "To rule?"

Bull sends a vid of a mouse banging its head with a hammer. "No, for the refectory. Of course to rule. What else matters with these Abbys?"

I send back static for the insult. "Why not?" I ask then.

"You can hide a freehead's face, but never his rep," Bull streams.

"Scary stories about that one. I warned you. Those things add up. Even for a dictator, erk—" There's a pause, and then: "For a spiritual leader, I mean."

I recall what Damali told me. *Monster*, she called him. It isn't my business. Not something that should concern me at all. But there is a feeling I can't deny. I push it toward the implant, this feeling. I get a tweak in return. I fight it off. Push against it again. The tweak seems to move through my body until every nerve ending lights up.

Then the feeling dissipates.

"TheadBare!"

The prince is scowling and both eyebrows are raised.

"Yes, Master?"

He looks at his father and snorts. "Do you get this with yours? The times when they just leave?"

The Imam shakes his head. "I'm not aware."

The prince looks at me again. "I have been lax with your training. I left it to Jahm, that idiot."

"I am sorry." I bow. "What do you require?"

He snorts. "I asked what you thought of my proposition. Of letting you two control the bots...?"

I shake my head, then glance at Bull. "BullHammer and I? I would not know how—"

"Nonsense," the prince says. "You're created to control bots."

I force a bow. "But I know nothing about this..." I glance at the octagon and the now-motionless bots. "Sport."

I message Bull for his support. He sends back a shrug. Not much help.

The Imam raises a hand. "This isn't what they are for, son. They have other uses."

The prince smiles. "Come, it will be fun. Just once." He indicates BullHammer. "Your DR is ready. Look at him, he's ready." He raises his glass. "We will put a wager on it. Perhaps a case of this drink. You enjoyed it, yes?"

The Imam frowns, but relents, nodding slowly.

NO, NO, NO. This isn't going to work.

I look at BullHammer again. He's standing behind the Imam, pack on the ground. I can't read his expression, and he won't answer my messages now. Wouldn't make sense to, though, would it? We're adversaries. Competitors.

The prince holds his bot controller up, smiling. "I assume you won't need this?"

"We won't," BullHammer says. "There's a stream tap. We can link to them." He looks at me. "We don't need controllers."

The prince resets the scores and the timer. "Another three minutes. I expect good things from you, ThreadBare."

I bow my head, but inside I'm anxious. Worried.

"Did you find the tap?" Bull streams.

"Now you're talking?" I ask. "Where were you—?"

He sends a cheesy grin. "Only streaming to know you're ready. Master privilege, remember?"

Then the wall between us goes up. I close my eyes, and finding the prince's bot in the stream, pull its tap toward me. It appears like a ring of levers. Hard to describe, but I can manipulate each lever—representing a posable section of the bot—with a thought. But there are hundreds of levers. The range of control is better than the prince could manage on his controller, but the possibilities are almost overwhelming. This isn't one of my specialties. I'm not sure I can do it.

Of course, it isn't Bull's specialty either. At least, I don't think so.

I can see through the bot's optics now, live the match from inside its head. Is that good or bad?

The timer starts. Bull charges his bot towards mine. There are so many choices. I hesitate a moment before deciding to turn the bot and sidestep. Bull lands a powerful blow on my mechanical's right shoulder. It flashes brightly and I feel its scream in the stream. Worse yet, the arm's power has been decreased by 50 percent. I locate the bot's feet and make it dance away, putting some distance between it and the other bot. A chance to examine and recover.

There are a number of minor injuries from the earlier bout too, I notice. Things that make me wish we'd been able to repair first. This bot doubtless got beat up worse. There is damage to its left chest, its midsection, and its right optical processor. I try to categorize those and prioritize. Some of it I can address from here, I think—

Bull charges again. This time I try ducking my bot's head, turning, and aiming the right—no, the left—arm for the midsection. I take another glancing blow, but I also connect. The Imam's bot bends over from the impact. That has to be good. Seems good.

Bull lands a counterpunch on my bot's jaw. The optics shiver and waver, plus I'm reading another power loss. Then another and another. He's still coming at me—

I push his bot away, clearing the area to get some space. I try to remember what I saw the Imam do. The things the prince did wrong. I bring up the bot's hands to cover its face. Put bounce in its step. Circle slowly.

The stream! There has to be some fighting examples there, right? I start a streamwise search. I manage to get lots of new terminology. A sport called "boxing." Words like: clinch, bob, weave, and jab. Not that helpful. Need more!

Bull appears to be matching my movement. He *jabs* and I *block*. He jabs again. I block and counter, aiming first for the head, and then the torso. We are going toe-to-toe! I manage to get a few shots through, and he does too. Power level on my right arm is at 40 percent. Need to shift away from that.

Southpaw? What is that?

Oh! A left-handed fighter! It will flip my brain, but I might be able to do that. I shift the bot's stance, moving the other side forward, then start jabbing with that hand.

Bull seems confused by the move. Excellent!

He responds, though. He slowly shifts his stance, and tries a jab.

I attack with the left. He brings the bot's hand up to block, but it isn't complete, isn't solid. My left makes it through, scoring. Bull's bot staggers back.

I'm starting to emote through the bot. I'm starting to remember the times Bull has prodded me over the years. The triggers he has pulled. The bot levers are moving as extensions of all that. Jab, jab, move, roundhouse, hook. This could be fun. It *is* fun.

Blam! Bull lands a hit to my bot's jaw. Power levels are dropping everywhere. I manage to bring the hands up, but they are weak. Hardly any protection.

Blam! I'm hit again. I'm getting lots of warnings. I don't have time to address them all.

Rails, this is too much! My implant might explode.

I back up against the ropes and simply try to hold my own. To keep my arms up. Bull is wailing away at me, at my bot. Strike, strike, strike. I stream out, looking for anything to help me. Something for just this situation.

I find something. A technique called "rope-a-dope." I crouch against the rope, balling my arms and hands even closer. Bull keeps wailing. How much damage is he working with? Not enough.

The power level on the right is worrying me.

He has to be expending power too, doesn't he?

A long piece of plating breaks free from my right arm. Seesaws to the ground. That arm will fail soon.

I peek at the prince. He is bent forward, hands cupped together. Sweat beads on his forehead and neck. Rails, I can smell him now that I think about it. His hands separate and his right reaches for the bot controller. He thinks I'm in trouble. He's going to intervene.

I wouldn't blame him. The bot body is lighting up all over. I'm seeing power losses everywhere—arms, chest, abdomen. I need a new strategy.

I shut my eyes and try to get in it. If my levels are down, so are Bull's. He's been pounding away for most of a minute now. I've got lots left inside. Lots in the bot's motivators. I wait for a pause in Bull's strikes. I see it—

I bring up both arms and push him back. I throw the left hard, and follow up with the right. Both find bot face. Both rattle plating. His head looks like a lightbulb. I block, and swing again. Bam, bam.

There you go, Bull. Call me BareBare. There you go. Now who's hammering?

His arms are drooping. His bot's head is moving with my every hit. He's backing up. Trying to recover. I'm moving along with him. Urging the bot into his space. Have to keep at him while I can. A piece of his plating falls to the ground. And then another. Inner workings are exposed. Conduits and pathways. My power levels are stable. I press ahead, swinging again and again.

Everything stops.

. . .

Our time is up. I release the bot's tap and watch as the circle of levers fall away. It is like a weight dropping off my shoulders. I suddenly feel tired, and a little ashamed.

"Excellent!" The prince claps his hands together. "Impressive performance, ThreadBare. I knew it was a good idea. You are made for it."

Bull looks tired too, but he's eyeing me suspiciously. Like I've been masking something for years. He hasn't messaged me, he isn't taunting me, so that's something. A welcome change.

The Imam watches me thoughtfully. He doesn't look upset. I doubt bot boxing is one of his most important conquests. He has adversaries for that. Antitex and the like.

But Prince Aadam? Rails is he happy.

"Would you like something to drink or eat?" The prince raises a hand and one of his guards appears from the shadows. "Get him something." He looks at me again. "What would you like, debugger? You look exhausted."

The Imam stands and hands his controller to his son. "I should go to my room," he says. "My wife."

"Of course," the prince says. "We can play another time."

The Imam smiles. "Of course. Perhaps we'll invite your brother next time."

The prince bobs his head. "Yes, yes, that would be good." He chuckles. "I would like to beat him."

The Imam nods, but says nothing. He and BullHammer exit the rows of seats then walk around the nanoscreen. Disappear from view.

"Bull?" I stream. "You all right?"

There is a millisecond of delay. Did I hurt him? Injure him somehow? It wasn't us fighting, after all. Only machines.

"Yeah," he streams finally. "You upped me again. Nice work."

"Again? I count once."

Another pause. "You don't know how it is, is all. And I can't tell you."

"Rails, Bull, it was only a game."

"Was it?"

The connection ends and repeated resends gets me nothing more. Nothing but static. Bull is not happy, and possibly not well.

I did something good here, didn't I? I obeyed my master and I succeeded. That has to be good. It is supposed to be good. Why does it feel like I failed? I didn't fail.

The prince prances around the room, smiling and laughing. He moves from one guard to another, slapping backs and squeezing shoulders. Occasionally he pauses to check one of the vidscreens. There's a lit smokestick in his mouth. Tendrils of smoke trace his path.

He has a contraband drink in one hand. He's being reckless with that, much of it spilling onto the floor. I notice traces of food on the floor everywhere. Small items—crumbs and missed bites—things only a debugger or a mouse would notice. The smell in the room is becoming oppressive. The mix of smoke, food, and drink. My stomach complains.

The prince approaches me. "That was incredible. Your moves—it was like you were inside the machine." He sips his drink. "Gripping entertainment. Did you surprise yourself?"

"A little," I say, "But—"

"Yes, of course you did! No debugger gets to do what you did. To taste greatness." He gestures toward the bots, then sips his drink again. "The bots will need some attention. Can you handle them?"

I'm exhausted. Really, really tired. "Yes." I find my bag in one of the seats in the back row. I don't even remember placing it there. "I may need supplies. Parts."

I also need a nap. Both are in my room.

Four women walk around the curtain—the three I know from the pool, along with another, red-haired, woman. They are dressed provocatively. Formfitting dresses with low necklines. It stirs a range of emotions. Ripples along the surface.

The prince looks at them and smiles. "Ah, beautiful, beautiful."

One thing is certain: little about his life follows the scriptures. The rules written in my head. It's no surprise that portions of the population loath him. That he may have lost his position due to graft and treachery.

The prince waves his drink at me. "Perhaps you could give them a demonstration, Thread?" He indicates the octagon. "Show them what you can do!"

I say nothing. Only wait for his next command.

He raises his drink, studying me. "You know...I should reward you first."

"I need no reward, Master."

"Of course you do! Everyone needs a reward." He holds out his drink. "Would you like some of this?"

I shake my head. "I can't."

The women huddle next to him. Damali gives me a sad smile before glancing at the prince and appearing happy. The other women beam, but I suspect they are acting too. At least for the women I know.

The prince brings his drink closer to my face. "Come now, a taste will not kill you."

The smell of the drink alone bothers me. "It will hurt a great deal." I'm curious, of course. As I am with a lot of things. We're made to be curious, debuggers.

"I order you to try it." He glances at the women, then puts his free arm around the nearest, the redhead. The smokestick still rests in the corner of his mouth. There are large patches of sweat under both arms. "That is all it should take, correct? My order?" He laughs. "Or do I need your controller, as well?"

"I've never been ordered to disobey my stops," I say. "The conflict never arises."

"Well, we have no stops in my home. We're royalty." He laughs, then raises the glass to my face and tips it. Fluid runs down my lips. I resist, but he keeps pushing. Finally, I let some in.

I feel scorched. Like that Model 153-432, rev D missile went straight down my esophagus. It explodes when it hits my stomach. Then comes the headbuzz, and it is a doozy. It forces my eyes closed.

He snorts. "That really got you there, didn't it?"

Everything collides—my exhaustion, the liquor—even Damali's presence. I find myself lurching, expelling everything that is in me. It splashes onto the floor.

The prince and his women leap back, away from me. The pain, both above and below, continues until I'm on the floor too.

"Get something to clean that up!" the prince says.

I'm sitting in his crumbs. I can literally feel them through my suit. And the smell...overwhelming. In my mind I'm bot boxing again. Except I'm feeling every punch, and they're alternating between my head and my gut. Bull has me. The prince, Damali, Sandfly...everyone has me. The walls spin.

I'm out.

WHEN I WAKE UP, I'm in my chute again. I feel better, less tired, but my head still aches. The rest of me is functional and pain free. Rails, that was bad.

The illumination filtering through the lid suggests that the room lights are on. So is it night or day? Implant chronometer says it is still day. Late afternoon, but still daytime. Feels later, but I should get up.

Air quality in the chute is fine. I don't smell anything that makes me want to get sick again.

I glance down. I'm not in my jumpsuit. Only my undergarments. Who took off my suit? Who touched me?

Shadows move outside the chute. Someone is sitting on the couch nearby, waiting. It's eerie to be watched while you sleep. While you're vulnerable.

So who is it? The prince again? I hope not.

Plus, I'm in my underwear again.

I can't hide in here forever. I send the chute an open command. The lid begins to rise and I feel a burst of cool air on my legs and chest. They could've at least given me a blanket.

The person on the couch moves, and then stands. The lid retracts enough that I can see: It is Jahm. I'm relieved.

Jahm is dressed as he was this morning: Formal beige thobe and headdress. His face is difficult to read, but he doesn't look angry. He hands me a jumpsuit. "Works every time," he says. "Put the debugger in the chute, and everything will be fine. Everything will function again. Like restarting a machine."

I climb out of the chute. "Not always," I say, "but I feel better. Thanks." I clumsily begin to dress myself. "I will be ready to serve in a moment."

Jahm raises a hand. "You need do nothing more today. The prince insists."

I shake my head. "No, he wanted me to repair his combat bots. I can do so now, provided I am still permitted in the room." I walk toward the wall closet, and opening it, start scanning for parts. I wind back my implant storage until I find the damage lists for both bots. They are fairly extensive. I will need more shapers to start, and forming solution. Sheets—

Jahm draws near, motions for me to move back, then closes the closet door. "You have been given a reprieve. You shouldn't waste it." He studies me. "You are certain you are all right? Have you run an internal analysis?"

"I can if you like," I say. "But I don't think it's necessary. I know when things are right."

He nods. "I will take your word for it." He walks toward the chute again. "I'm grateful we didn't need to send you to Bamboo. The prince despises him. Finds him arrogant and conceited."

My throat still aches from the prince's drink. I drift to the kitchen, open the cupboard next to the sink, and take out a glass. "He is both," I say. "But he's also a fair teacher. Wise and brilliant."

"He is irreplaceable." Jahm places a hand on my chute, then runs his fingers down it. He smiles as if admiring a new vehicle. "Still, I am grateful his help wasn't necessary. Less complication." He turns to me and smiles. "We're independent here, as you've seen."

I fill my glass and take a long drink. It hurts to swallow, but the water helps. Seems to smooth over the pain.

"You have impressed the prince," Jahm says. "Impressed him very much."

I bow. "It was my pleasure to do so."

He squints. "I suspect you've made an impression on others here, as well."

I stifle a cough. "I have no idea what you mean." Why would he say that? Who is he talking about?

He smiles, and turning, leans against the chute. "No, I suppose you don't. Why should you?" He touches the side of his head. "You're a debugger. You have other problems on your mind."

I take another sip of water and set the glass down. "I have many things on my mind, yes." I lean against the counter. There is comfort in its coolness. I still feel...vague. "Are you sure you have no task for me?"

His eyes are still narrowed. "When you collapsed, one of the prince's companions attended to you. I arrived and found that she'd placed a pillow under your head. She was fanning the air around your face, in fact."

I shake my head. "I don't remember any of that."

He pats the chute lightly. "That's why I'm telling you."

Jahm's contact with my chute bothers me. It is borderline rude. Would I go into his room and touch his bed?

"She wasn't alone in her activity, of course," he says. "Others helped clean the mess, but I'm told the prince ordered that. They were only trying to please him."

Where is he going with this? "I remember that," I say. "He ordered someone to clean." You'd think with all the crumbs he might've done so earlier. Guy is a walking mess, let's face it. He's like the anti-debugger.

Jahm studies me. "You have no interest in knowing who favors you, do you?"

The truth is, I can make a fair assumption. "If I did," I say, "it would only be so I could know who to avoid." I force a look of disgust. "There's no future with a debugger. Everyone knows that." My insides betray me, though. Not like before, not like I'm going to get sick. But I don't feel especially well, either. It makes me want to analyze myself more than anything that happened before I passed out. It is out-of-spec strange, and I know it. Dangerous strange.

Jahm nods. "That's good. It would do you no good to create...unhealthy attachments here."

"I'm incapable of doing so," I say. "The stops, remember?"

"Yes, the ubiquitous *stops*," he says. "Another gift from Bamboo."

I take another drink then push away from the counter. "Well, they work," I say. "Believe me." I'm starting to feel hunger now. I could stream the food conditioner, but would that be rude? Have it spinning and clicking while Jahm is here?

Do I care if it is? Why is he still here, really?

"I will take your word for it," he says.

"They. Work." I feel a tingle of a stop there, but I had to say something. He's prodding me without reason. Plus, I'm hungry.

He nods again. "Very well." He moves away from the chute. "I'm glad you're functioning as you should. You've impressed the prince. He will expect more from you in the future."

I feel a twinge of concern. "The combat bots, what I did there, it isn't a specialty. Isn't really part of my training." I glance up and notice the ceiling's painted animals, and the Ark. The animals don't look docile in this rendering. They are growling and frothing, threatening to bite. "I can't do it again." I shake my head. "I shouldn't."

Jahm is near the door now. "I wouldn't worry about that. The prince is..." He frowns and waves a hand. "His tastes blow like the sand in the desert. What you find today you won't find tomorrow." He forces a smile. "Though there will be similarities."

* * *

My period of rest is anything but restful. I contemplate asking for a ride into the nearest town. A short trip to clear my head. I miss the clang and clicks. I miss the strings. Rails, I almost miss my old garage.

But I doubt my request would be granted. As Jahm said, the mansion is "independent." My presence is part of that independence. Slaves don't go on joyrides.

I consider exploring more of the house, or even sneaking down to fix the combat bots, regardless of Jahm's orders. I'm a little concerned about being around the house without having work. I could run into the prince's harem again. I could see Damali. That would be troublesome.

Plus, Jahm suspects something. Suspects *what*, I'm not quite sure. But something with me and her. I know he can't see my insides. I know he can't read my mind or see how many times she's induced stops. Praise A for that.

It isn't my fault she's taken an interest in me. He should be threatening her, right? Isn't that the way it usually works? The woman bears the blame. Otherwise, why the coverings? Why the restrictions? In most cities they can't go out unescorted. My mother used to wait half a day for father to come home, only so she could visit the market.

And *I'm* the slave...

An hour of introspection goes by. I even miss afternoon prayer time. I was reminded, but I chose to ignore it. What sort of disciple am I?

Now reclining on my couch, I try to contact BullHammer again. I'm concerned about him. His demeanor, his face. There were feelings in his last message. Not only anger and shame, but something else. I didn't recognize it at first, but now I do: trepidation. A glimmer of fear.

He isn't responding. Rails. I don't like him, but I still hope he's okay.

I stare at the ceiling again. Noah is portrayed there as larger than his fellow survivors. He's wearing a blue robe and a white turban. The boat is curved, colored red and purple, with a large, white sail. It appears barely large enough to hold all onboard. There with Noah are three men, three women, and two floors of animals, all staring out the windows.

The animals are from legend, I know, because our scriptures don't specify that the animals were there. Only that Noah was to bring "of each kind, two, male and female." It is a point of contention whether that meant animals or other believers. Some depictions show animals, some do not. I typically like the ones that do.

What this picture *doesn't* show is Noah's wife. Scripture teaches that she was left behind because she was an unbeliever. She is commonly equated with Lot's wife who was turned into a pillar of salt in another story. Noah's wife drowned in the deluge that followed, along with one of her sons. The size of the deluge is a point of contention as well.

I think it was catastrophic. I think it was worldwide. It would have to be to wipe away all the bad parts.

I try Bull again. No response.

I need a datamix. I need a change of location.

I message Front and he answers on the first try. We connect Full Impact. He's feeling good. He's on a downrider somewhere. It has a

165

red interior and looks very clean. They almost always do. I glimpse buildings moving by in the windows around him. Blurred civilization.

Front grins at me. "Still living the life?"

"I'm living something," I say. "Lots going on. Lots filling my cycles. I wish I was where you are now, though. Strings, yeah, I miss them."

"Isn't so great," Front says. "Another shop got bombed yesterday, did you know? *Little Thinkers.*" He shakes his head and I feel the sense of loss. "The place was small, but it had the best chews. Kept in a fishbowl near the checkout. Used to grab a whole handful on my way out. Grape and mango. Rails, I loved those."

I sigh. "Flipping antitexs. Always bombing."

"Yeah," he says. "At least you got sent a real missile, not some wrapped on, walking, pyrotech Abby. Missiles are cool."

"No," I say. "They aren't. Not really."

"Whatever," he says. "I'm toasted about it. No more chews."

"Are the owners okay?" I ask.

"Yeah, they got out," he says. "Small bomb. Only took out the front half of the store. Other freeheads got burnt. Pedestrians."

"That's unfortunate," I say.

"Is it? Sometimes I wonder. Wonder if it wouldn't be better if it was just us. We could never hurt anyone. Never bomb anyone. We only do our job. Keep the bits flowing."

I don't say anything. Can't help but think of Bull. Remember his fear.

"You need to live someone else's life already?" Front asks.

I open an eye and look at my chute. I can see the smudges from Jahm's hands. Freeheads. "Do you have something?" I ask.

Front narrows his eyes. "From the list?" I recognize a black TreArc building in the window behind him. There are two domed temples in the scene, as well.

"If you can."

"You're lucky, Thread. Did I ever tell you?"

"Probably." I stroke my couch's surface. Seems like real leather. Soft and cool to the touch. Warm on the body. Remarkable. It might be my first time having a leather anything, ever. I might be able to sleep here, even without a chute.

"Well, I do have something. DR 157 went missing three months ago. Turns out he has a strong rep before that. Almost a perpetual fourteen. Sharp and sleek. Are you ready?"

"Sending credits now."

His eyes widen. "I'm seeing them. Gorgeous. Prepare to step into his mind."

"I'm ready. Really ready."

I HEAR THE SCREAMS all day, and I love it.

Right now I perceive four distinct downriders. If I close my eyes I could identify each of them. In fact, I think I'll do so now.

To the south, an Elixir 750. It is a two-year-old model with re-duced-noise braking system and a single acceleration node. To the east are two models—a Savron TX-80 and another Elixir. The latter is last year's 900 update, which is essentially the 750 with sleeker lines and more colors. They added sapphire and emerald.

The TX-80 is a double hump downrider. It has twice the engine output of the Elixir, with half the noise. Originally they were so quiet a few debuggers got inadvertently smacked by them. The next update increased the noise level so they would be safer. So far, fewer smacks.

The fourth downer is a little harder because it is a Krindle mod. I'm fairly certain it is built on a Coniqe chassis and engine house, but all Krindle's sound alike. They have this distinct two-note whistle as they move. They make birds fly and dogs howl, but rails are they fast. I could build something that would look better, but not sure if I could beat the performance. Krindle is an icon. A mythical being.

"Did MadOck find you?"

I open my eyes.

CoolRun is standing in front of me. He's a level twelve trainee. Blue eyes and a head smooth as a baby's and probably as soft. Lowest man in the shop, but he's okay for a kid. Likes to walk in my shadow, and I don't mind. He'll be good someday. Maybe take my place.

Behind him is a meter-long scale model of my latest design. A new gravity assisted interplanetary. A glorified ore mover, but without some of the chunkiness of older models. It still looks like a large pinecone, but I removed a lot of the unnecessary lines. Smoothed it out. Doesn't add anything to the overall speed—at least, not in the vacuum of space—but it looks better. And when we're slingshotting the gas giants, yeah, we should get some boost.

Downriders were my first specialty, though. That's why I love them. Why I still pay attention to their movements on the strings.

Plus, up here that isn't a difficult hobby to have. All around us are windows. Our design floor is the nicest on the planet. We have the whole city of DT surrounding us. The tops of every building, and beyond, to the north, the mighty lake. The surface appears to go on forever. All ice now, though. One big rink of forever. There are people out on it, in fact. Hope they got nanos in their suits, or they'll freeze.

"MadOck?" I say. "Haven't heard from him. Not even a message. Why?" MadOck is our freehead liaison. He's a stocky man with dark, thinning hair. Generally pleasant for an Abby. I like him.

Cool's eyes are wide. A common look for him. "Because something big," he says. "Planetary government big."

Our team has government types show up occasionally, but usually we're only plagued by company reps. We're company owned and maintained. The details I don't understand. I don't want to understand. I understand the math and the science. I get food and clothing. I have a nice apartment. Plus, there's this view complete with downer screams. Can't forget those. They help me work.

"They aren't asking for weapons again, are they?" I say. "Because they've been told to stop."

Cool shakes his head. "I don't think so, sir. It was an older man with two companions. He said he represented the ruling family."

"The Imam?" Now that *is* exciting. Not Krindle engine exciting, but enough to stir my implant. Get me wondering all sorts of strange. "What would he want with us? I don't think he trades in ore or stone. But I could be mistaken."

I look past Cool to scan the entire floor. The layout is an open one, with dozens of design stations and few walls anywhere. There is activity at each station—debuggers hovering over desks or sculpting prototypes or manipulating holographic displays for freehead engineers to view. There are a few walled offices near the opposite end of the building, but even those have transparent fronts. Little is hidden here.

"I don't see MadOck," I say. "No wait, yes I do. He's in one of the conference rooms along the south wall there." It is a little far, but I think I count three people with him. If he needed me why wouldn't he message me?

Of course, Mad is only an honorary debugger. Not the real thing. No implant, so streaming isn't natural. We only gave him an easy name so he would fit in. Ock is short for Octopus. Hands in everything, that one.

"He looks distressed," I say. "I'll go check on him."

"Want me to go with you?" Cool asks. "I can be your backup." He shrugs. "In case you miss anything."

I smirk. "My eyes work. Implant works. Won't miss anything, thanks."

I pass four design stalls on my way. Lots of amazing creations. Prototypes for all sorts of mechanicals and conveyances. Servbots, hoppers...I even spot a new space elevator design. I had no idea we were working on one of those. The debugger's name there is Data-Bind. Light skinned and temperamental. Doesn't even smile when he looks at me. Face is a mask, and inside—turmoil. Every design shop has one.

I walk by the conference room once to scout things out. MadOck is there with three other men, like Cool said. Mad sits at the head of the table, and the others are on either side of him. They are dressed in more formal garb than we typically wear here, complete with head coverings. Actually, even Mad is looking spiffed today. His head isn't covered, but his pants and shirt look clean and pressed. Most presentable I've ever seen him. His remaining hair is even combed.

Too interesting. Yeah, I have to get in there. Why aren't I in there?

I turn and pass by the conference room again, but this time I go slower. I take the time to study everything. The older man has the look of someone used to giving orders. Straight posture and a sort of regal, yet casual, demeanor. The other two men are underlings, or if not, they still defer to the older gentleman.

Mad's face is intense and a little pale. Whatever they are saying is not something he wants to hear. He's even tapping his thumbs together at the table. That nervous thing he does.

I have to get in there. I don't know that Mad would get a message if I sent one. I don't see his com device with him. He isn't looking my way either. Still focused on the client.

Whatever. Cool said Mad might be looking for me. I'm entitled to interrupt, right?

I pause near the door and simply wait there. Finally, one of the other men notices. Then the older gentleman. I raise a finger. An interruption finger. Useful tool. Opens nearly any door.

Mad glances at me, but still looks uncomfortable.

No going back now. I open the door. "Sorry to interrupt. Cool said you might want to see me?"

Mad looks at the other men, then nods.

The older man stands, and the other two follow. "And who is this?" he asks.

"One of our designers," Mad says. "Kicker."

"And what level is he?" one of the younger men asks.

Mad looks at me, seemingly nervous. "Oh...I think he's a thirteen. You're a thirteen, aren't you?"

I frown. "Fourteen, thanks. Been at this awhile. Went fourteen last month."

Mad chuckles nervously. "Of course, how could I forget?" He swings a hand toward the older man. "Kick, this is Jahm Chahine. He comes to us from the prince's retinue."

I bow. "Peace be unto you, Jahm."

He returns the bow and the greeting. He has a bemused look on his face, as if he knows something that I do not. That's impossible, of course. Here I know everything. Or almost everything.

"My associates are Ibn and Naadim," Jahm says.

I mimic their bows.

Jahm returns to his seat. "Please, won't you sit with us...um...Kicker, yes?"

"Kick is fine." I walk to the foot of the table and take a seat. That leaves me a couple chairs from any of them, but I like that buffer zone when I can get it. Plus, it means I can see everyone comfortably.

Mad doesn't seem to like it, though. He's giving me the squint-eye. Makes me want to laugh.

"So you're one of the designers," Jahm says.

"Righto," I say, glancing at Mad. "What has Mad told you?"

Jahm folds his hands on the table in front of him. "He has told us nothing about you specifically."

Now I'm a little miffed. I look at Mad again. Feel like frowning, want to frown, but don't. "Well, I like to think I'm one of the best," I say. "I've been at it for nearly twelve years. I have my name on a handful of secured designs. Won a Selza award in '98 for an orbital. One in '96 for a downrider. Perhaps you've heard of it? The HeavyKick by Alonsic? That's mine."

"Very impressive work," Naadim says. He's a skinny guy that seems too small for his clothes. And also a little nervous. A little twitchy. "We are aware of that model. The Imam has one on his personal circuit. Very impressive, very fast."

I grin. "Right, fast. That's part of my operating procedure. The tightest, cleanest lines and the best output per grams of fuel. Tight, efficient and fast."

Jahm is still smiling. "Your liaison has told us about some of the other debuggers here. About a CoolRun, a DataBind, and—"

I frown. "What sort of design are you after?" I ask. "Those two, well, they're good, but I don't know that they are what you need."

"And what do we need?"

"Depends," I say. "But if you want lines and perfection I think even Mad would agree they're not there yet. Cool is only a twelve. Needs some seasoning." I feel a twinge of guilt and find myself glancing out at the studio proper. I can't see either Cool or Bind, but I would hate the former to think I didn't mark his talent. Because the kid has talent. He simply isn't ready for a full job, like it seems these guys want. What do they want, anyway? What would the royalty need? Another vehicle? Another luxury yacht?

"Yet someone like you," Jahm says. "You would have the skills necessary—"

Time to play a little closer to the vest. "That's up to Mad," I say. "He's the most impartial judge."

Mad is tapping his thumbs on the table now. "Yes, Kick could handle almost anything," he says. "Sure."

"What is it I would be handling, precisely?"

Ibn shakes his head. He's larger than the other two. Fits his clothing better. "We cannot say here. It is a special project."

"A new design or a refinement?" I ask.

Jahm nods once. "It is a new design, yes. A bit of a revolution."

I feel a tingle in my chest. Warm and cool at the same time. I move forward in my chair. "A new design?" I say. "I love new designs."

Mad's drumming stops and his fingers splay out like tines on a rake. "You have plenty of those here, though," he says. "Many projects in need of completion." He indicates Jahm. "What they are asking for is a long commitment."

"How long?" I ask.

Jahm shakes his head. "We are not at liberty to say. But realistically, it is indeterminate at this time. We must first assemble our team."

"Team?" I glance out at the studio, noting all the busy stations. The incredible designs. "We have a team right here. You don't want that? I mean, even Bind is better than ninety percent of the design DRs out there. Grumpy or no."

"Kick... ," Mad says.

I shrug. "I'm only trying to understand. Why would someone want to pass on this team? This facility? Best in the world. We've won dozens of awards—big awards—hundreds of contracts and completed tasks. Why wouldn't—"

Jahm raises a hand. "There are logical reasons for what we are doing. This project requires a special environment. A special team."

"And we have a special team. That's what I'm trying to say."

Jahm clears his throat. Smiles. "I would not dispute that. But we have unique requirements. Until the DR is transferred to us, until they are under our temporary ownership, we cannot go into detail."

I lean back and bring a hand to my chin. These guys are baiting me with their secrecy. I hate that. On the one hand, whatever they're creating has to be big. Important. But leaving this place? This team and the downrider screams? That's a big hurdle.

"You appear to be in deep thought, Kicker," Jahm says. "Does that mean you are considering joining us?" He looks at Mad. "Am I correct to assume he *is* your best?"

Mad nods. "Sadly. Yes."

"What sort of project requires a special location," I say, "when the stream is everywhere? When DRs can visualize everything inside their head?" I frown. "There's only a few situations I can think of, and even those are borderline. One is aquatic, like if you were designing a submersible, or a new underwater city, maybe. The other possibility is space, but like I said, most of that can be simulated, either through the stream or through altered graviton fields and the like. Expensive, yes, but possible. We have a small field lab downstairs, in fact."

Jahm is still smiling. He bows his head, but says nothing.

"It isn't the ocean work, is it?" I say. "Because I have problems with depth. Depth and fish. I hate them."

"There are risks," Jahm said. "But there will be no fish."

Ibn scowls. "He is clearly not interested. We need someone right away." He looks at Mad. "Please bring us someone else."

"I don't think he has the temperament," Naadim says. "He is an egotist."

I sigh. "Don't get stirred there. I'm still thinking."

"With all due respect to these gentlemen," Mad says. "I would rather you don't do this, Kick. You'll make my life harder."

Times like these I really wish Mad had an implant. I want to know what he really thinks. Reading facial expression and body language isn't the same as a good ole Full Impact message. I know he isn't saying everything.

Something about this feels right, though. Fourteens should be working on monumental things. Earthshattering things.

Plus, it is a chance to impress royalty.

I hear another downrider scream. A close one. Another Krindle mod. Gotta give it to Krindle. He's made a significant impact.

"Fine," I say. "I'll do it."

I SNAP AWAKE.

I stare at the ceiling for a moment trying to orient myself. Noah gazes down on me, larger than life. The other passengers are huddled in groups, looking frightened. And all around them the waters rage, rage. The animals at least look content. A little savage and possibly angry, but they're still just being animals. Still know their place.

I don't know my place.

No wait, of course I do. It is wherever they put me. Doing whatever they want. That's my place.

Jahm...Jahm was there. In Kicker's mix. Big revelation.

So what have I learned so far?

And why do I care?

I care because it is a mystery, and debuggers solve mysteries. Back to the first question.

What do I know?

I know a group of masters and the royal family were creating something. Something in space. Something that required a team of high levels. Designers, engineers, and debuggers interested in astronomy. All of them went top secret as soon as they started. At least, none of them ever posted another mix, assuming Front is giving me their latest. Which he probably is. I also know that they're all missing and possibly dead. Or maybe still in space. But if that's the case, why add them to the offline list?

Who knows?

Jahm. Jahm knows. And probably the prince. And the Imam.

All this time dreaming, and the reality is right here. In this very house.

Figures.

No talking about it, though. How would I bring something like that up? Hey, Jahm, where are all those debuggers you gathered? Haven't seen 'em around in a while. Where in space are they, really? And what were they, or *are* they, doing?

It is none of my concern. None of it. I'm nobody.

Is Sandfly a somebody? Prying chute lids and dropping barge arms? Saving people? Even though he's like me? Controlled like me.

Maybe.

Should I try to message him? Try to understand?

It would be strange. He already thinks I'm subpar. And after I've viewed a mix of him? It would be out of bounds. Never discuss mixes with the people in them. It is too intense. Too bright and squishy.

You know who's somebody? Damali. She's somebody. She's like me, trapped here, but unlike me, her head is free. Simple and unconnected, maybe. But free.

I wonder where she is right now. Is she still with him? I don't like it that she has to be. She shouldn't have to be...

A tweak begins, but it is mild. Or perhaps I am truly growing accustomed to them. I wish there were a measure, a scale somewhere that would measure the pain I'm enduring with each tweak. I know the master's controllers have settings, so there is a measure. But internal stops have no indication of their severity. They simply hurt.

I find myself wanting to talk with her. Right now. I would share something about myself. Tell her about my life. Then she could tell me about hers. Except the prince parts. I don't want to hear about those.

How would I reach Damali? How could we meet? I can't do anything to contact her. Even if there was a way to message her, I couldn't easily do it. There would be pain involved.

I can't break a bot and have her come running to me, obviously.

I look at Noah again. He's all alone on that boat. Part of his family is there, and the animals. But no wife, scripture says. That seems a little sad, and perhaps a little unloving of A. Wouldn't A want Noah to take part in repopulating the Earth? Why is the great patron the only one on the boat without a mate? Did he have an implant? Was he a slave like me?

I can't sleep now. Perhaps if I go to the arboretum again, she'll be there. Wouldn't that be interesting?

I stand and look myself over. My jumpsuit is a little wrinkled, but it is otherwise clean and stain free. Should I check my appearance? Is that what freehead people do before they meet someone? I wouldn't know. I have no hair. The amount of things that could go wrong is therefore greatly reduced. I run a hand over my face and head anyway.

Teeth! I should check my teeth!

I walk toward the reflective portion of the wall near the chute. I'm still a debugger. Still a nobody. Lonely and unlovable, like a robot made of flesh. Except I'm worse, because I feel. I try not to, I'm conditioned not to, but I *do* feel.

I return to the arboretum. I climb into my favorite tree and stare out at the fields. The sun begins to set.

No one comes.

A DAY OF NORMALCY has come and gone. I've fixed seven mechanicals. Three were routine maintenance—simple code refreshes and diagnostics of all systems. A couple required larger services like core updates and nano blends. Still nothing major.

The other two were prince parties. The first was a cleaning bot found inside a freezing unit that was literally a block of ice. I have no idea how he pulled that one off, because it would've required the bot to be within a container of water. There were no containers around, though. Only a frozen bot cube. Like someone's idea of a party prank.

The last bot was the worst. It was painted in blood and had large puncture wounds in its chest and abdomen. The sort of wounds that a projectile weapon would make. It was as if the bot were holding someone...who also got perforated. I tried not to focus on that as I worked, but it was difficult. I had to stop and start a few times. Drive flying head dreams away.

I hope it wasn't someone I knew.

I haven't seen Jahm or the prince in all that time, but I know the Imam has departed. He left yesterday morning.

I haven't seen Damali either. I've been to the arboretum two more times.

Right now it is late afternoon. My list is clear and I'm in my room. Where else would I be?

I'm hungry, but the matter store on the food conditioner needs filled. Generally, one of the servants is responsible for filling those, but most of them are afraid to come to my room. Probably think they'll catch whatever caused me to lose my hair. You get a lot of that in human servants. They think everything is leprosy.

I walk over to the food conditioner. It takes cubes of proteins and other essentials. I know it is low on the former because it has been stream humming about it for the last day. But where would the replacement cubes be?

There is a heavy thump on my door, then it clicks open. The prince and one of his bodyguards hustles in. The guard lingers near the door, but the prince is soon halfway across the room. He's now standing near my chute. Smiling, he pats the canopy. His eyes flit everywhere, looking at everything—the walls, the ceiling, the furnishings. He circles, touching and looking. He then walks to the supply closet, and swings open the doors.

I simply watch as he moves through my hanging jumpsuits, sliding one aside, and then another. He starts pulling out drawers and examining the items on the shelves.

"Master?" I say after a few moments have passed. "What do you require?"

He turns and smiles. "Ah, ThreadBare, there you are." He presses his hands together in front of his face. "I require you, of course. I have a new task."

I bow. "Of course."

He looks at the closet again. "Yes, gather the things you need and come along quickly." He drifts toward the door again, still examining everything. He picks up a decorative crystal from an end table and turns it every which way, then scowls. "This is garbage." He tosses the crystal across the room. It smashes against the floor.

I gather my bag from the closet.

The prince removes a framed painting from its stand. I expect him to hurl that too, but he notices me, and places the painting back where it was. "Are you ready?"

"Yes, Master."

He nods once. "Let's go then."

We walk briskly through the house. I stay behind the prince before he beckons me forward. The guard takes my former position. We walk south through the east wing of the home. We pass the large foyer where I first entered the building, then comes one of the smaller pool areas, then the museum I discovered earlier.

We're headed toward the back of the building. I can't help but think of the arboretum. Does the prince know I go there? That Damali has met me there?

I feel my feet grow heavy. I begin to lag.

"Please, stay with me, ThreadBare," the prince says.

I force my feet out of the mud they've found, taking longer steps to draw even. "Yes, Master."

He squints at me. "What do you think of my father's sentinel?" he asks.

"I know little about that model," I say. "They are a closed design. Proprietary."

"Of course, I know all that." He scowls. "I wasn't asking whether you could fix one. Only what you thought of it. Debuggers have thoughts and desires, do they not? A sense of what is beautiful or lovely?"

"In some form," I say, "yes."

He chuckles. We pass a group of female servants dressed in white, but with faces visible. They bow and the prince studies them. His eyes linger especially long on two of the younger ones. "In some form. Such a good answer." He looks at me again. "So, your thoughts on the sentinel?"

"It appears functional and well designed," I say. "It would be a privilege to maintain such a device."

"But you don't like the company policy," he says. "That they keep it to themselves?"

"It is not my decision. If that is what the Imam requires, then it is good."

He scowls. "How much of what you say is implant controlled, debugger? Eighty percent? Half?"

"Are you talking about my stops? They—"

"No, not your stops. Not what you are disciplined for. What you keep yourself from saying to avoid being disciplined. This is what I mean."

We're near the home's southeastern corner now. There's a large library here filled with vidscreens and holographic displays. These are built into shelving with a selection of bound manuscripts. There is a functional fireplace as well. The area has a musty, aged smell. I doubt the prince goes there often.

"I have no way of knowing, Master."

"You should keep track of such things," he says. "I would guess it's a large number." He leans closer and smiles. "I have no such restrictions."

We take a turn toward the building's interior. We walk down a short hallway that has two unevenly placed chandeliers and dark paintings of a style I don't recognize. Each one seems to use black as the primary color. The subject matter is of mythical creatures. Dragons and giants. In every one, someone seems to be in mortal danger. Either tied or pursued. We take another turn into a narrow hallway. The walls are strikingly less ornate, almost bland. The lighting is dimmer too, and the musty smell returns. Thicker. It bothers me a great deal. It's a lonely place.

Finally, we stop beside a beige door. There is nothing remarkable about it at all. I couldn't access it before...but now, testing the stream, it appears I can.

"You've impressed me, ThreadBare," the prince says. "You are more resourceful than you're given credit for. Underappreciated. We have a kinship in that, I think." He rests a hand on my shoulder and squeezes. It is an unwelcome feeling, but I have little choice.

I bow my head. "Peace be unto you, Master."

He laughs. "Yes, peace. Peace is a word with no meaning, debugger. A spoken nonsense."

He touches the door and it slides open. The room beyond is very small. No, it isn't a room at all! It's an elevator. Rails, Thread. Obvious.

The prince walks in and motions me inside. The guard and I join him, the doors close, and we begin to descend. The elevator has a heavy, chemical smell. Strong enough that my eyes water.

We ride down for some time. There are no distance indicators, but the time is long enough that I estimate we've traveled at least two floors. Then the elevator stops and the doors open. Numerous scents confront me. Biological scents, like having walked into a zoo or a barn, are present along with the masking aromas of perfumes and cleaning agents. I detect the acrid smell of smokesticks, as well.

The room beyond the elevator is bare, aside from a large sink on one side, heavy hooks in the ceiling, and a vidscreen on one wall. The walls and floor are slate grey.

The stream's emanations are omnipresent. I sense new appliances. Things I've never encountered before. I try to get a handle on all the devices. There are bots down here—servs and other common mechanicals—but those aren't what holds my attention. The other machines...I have difficulty even locating their model numbers. And those I do find, don't seem to have specs in the global stream. I see only individual components specs, but not the devices themselves.

Very strange. I'm afraid to ask what this place is. But I can theorize.

"I call this my playground," the prince says, stepping into the room. "As I'm sure you know, the Imam, my father, has enemies. We *all* have enemies."

He sweeps a hand in the air. "This is one of the places we learn about them. Where we try to discover their motivations." He looks at me and grins. "You should have some appreciation for this. Solving mysteries is part of your design, correct? Think of this as your debugging process in a more biological form."

"There are unknown devices here." I'm not sure how much to say. Not sure what is safe.

"Oh yes," he says. "Many, many machines."

I study the room carefully. I notice stains on the floor beneath the hooks. There are discolored portions of the walls and fiber strands in one of the corners. Nothing tech aside from the screen. "But not here," I say.

"No, no, this room is a bit of a throwback. A place of mundane labors." He looks at the guard. "We won't spend our time here. Come along."

We cross to the opposite wall and another sliding door, which the prince opens. Beyond it is a long hallway with doors on either side. Between each door is a pane of glass for viewing the area past the door. The panes of glass are strangely shaded. They might be invisible from the other side. Possibly nano shielded.

The prince pauses at the first pair of rooms. "I have many responsibilities for my family. This solving of mysteries is one father says I'm best at." He nods at the pane to our right. "I'm especially proud of the technologies we've developed. Come, what do you notice here?"

I approach the glass. Beyond is a long, dimly-lit room. It stretches many meters away from us. Far enough that it's furthest corners are quite dark. It is empty aside from a few metal plates in the ceiling. The floor is divided by a series of evenly spaced lines. Almost like markers in a sporting event. I describe all this to him.

"You don't see the machines then?"

I shake my head.

He manipulates a small controlpad between the window and door. A few seconds later plates in the ceiling move back and two metal arms drop through. "A new model of sonic inhibitors," he says, smiling. "Invisible to all sensing equipment, including implants."

"And the lines on the floor?" I ask.

"Used to test their effectiveness, of course."

"And on what is it tested?"

"Why, the Imam's enemies, of course."

Like the heavy I worked on. The heads sticking out of the desert. "Human subjects," I say.

"Is there a better choice?" he asks. "The Imam is A's representative, is he not? Fighting him is like fighting A himself. It is the work of Shaytan. The worst of all heresies."

"But aren't such judgments made in our courts?" I remember the many public punishments I've witnessed. Beheadings and stonings. "The displays—"

"Yes, all necessary. All according to our laws." He smiles. "But the courts cannot take care of everything. And the Imam is the embodiment of the law."

He walks to the next window on the left. The lights inside are off, but he turns them on with the nearby controlpad. This room is stark white. In the exact center is a man encased in a large, silver bubble. The bubble is shiny, and appears pliable, but the man is not moving. He's facing us and sits within the silver blob. Only a portion of his body is visible—his head above the chin, part of one arm, and both legs below the calves. His face is very thin and there are circles under his eyes. There are red streaks on his brow and arms. I can't hear him, but his mouth is moving slowly. As if he were moaning.

I'm disturbed by the scene, but the silver substance intrigues me. What is it? Not metal, not with him still being alive. A synthetic of some sort? But what?

Oh, wait...

"Are those nanos?" I ask. "His restraint. It is composed of nanobots?"

"Very good!" the prince says. "See, I knew you were better than you let on."

"This is another, um, experiment?" I say. "Another test?"

"Yes, a restraint system. For tech areas where more...hands on approaches might be dangerous. In space, for instance."

I look at the trapped man again. He's very pale. "How long has he been in there?"

The prince folds his hands behind his back, looking in. "Yes, he's especially resilient. It has been over a week now. Sitting there, staring at the window." He shakes his head. "Can you imagine?"

"And what has he done?"

"We suspect him to be an antitex agent, though his arresting crime was less severe."

"And what was that?"

"He was in a state of seclusion." The prince looks at me.

"Found with an unrelated woman?"

"Yes, of course. A mutaween brought him in."

I bow in recognition. Mutaweens are officers of the Ministry for the Promotion of Virtue and the Prevention of Vice. They ensure that freeheads follow the rules of our faith. The only places they don't have jurisdiction are the homes and offices of the royal family. I think I know why.

The tour continues for twenty minutes. The prince doesn't stop at every room, but he stops at many. Each features a different brand of freehead "testing," though most would call it torture. All the subjects are in bad shape. Emaciated, bruised and sometimes missing limbs. Some are hung from the ceiling, others are bound and gagged. There is usually a tech angle. Another machine that's been twisted.

It's all I can do not to be sickened. I'm no longer a freehead, but I know what it's like to be them. I was implanted only a few years ago, though it seems a lifetime.

The hallway turns to the right, and the doors become less frequent. There are only three large ones ahead, and no windows. Only one wall-mounted controlpad.

"I expect new testing subjects soon," the prince says. "An unusual case. It may be difficult to learn all I need to know." He pauses in front of the first door. "I like to experiment here, obviously. And you've inspired me, ThreadBare."

"I've inspired you?" I say. "I'm a debugger. I'm nobody."

He frowns. "Please, I think we've already established that isn't true. We are both special, you and I. Your performance the other day. How you worked the combat bot. I could ask for little more." He places an arm on my shoulder and squeezes. With the other hand he works the controlpad. The door opens to reveal a darkened room. A large room, if the breeze I feel is any indication. I hear moans and smell the scents of human waste.

The lights come on.

There will be similarities. Jahm's words.

He was right.

THE ROOM IS THE largest one I've seen. Doubtless the largest room on the premises. It is at least sixty meters across and seventy wide. It has the feel of a small amphitheater, except without the rows of seats.

In the center of the room is another enclosed space, similar to the one used for the combat bots, except smaller. It has more the look of a cage. Closed in and inescapable.

There is a singular bot in that central cage, painted red. It is more refined than the one I manipulated before. Sharper. Not the same as the Imam's sentinel, but made along the same lines. Formidable and quick.

Positioned around that central cage are smaller cages, stacked three high. These are only partially full, but there has to be at least forty prisoners present. There are three climbing servbots in the room. Bots built with prehensile limbs able to grip the bars like monkeys. They are less humanlike in other ways too—their faces and bodies are narrower, and their skin is greyer. They're designed to service the menial needs of the prisoners, except, judging from the smell, I don't think they're performing up to spec. Or maybe they've been instructed not to.

What is worse? To have a need and seeing no way for it to be met, or seeing the provision, and having it purposely denied? Being thirsty, seeing water nearby, but being unable to reach it?

The prince leads us into the room. "You touched on something important when you mentioned our public displays," he says. "Such displays serve as a deterrent, you know. They keep others in check."

And sometimes spark rebellion.

He raises both hands. "Do you like what we've done here? You partially inspired it."

"What is it?"

"It is a display too, of course." He addresses the bodyguard. "Pick whichever you like."

The guard nods and produces an orange, meter-long stunstick from his belt. He walks toward the cages to our left. He stops at the first and studies the person inside. He then strolls casually to the next cage and the next, looking both high and low.

"Do you plan to stream from here?" I ask.

The prince looks irritated. "Oh, no, no. Of course not. This place is secret." He watches the guard. "Don't take too long, Ghazi."

The guard nods again, then pauses where he is. He grunts and motions for the nearest bot, perched a row above him and two cages over. The bot scrambles to the ground, then walks to the cage near the guard and manipulates the front locking device. The door clicks free and the guard enters with his stick. He comes out, pushing a thin, old man in front of him.

The man's hair is disheveled and dirty. His hands are bound. There is a hint of purpose in his stride, though. "What is this?" he says, sneering. "Tired of getting blood on your hands, Aadam?"

The prince giggles. "No, I simply like variety."

"You and your machines," the man says.

The prince raises a hand. "Gag him, please."

The guard taps the man with his stick. There is a sizzling sound, the man screams, then doubles over. The guard moves him away, passing between the row of prisoner cages toward the central one.

"I'm sorry," the prince says. "That man made an attempt on my father's life. He deserves whatever he gets."

The other prisoners start to yell and moan. It becomes deafening.

The prince winces. "Shut them up!"

The outside of the cages start to shimmer, and the noise ends. A translucent nano-filter of some sort. The prisoners still appear to be yelling, but I hear nothing. The human smells have abated some as well.

"That's better," the prince says. "Now, what were we discussing?

Oh yes, the stream! Always the stream with you debuggers." He smiles and begins to walk to the left, following the row of cages. "This display is for the local audience only. For the refuse in these cages."

"To deter them," I say.

"Yes, as my father likes to say: Crush one and the rest become brittle." He raises both hands exuberantly. "This will be an incredible timesaver. And we get to have fun too."

We reach a break in the row of cages. Ahead of us, closer to the central cage, are four comfortable seats and a table with drinks. There is a slender controller on the table, as well.

"Do you know why you're here, ThreadBare?"

I'm hoping it isn't to run the combat bot. The stops might allow me to, if ordered. But it would be complicated. Another boundary that is rarely tested. I don't want to test it now.

"There are mechanicals that need repaired here," I say. "One of the climbing bots, and four of the machines we passed on the way in."

The prince glances toward the door. "Well, that's one reason, yes. We should definitely have you check everything over. You've been given access, so you can do that at your leisure."

I loosen the pack on my back. "Would you like me to—?"

"Not now!" he says. "No, no, not now." He walks to the seat nearest the table and sits down. "Right now I want you here with me." He motions toward the other seats. "Sit there if you like."

I put my pack on the floor. "I would rather stand."

He makes a fist with both hands. "Always ready for trouble. I love that in your people. Skins of action." He picks up the controller and turns toward the central cage.

The prisoner is inside the cage now. He looks very small and frail next to the bot. It dwarfs him by at least a meter, and its arms are larger than his head. They are also made of plastisteel—a thousand times stronger than bone.

"His hands are still bound!" I blurt out without thinking.

The prince glares at me, but then his features soften. He looks at the cage again, squinting. "Yes, that doesn't seem right does it? Let's have a fair fight." He claps his hands over his head. "Ghazi!"

The guard quickly joins us, still holding the stunstick. "Yes, sir?"

The prince puts out his hand and the guard places the stick in it. He pokes the guard with the stick. It sizzles and pops while the guard shrieks and clenches his hands together. The prince then removes the stick and the shrieking ends. The guard bends over and breathes hard.

"What were you thinking?" the prince says. "How do you expect him to fight like that? Unbind that poor man." He hands the guard the stick.

The guard bows, and walks—haltingly—away.

I soon see Ghazi on the far side of the cage. He calls to the prisoner and frees his hands. The prisoner attempts to grapple with the guard, but only gets the stick again. He's left inside, free, but on his knees. The bot casts a long shadow over him.

I don't like this. Not at all.

The man is a traitor and an infidel, right? He deserves nothing. That's what the rules say. What the prince says.

Plus, it isn't my business. I can't do anything but what I'm told. I'm stopped. Forbidden. I have to obey and watch it happen. That's my lot.

Sandfly didn't watch. GrimJack didn't watch. Last time you watched: pop, pop, pop.

My chest feels hollow.

"I've changed my mind," the prince says, looking at me. "I would be more comfortable if you weren't hovering over me. Come and sit."

I nod once and take the seat on the other side of the table.

"That is a fruit drink, by the way," he says, indicating the glass nearest me. "I know you don't like the hard stuff." He laughs, childishly.

He brings up the controller. "The reason I invited you here is for your access, Thread. I may need your help. You're like a walking library. I don't want to assign the fun to you, but I would like you here...just in case."

He activates the bot. It straightens and raises its hands in a stretching motion. Its head moves first toward one shoulder and then the other, simulating the movements of an athlete. Like the "boxers" I saw on the stream. Its hands come up defensively. An unnecessary movement.

The prisoner is in a crouched stance. I'm not sure if he plans to run or attack. To fight or flee. Either strategy is a losing one, I suspect. The bot is reporting its specs on the stream. The power, the speed. No man could compete.

The prince smiles and works the controller. The bot charges straight at the prisoner and strikes downward. The man dives to the right, barely avoiding the arm. He then regains his feet and scurries to the left, attempting to get behind the bot.

The bot shifts left, and swings again. It misses the man by centimeters, but it manages to stop his escape.

"Well, that wasn't very good," the prince says.

The man is pressed against the ring. He attempts to scurry to the right.

The bot connects this time. The man is thrown hard against the cage, lurches to the left, and is hit a second time. I see blood fly through the air, and feel a little of his pain. The man impacts the floor, yet manages to get up on all fours. He glares up at the bot, hurt, but defiant.

"That was a bit better," the prince says. "I believe that would qualify as a one-two punch, correct?"

I stream the phrase to be certain. "Typically it is a shorter punch followed by a longer, more damaging blow," I say.

"And isn't that what I did?" he asks. "Look, he is damaged."

"That might pass as an informal definition," I say. "Yes. Two punches."

He works the controller and the bot does a series of quick jabs with its left hand. "Is this what you're talking about? The short punch, yes?"

I don't want to be a part of this. "Yes," I say. "That is called a *jab*."

He manipulates the controller, producing more jabs with both hands, and then a slower, more powerful-seeming punch with its right. He next starts a series of double jabs with the left followed with the same heavier punch with the right: jab, jab, punch, jab, jab, punch.

"Like this then?" he says.

I nod. "I believe so, yes."

The prisoner is back on his feet and is circling behind the bot. He isn't attacking, though, only waiting. Planning. His face has a large welt on it.

The prince sips from his glass. Smiles. "Very good. I'll continue with more of that combination then." He pushes a button and the bot quickly spins so it faces the prisoner. "Aha!" he says. "I see you."

The prisoner acts surprised and nervous. He crouches and glances both ways.

"Which way will you go?" the prince shouts. "Right or left!" He chuckles. "Maybe the question should be which way will *I* go...?" The bot starts to bounce on its toes. "This is what is called footwork, ThreadBare," he says softly. "The goal is to confuse the opponent. To get him out of his rhythm." He smiles again. "You see, I *have* been studying."

The bot throws more jab combinations. It is barely a meter from the prisoner, but moving steadily closer, despite his attempts to elude. The man puts his hands in front of his face. The bot mimics the movement, but continues to jab, punch, and bounce.

"Do you think he's ready?" the prince asks. "Do you think he can elude me this time?"

"I have no way of—"

The bot fakes to the right, and when the man dodges, the prince swings hard with its left hand. It smashes into the man's shoulder. The man's arm drops away from his face.

"See there," the prince says. "He is partially exposed." He looks at me. "What should I do now?"

I shake my head. "I have no idea."

"You have a million ideas!" he says. "That is why you are alive. Now find me a good one!"

I halfheartedly stream a list of boxing moves. There are many possibilities, especially on a tiring opponent. I don't like any of them. I'm not...this isn't what I'm made for. I remain quiet, stalling. But I can feel the beginning of a stop. A warning for disobedience. What choice do I have?

He snorts. "Please, there is no need to be shy here. We are confidants."

"There are many possibilities," I say.

He takes another drink, and grimaces. "Yes, I'm sure there are. But which one would you use? Life is full of decisions, ThreadBare. We must make the best one. Now give me a move."

The man attempts to sidestep to the right, but the prince presses the controller. The bot reacts with a right to the man's left arm. I hear something snap and the man scream. He drops that arm and shuts his eyes.

"Now he has no defense whatsoever," the prince says. "There must be even more options. Give me a suggestion!"

I remember the artwork. The detonator I helped arm. Beauty gone forever. It wasn't my doing. Here, with the prince, I've assumed a more active role. I'm forced into it. The activities I've been a part of: the bombing, the trampling of those people in Delusion—even the man in the prince's office—those I could abstract. But this, this is much harder.

"Do I need to find Jahm?" the prince says. "Have him bring your controller?"

The man's eyes are closed and his lips are moving. It looks like he's praying. To whom? If he's the infidel the prince says he is, would A even listen?

What would be mercy in this case? To sustain what is happening, or to finish it? To give it its own End of Task Report?

I hesitate. Another stop builds.

"Straight jab, followed by a roundhouse," I say.

"Roundhouse? Ooh, I like the sound of it. Describe it, please."

"The arm pivots on the shoulder joint while the body steps forward. A merging of weight and momentum."

He bobs his head excitedly. "I do like that. I like it very much." He looks at the controller. "Let me see...I want to get this right..."

The prisoner is sobbing and his legs look unsteady. I want him to run. In fact, he tries to stumble away, but the bot hooks his shoulder and swings him back in front. He screams at the contact.

"Ah yes, I have it now. Let's warm him up, shall we?" The bot throws another series of light jabs: one, two, three, four, five. The prisoner's head didn't move. I don't think any of them make contact. His eyes are still closed.

The prince leans toward me. "He was one of my father's advisors once. A cousin from my mother's family."

"The prisoner?"

"Of course! He didn't agree with our security policies. Father thinks he was planning a coup over it. Working with antitex." The prince smiles and winks. "It was a rumor I planted. The seclusion charge was only to distance him from the family."

His attention returns to the controller. "Now this!"

A straight punch connects with the prisoner's chin. His head snaps back, then the roundhouse slams the side of his face. More blood, and his features seem to fold inward. He drops limply to the floor.

The prince jumps from his seat and claps loudly. "Aha! That was wonderful!" he says. "Wonderful!" He looks at me. "Excellent choice, ThreadBare. Astoundingly excellent."

I don't know what to say. There is a pool of blood forming on the cage floor near the man's head. I can't tell whether he is alive or dead. "Are you done?" I ask finally. "Can I go?"

"We are celebrating, ThreadBare." He motions toward my drink. "Look, you haven't touched what I prepared for you. Would you like something else?"

I shake my head. "I didn't sleep well last night. I would like to rest."

He frowns, but then nods. "Yes, I will allow that. We will do this again, though." He looks at the prisoner cages. "This was a good demonstration, but we will certainly need more." He nods repeatedly. "Yes, many more."

Images flood my mind. The artwork. The heavy. The popping sounds. Broken bots. Damali. The Noah in my room. I feel light-headed. "Master, may I go?"

He waves a hand. "Yes, yes, you're no fun. Please, go. Go get your rest."

I bow and turn. Focus on the door and the way out.

"Turn their sound on again," the prince yells.

I RETURN TO MY room and fall into the couch.

I try to reach BullHammer again. I don't know why. We've never been friends. Even as implants, we're not that similar. But of anyone, he would understand my position. I can't come right out and tell him anything. But he might be able to guess. He seemed to suspect things before. Maybe that's why I dislike him. He gets things before I do. Even dumb things.

There's no answer from him, though. Not even Easy Impact. Not even a single character of text. Nothing.

I think about Bamboo. We debuggers, we never know what all the rules are. We never know the perfect path through the maze that lives in our heads. Bamboo didn't train us on it. Nor would he explain it now. But he should at least be able to tell me why I don't get more stops. Why I'm even allowed to be in the cage room with the prince, much less participate in his torture. This has nothing to do with debugging. What part does my will play in this? Do I bear any guilt?

Would any parent submit their child to this if they knew what it would make them? Is the assurance of a reward after death worth a life as someone else's puppet? Is that even what A wants? Does he want puppets?

I'm my master's property, Bamboo would say. I must obey him.

Killing is an offense, I know, but the corrupting of the world—of our faith—is considered worse. Someone who tried to kill the Imam is fair game for killing. As are all unbelievers. But that prisoner, the prince's admission—I don't think he was guilty at all.

Am I a puppet of death?

I message FrontLot a single question: Are we puppets?

He responds with: Yeah. But so is everyone. Everyone bows to someone.

"What about the Imam?" I ask, sending voice and text. "Who does he bow to?"

"To A, right?" he says. "To the law."

"Does he?"

"You know better than I, Thread. You always know better." A pause. "Need another mix?"

I need to live someone else's life, I really do. But I find myself saying "No." I also say "Goodbye," which is strange. And Front says it back. If nothing else, the guy is polite. Efficient.

Rails.

My door chimes. I'm still hungry. I never ate! And I don't want company now. I don't want Jahm or the prince or this place. I want out, that's what I want. Just give me a garage somewhere and an endless stream of nominal bots to fix. Everyday bots with everyday problems. Preferably the two legged models, but I can be flexible—

The door chimes again. Probably isn't the prince, because he would be in here already, sniffing around my stuff. I've never known Jahm to wait either.

Who is this? My back is to the door so I can't see who it is, but I'm curious. Are the servants finally coming to fill the foodcon?

I stream the door open. I'm too worn to move. Too frayed. Plus, if it *is* the servants, they won't want me near on account of the leprosy. I groan and sink into the couch.

I hear the door close again, but little else. Whoever it is, they are being really stealthy. I hope it isn't one of the prince's enemies. Someone who's come to kill him and found me by mistake. I might not be able to direct them properly in the state I'm in.

Ouch, little tweak there.

Seriously, who is it? I raise up and glance at the kitchen, at the foodcon. No one there. "Yes?" I reposition myself so I can see the entranceway. "Is someone—?"

Huddled near the door is a figure dressed completely in black. A woman, I think. It still could be an assassin, but I don't believe it is. I don't see a weapon, anyway. She could have explosives under her clothes somewhere...

"ThreadBare?" Damali's voice.

I'm alert now. Delighted but also frightened. Darkly frightened.

I stand. "Why are you here?" I ask. "You shouldn't be here. I mean, I don't think you should be. How did—?"

She rushes forward. "I went on a walk, is all. I'm allowed a walk. I only happened by."

I shake my head. "No, this is not good. Not allowed."

She indicates her coverings. "I'm perfectly compliant. Completely dressed."

"You're unescorted," I say. "And you're the prince's woman."

She moves closer. "One of too many." Her eyes narrow. "And you can be my escort. Everyone knows that debuggers are safe."

Except me. "You should return to your quarters," I say. "Immediately."

She stretches out a hand. Grasps my arm. "I will," she says. "But I need to see you first."

I check the door to be sure it is shut. "Another broken bot?" I ask.

She chuckles and shakes her head. "No."

I turn so her hand slides off me, even as I wish it would remain. "Then you don't need me."

"But you're made to help. I *want* your help."

"I am a servant," I say. "But not of you."

"Then who?"

I grimace. "Of whoever owns me, of course. Of wherever I'm placed." I feel the start of a stop. Another warning. "If you stay here I'll need to report you. Whether I want to or not."

Her body grows rigid. "Are you that weak?" she asks. "That much a slave?"

That throws me. "Weak?" I say. "Maybe. But I'm...I'm nobody." I turn and try to focus on something else. The mirrored section of the wall, or my chute. Something.

I worry that she won't go away, though. That I'll be responsible for her ill if this goes on. I don't want that. "What do you need?"

She walks in front of me again, standing between me and my cinder chute. "I want to escape," she says. "I want to leave."

196

"I can't help with that."

"Are you sure?" She draws closer still, enough that I can smell her breath. It is mango and peach.

I feel warm, intensely warm, followed by a synthetic cool. A result of the emotion stabilization that I think the implant generates. Not a stop, but an anti-go. "I don't know how I could," I say. "I'm controlled, remember. Everything, controlled."

Damali diverts her eyes, looking first at the floor, and then at my chute. "Is that where you sleep?"

"Yes, I—"

She takes a step toward the chute, bends forward and peers through the canopy, but keeps her hands folded. She doesn't touch. She then turns to me and frowns. "It seems cramped," she says. "Lonely."

"It is made for one," I say. "For only me."

Damali smiles and looks at the ceiling. "You have Noah up there." She studies the image for a few moments, then makes a clucking sound. "No wife, so completely wrong." She looks at me. "His wife was there, you know."

I check the ceiling. "I don't think she was," I say. "I see no indication she was painted over."

She laughs. "Not up there, Thread. On the boat. She was there."

I frown. "The painting is a proper representation of the story. Noah's wife was an unbeliever. Left behind."

Damali shakes her head. "There are other versions. Other histories. In them, she was there. On the boat. Along with all three of Noah's sons—"

"There were *four* sons," I say. "I've streamed it. I'll stream it now, in fact." I shut my eyes, touch the stream for clarification, then open my eyes again. "Four sons: Ham, Shem, Yam, and Japheth."

She moves the cloth away from her face. "There was no Yam," she says. "No son left behind."

Her features seem more striking now, here in my room. Why is that? I feel warm again, then cool. "You are mistaken, um, the stream says—"

She chuckles softly. "You believe everything you stream?" She waves dismissively. "No wonder you can't help."

I look at the kitchen and the foodcon. I'm really hungry. Plus, I'm a little angry now. Why does this...this *woman* bother me? I don't want to be bothered.

Her theory about Noah is intriguing, however. Where do people come up with such diversions? Such random heresies? Not on the stream. The Ministry makes certain of that.

Wait. What about the medieval images I saw? The glass Noah. What did that show?

I don't remember, but the implant always does. In an instant I'm paging back, dipping within the implant's storage. Trying to find the specific image I saw. What day was it? Seems an eternity ago. Before the missile, before Delusion...

"Are you okay?" she asks.

"Yes," I say. "I'm...just...thinking." I find the right time segment, my stint with Kadeer the demolition *expert*. Where is it? Where did I see the glass Noah image?

"Of course, you don't believe me," she says. "I'm a woman."

She turns from me, hands locked together. "When I was a child I found something. I was playing on some rocks near our home and found a little crevice. A place only someone like me could tuck into. There were little treasures there. Small candles and scraps of things. The find delighted me, my little cave.

"There was also a tiny book, a picture book. It had Noah in it, and the animals. In that version, Noah had only three sons, and none of them were left off. None of the family, I mean." She smiles at me. "I liked that telling better. Everyone together. Everyone important."

"Except the people who weren't on the boat, you mean. The others who were drowned."

She shrugs. "The story said it was their choice. That they were warned and chose to mock instead. They didn't reject Noah, but A himself. They chose sin."

I finally find the glass image in my storage. It presents Noah's family exactly as Damali describes it. Three sons, all with wives. And another woman too. Older. Probably Noah's wife. Plenty of happy animals. Interesting. Heretical, but interesting.

"I had a brother," she says. "He disappeared. Maybe that's why I don't like the idea of a lost son. I'd rather they were all together again. On the boat."

What? I'm still analyzing Noah's family, and she said what? "Disappeared?" I say. "How did he disappear? Was he a debugger? Like me?"

She shakes her head. Draws closer again. "No, but he was really smart like you. Loved science. Loved the stars."

The stars? Space? "But he wasn't a debugger? He wasn't taken for implantation?"

Her forehead wrinkles. "No. He was older when he left. I mean, he went to school for astronomy. Wanted to fly one of the delivery ships. You know, the ones that go to the giants? The large planets?"

"Jupiter and Neptune. I'm familiar with the ore trade. Some of my classmates maintain those ships. CrazyTrain, is one, I know. He works on the graxin collectors too. Haven't streamed him in a while. I wonder if he mixes..."

She stares at me, looking puzzled.

I shrug. "Your brother disappeared in space?"

"I don't know if he ever had a ship. If he ever went somewhere." She touches me again. "The prince is in charge of the program. I thought, by coming here—"

"So coming here was your choice?"

Her eyes widen. "No, no, never. But I hoped, if I was going to be in his service, maybe at least I'd hear something. Maybe it wouldn't all be for nothing. That maybe I could give my family something."

I shake my head. "I thought that too." Another warning tweak. I turn so she can't see me as I fight to push the pain away. "I mean, I've heard that he was in charge. But I don't think that now. I don't think he has anything to do with space. Maybe Jah—" I'm hit again. This time harder and stronger. Rails.

"Maybe what?"

I wipe my face with my hands. It feels damp, sweaty. "I've heard what you've heard," I say. "But I've seen little evidence. The prince has...other projects."

There is silence for a few moments. "Then maybe it is for nothing." She walks so she can see my face then bows. "I'm sorry."

"No," I say. "I'm sorry. I'm not—"

"Would you like me?" she asks. "If I weren't his, if you weren't a debugger, would *you* like me, ThreadBare? Even a little?" Dark eyes stare at me, imploring.

Again, I'm stalled. Torn up. "A freehead?" is all I can say. Which is sort of flipped, if you think about it.

Her head drops. "Nevermind." She turns and hurries past the couch, heading toward the door. "It was foolish of me to come here."

"Yes, but—" I follow her. Conflicted, confused, and empty. Seeking for something I can never find.

"I won't bother you again." She drapes the cloth back over her face, and raises a hand to the door's controlpad. She pauses and looks at me. "Can you open the door?"

I nod and stream it open. "I'm sorry..."

"No," she says. "Nothing is your fault. Forget I came here, okay?" She looks at me again. "Right, you can't do that. But try not to...whatever you could do." She rushes outside, turns right and disappears, only to hurry by my door again a moment later going the other way.

Curious, I walk to the door. I catch a glimpse of her dark robe as she passes around the corner to the next hallway. I frown and then look to the right, in the direction she first went. The hallway itself is empty, but at the far end is a large, well-lit foyer.

There is a small group of men there. Among them, and looking directly toward me, is Jahm.

• • •

Jahm visits me later. He says nothing. He only tests his controller on me. It works very well. And even after I assure him of this, he tests it again. Over and over.

I have a fitful night of sleep. Pain even the chute can't take away.

But the topper? The new offline debugger list arrived.

Sandfly and HardCandy are on it.

THE TORTURE ROOMS ARE part of my routine now. I try not to think of them as that. I think of them as the advanced processing labs. But let's face it, they're for only one reason: torture.

Generally, I stay in the examination rooms and fix the machines there. I needed a quarter level increase to manage the sonic inhibitors, but the prince had no problem authorizing that. Interesting devices, inhibitors. Seemingly simple, but with many interdependencies. In comparison, bots and even his nano restraint bubbles are less complex.

The torture rooms are filled with unique devices, and many of them are in need of maintenance upgrades. I'm grateful for this, because it means I'm alone while I work. It also means I don't have to see the prisoners. Don't have to smell them or otherwise interact.

That's doubtless a coldhearted attitude. An inhuman one. But, as we already covered, I'm not really human. Many things would be different if I were.

Today I have to go to the cage room, though, so that's why it's on my mind. I need to address one of the bots there. It has been throwing errors for weeks. Now there is finally someone around to catch them. Me.

The cage room door clanks and slides open. The room is dimly lit. Enough to make out the outlines of the cages and the prisoners within. I feel the same gust of wind as before, smell the same foul scents. I shift my bag higher on my shoulder, fight a twinge of apprehension, and step inside.

I order the lights up a level. Still not bright, but light enough that

I can see everything. I see two bots perched on the cages in front of me. I identify the highest bot as being the one I'm here to service. I stream it a command to come down. It starts to descend.

I wait, still a good seven meters from the nearest cage. The bot reaches the ground and pauses, as if I will come to it. I shake my head and stream it a command to come to me. It click-clacks its way across the floor. The feet of these bots are made for grasping. They are narrower with three long toes. Bird-like. And so, the clacking.

The primary error on this bot is in its left leg. One of the nanopaths is stinted, causing performance issues. A problem more likely to happen in bots with narrow construction, obviously.

I direct the bot to a spot a few meters left of the door, directly under one of the overhead light sources, then ask it to lie down.

The bot gets into a prone position. I stoop next to it, placing my bag on the floor. The bot wears a suit, reminiscent of my own, though his is green. I release the cuff around its heel and pull the material back. The blockage is in the left calf. I dig out a sheet and start to smooth it on its leg.

"It's a skin!" a prisoner yells.

There's a small chorus of laughter, then another one says: "Don't call him that. They don't like it."

"Oh, right," the first says. "Debugger! They like *debugger*. Makes them sound like an exterminator. Don't squash us, debugger."

"No! Get us out of here!"

There's a snort. "He can't. Can't do anything except what you see him doing. Fiddle with machines."

"Yeah, he was with the rat. Helped him beat Ehan. Poor Ehan."

"Poor us."

Another voice, this one sounding more strained than the others. "Could you help us, debugger? None of us are guilty. Our crimes are only offending royalty, but you must know they aren't royalty at all."

"Ehan," another says. "Ehan was here because the prince wanted his wife. Poor Ehan."

I shake my head, focus my attention on the bot. I can see where the blockage is. It shouldn't require opening him up. I'll create an access port as close to the block as I can, shove a probe in and hopefully free the nanos.

"He'll kill us all, debugger. You know that? That's what he does."

"The rat son," a low voice says. "He thinks he's untouchable. That no one knows his face." A broken laugh. "But there are those who see. People who will kill him."

Of course, it could be a software thing. Probably is a coding thing. I look at the blockage again. The pathway looks fine. Not pinched or anything.

"He doesn't understand," one prisoner says. "They are mute, I think."

"Mute!" There are a series of loud coughs. "What do you think mute means?"

"Well, what's wrong with them then? Are they neutered? I don't know what they have or don't have."

I shake my head again, then whisper, addressing the bot. "You can close them off, right?"

The bot nods and streams out a command. The nanoshields come down, bringing silence. I'm sure they are still talking within their cages, possibly screaming at me now, but I can only take so much. None of them know me. Not the real me. If they did, how would they feel? Would they realize we're all imprisoned?

I sing out for the nanos in the bot's leg, referencing them by their location. I collect a list of those that aren't moving, and dive into the code of the most stationary one. Next I search for the specific routines for motion. They appear fairly standard to me. Maybe that's good, maybe not. The bot is a little off-standard, it being a cage creeper. Maybe I simply try to push the nanos and see what happens.

I search for a small probe and a cutter. Still feeling uncertain. I find the tools I need. I place the probe on the floor and bring the cutter close to the leg.

I glance at the sheet again. Wait, where's the blockage now? I think it is gone! Rails. Hate when the mystery up and leaves.

I hear a clunk and the door to the room starts to open. I lose my grip on the cutter, then glance back. There is a group of six men at the entrance. Two wear the dark suits that the prince's guards typically wear, though I don't recognize either of them. They both hold stunsticks.

The other four men are in matching beige pants and shirts. Their clothing is ripped in places, but it appears to have lots of pockets and patches. One also wears a dark brown cloak. Heavier material, and with patches sewn onto it. Their hands are bound behind them.

One of the guards notices me watching. He seems surprised to see me at all, but I shrug and return to my work. I want him to ignore me.

The guards prod the new prisoners forward using their sticks. I don't look, but I hear an occasional crackle or pop as the sticks are used, and hear one of the prisoners cry out. I next hear cages being opened and the men pushed inside. I can't help but feel sorry for them. No matter where they've been, this is their last stop.

The guards walk past me to the door. I glance up again and one says "Keep an eye on them, skin, all right?" The other laughs, and they walk out.

The blockage. Have to deal with that. What caused it? I look at the bot's leg again. It still appears normal. Nanos moving as they should. Weird. I command the bot to roll over and I place a sheet on the back side of its leg. I see more conduits. They tend to be thicker and more rigid than nano paths. The way they wrap the sinew in this model is strange too.

Maybe it is a positional thing? Blockage only happens when he's on the cage?

Ooh, that's some reasoning there, Thread! Might make level thirteen yet.

Something itches my brain. The brown cloak. It reminds me of something.

I glance at the cages. I don't see any of the new prisoners on this side, though I catch a glimpse of the brown cloak on the other side. Why does that seem familiar? It looks like a security design—especially with the patches. But most government security guards wear blue garments. That's why they are called "bluecoats."

I do a stream search. I find hundreds of images of security wear. Many colors and designs. Brown is used for lift security. That could be what he is wearing.

I've never ridden a lift, but I know they go beyond the atmosphere. Have the prisoners been there? In space?

Distracting yourself again, Thread. My life is one big distraction these days.

I look at the bot's leg again. Yeah, I think it is positional. One of the conduits is pinching the nano path. I zoom the sheet for a closer look. I detect a slight impression in the nano path where something might be crowding it. Then I notice a broken anchor point for one of the nearby conduits. Easy fix. Simply re-anchor the conduit.

I stand and approach the other side of the cages, keeping an uninterested distance. The new prisoners are on the bottom row near the middle. There's another disassembled and inactive bot by the wall on this side. Why doesn't that surprise me? There is also a double-wide silver foodcon. It is an Elitist model—one of the most expensive and fastest brands. The pedestal is larger around than I am, and the processing portion is hourglass shaped. I'm guessing the prince doesn't use that machine for the prisoner meals, but it certainly could handle them. Thirty meals? No problem for an Elitist.

I check the cages again. The new arrivals are standing, and are looking my way. One has darker skin than the others. One is older with thinning hair. The other two are standard freeheads, though one is stockier and shorter than the other. The shorter one wears the brown cloak.

Their expressions are strange. Almost like there's a jinn walking with me. Or they've seen me before.

I want to talk with them, I do. To find out if they're lift security. If they've been to space.

I take a few hesitant steps closer. I can see bruises and welts on their faces. Standard for guests of the prince. I identify the letters "C" and "A" on the brown cloak of the short one. That sparks a memory. A piece of one of the mixes I viewed. I close my eyes to think.

Yeah, that's right. The one with the boy. He rode the CA lift into space.

I glance at the men again. I wonder if they know anything about the debuggers who disappeared! The ones from the list? Probably that is asking too much, but I've seen stranger things.

They're still staring at me. The mouth of the tallest one is moving, but of course I can't hear him because the screens are down. Should I have the bot raise them?

I shake my head. I should get back to the bot. Finish it up. There's danger in knowing people. In starting a conversation. Soon relationships form, and then...caring.

I focus on the central cage. The combat bot is motionless now. Waiting.

This is not the place for caring.

Fifteen minutes later I send my EOTR to Jahm. Twenty minutes later I'm on my way to another part of the palace. Another job.

IT IS NEARLY EVENING AGAIN. My tasks for the day are complete, but my mind won't rest—even with the chute's help. So I'm here, in the arboretum again, perched in my favorite tree. The sky visible from here is filled with twilight color—traces of every hue of the spectrum. I can see stars, as well. Particularly apparent is the hourglass shape of Al Jabbar, the Mighty. It is thought to represent a hunter.

For fun I stream up a star chart and overlay it with what I'm seeing. Yad al-Jauza, the hand, is on the top left. As-Rijl, the foot, is on the bottom right. An-Nitaq, the belt, is in the middle. And As-Saif, the sword, is on the bottom left.

The sword...yes, the sword is always present. Even in the sky.

I notice something new on the local stream. There are frequent bulletins there, ranging from the curious to the mundane. The arrival of the Imam, for instance, resulted in thousands of bulletins. Everything from repair and cleaning operations to food preparation updates. There was even a bulletin about what side of the bed the Imam preferred to sleep on. The sorts of things freeheads busy themselves with. Things I typically ignore.

But now there is a flashing bulletin unlike any I've seen before. It is about a missing person. I open it and scroll through the details. The prince has requested a thorough search. Every room and hallway. All recreation areas.

The important facts are near the end of the bulletin. The missing person is a member of the prince's harem. A dark-eyed woman with equally dark hair.

Damali.

I feel a tingle down my neck, and a dull pain in my chest. There's also the hint of a stop in my brain, but nothing I can't ignore. I straighten and glance back at the pool area, then out at the fields beyond the house. The fields...and the moat.

The moat.

I slowly make my way back down the tree. On the way I replay all my conversations with her, all the moments we spent together.

If I weren't his, if you weren't a debugger, would you like me?

It was foolish of me to come here.

Maybe it is all for nothing.

I feel the ground on my feet. I turn toward the moat and slowly walk that direction. The sky is even darker now. The stars brighter, but somehow more distant. The moat looks particularly calm. That doesn't mean it is safe, though. It is deep, and there could be things in it. Biting things.

I know she was a good swimmer. I saw her in action. So would she try to swim it? The moat?

I sprint across the driveway to the moat's bank. I study the moist ground in both directions. I detect footprints. The impressions of smaller, bare feet. Damali's?

I stare across the water. She ran away. I know that more than I know anything. She swam the moat and snuck through the fields. She is gone.

I feel a hint of relief, but also something else. A confusing free-head-like pain.

Noah's wife. Did she survive the Flood or didn't she? I shake my head. I don't know. It doesn't seem possible.

The sword, Thread. It is always overhead. Don't look at the stars again.

I get a message. A vague "where are you?" from Jahm. I tell him my location, and that I'm merely relaxing before bed.

He says he is at my room now. That he needs to see me there right away.

The sword. I can feel it without looking.

But mostly, I miss her.

...

Jahm tweaks me even before I arrive. It is a small one, more of an itching between my ears than outright pain. But it is from him, not me. I know that.

He is poised on my couch. Only him in my room. He's dressed in beige and his legs are crossed casually. His eyes follow me from the door to the place I find before him, head bowed and hands behind my back.

"What do you require, Submaster?" I ask.

He coughs, crosses his legs, then brings his right hand to his knee. The controller is in it. "Are you aware that one of the prince's concubines is missing?" he asks.

I bow my head. "Yes, I've seen the bulletin."

"Then are you also aware that it is the same woman I've found you with on multiple occasions?"

A shiver traces my spine. "I've never been with her, my lord." I feel a tweak, but I'm not finished yet. "I've been in her vicinity, yes. But it isn't possible for me to be *with* her." I straighten my posture. "I'm not a freehead."

He snorts, then coughs. "You have a strange proclivity for a debugger. A strange and dangerous curiosity."

"I thought my service here was beneficial," I say. "To date I have repaired three hundred and sixty-seven machines as a member of the royal family's complement. Fully one third of those while under your supervision at the palace. I have met or exceeded the average—"

He nods. "You've been remarkably efficient." He pauses to look at the controller, then shakes his head. "I don't like to use these things, these controls. My position gives me that responsibility, but I don't enjoy it." He frowns. "Please don't make me use it now."

I bow my head once. "I don't know why you would, Submaster. Your previous reprimands have been gentle and fair, yet I've never understood why they were necessary. I've always been honest with you. Always did what was required of me."

He presses the controller. Pain splits my brain. I grit my teeth.

"Now," he says. "I'm going to ask you one question and I expect an honest answer. Do you know where the woman went?"

I take a deep breath and close my eyes. "I do not, Submaster, but you didn't need to shock me to learn that. You only needed to ask."

"So we've been told." He places the controller on the couch next to him. Smiles. "Then I will ask again without the prod. Do you know where she went?"

I shake my head. "I do not. She said nothing to me. I have no idea."

He watches me closely, looking for any indication that I'm struggling. Or that I've been internally stopped. Finally, he nods. "I don't think you're lying."

He hasn't asked me where I think she went. I hope he doesn't.

He uncrosses his legs and pats his knees. "Have I told you about your predecessor? About what happened to our previous house debugger?"

I feel relief at the subject change. I shake my head. "You have not."

"I must do so. That way you'll know that my ministrations are on your behalf. That I seek no harm for you."

I relax my posture and back toward the chute until I can lean against it. Jahm's stop was more tiring than it should've been. What did he have it set at?

"He was a good debugger," Jahm says. "A valuable asset. Perhaps better than you. But one day he—"

The door to my room opens and the prince rushes in. He's dressed in a shiny blue suit and he's jittery, visibly agitated—or excited. He looks at me first, and then at Jahm. There is a black-suited guard near the door. "What are you doing with my debugger, Jahm?" he says. "I need my debugger."

"My prince." Jahm stands and clasps his hands together. "I was quizzing him about the missing girl. I thought he might have seen something."

The prince scowls. "That harlot? Why would he know anything about her?" He clears his throat and spits. "She will be found. And when she is, I will deal with her personally." He waves a hand at me. "Regardless, she isn't worth *his* energy." He walks closer and puts a hand on my shoulder. "ThreadBare is above such things, correct?" He chuckles. "In fact, he might be the perfect man. He's certainly the perfect servant."

Jahm bows his head. "My apologies. I thought it was my place to—"

The prince turns and strikes Jahm across the face. "It is your place to do as I say. Like everyone in this house." He smiles at me again. "And someday, the world. Especially with servants like my friend ThreadBare here."

There is a red welt on the side of Jahm's face. He's not touching it at all, though. He bows again and remains still, arms straight at his side. There is wetness in his eyes.

"Now, my debugger," the prince says. "Come with me. We have work to do."

• • •

We move quickly through the palace. The prince seems to be bouncing as he walks. I don't know if he's taken one of his illegal substances or not. His eyes appear clear and his speech steady, but he is more animated than I've ever seen him. The guard and I have to jog to keep up.

"It has been a very busy couple days, ThreadBare," he says. "Many of my projects have taken unexpected turns. Not altogether bad turns. Some are unfortunate, some represent losses. But I think we can rectify some of that today. Here."

We arrive at the elevator to the processing labs again. As the doors close and we start to descend, I try not to dwell on what might come next. I try not to imagine. The prince, his state-of-mind—it could be something bad. He's happy. Almost jovial.

What did Damali call him? A monster?

She isn't here anymore. She's missing, possibly hiding, or even dead. And if she isn't dead, what the prince will do when he finds her? I don't want to dwell on that either.

I want my garage back. My stinking, dirty garage on the edge of Delusion. That's what I want. That's what I'm praying for.

We reach the ground floor and walk quickly across the initial room then down the hall. We pass the examination rooms with their nasty machines. Some of them are occupied. Most aren't. The prince has bigger toys to play with now. More grandiose ways of torture.

The door to the cage room opens. The prince smacks his hands together and takes a deep breath. "Oh, so much to do. Where to begin?" He looks at me. "We have new guests in our little game room, Thread. Did you know?"

I glance in the general direction of the new arrivals, and nod. "Yes, I was here when they were brought in."

"Excellent!" he says. "You were fixing some of the machines? Being proactive as always?"

I nod again, but say nothing.

"You're getting this place in shape. Wonderful. I plan on using it for a very long time." He leads us past the first row of cages, past the central fighting cage, to the cages on the far side. He stops near those containing the four men in CA security garb. "Do you know who these gentlemen are?"

I shake my head. "I don't, Master."

"They have been to the stars!"

I feel a warming in my chest. "On one of the lifts?"

He raises a finger. "Farther than a lift or an ore freighter. No, these four are true astronauts. Our bravest and finest." He walks to the cage holding the tall astronaut. "Tell him where you've been, spaceman."

The man says nothing. He instead retreats to the far side of the cage and sits down. The other three take similar positions.

The prince sighs. "See how they are? They stole security clothing and tried to sneak away, but we found them!" He holds out a hand and the guard places a stunstick into it. The prince then walks to the cage holding the older astronaut and jabs him through the bars. There is a crackling sound and the man shrieks. The prince waits a moment, then pokes him a second time. Again he screams.

The tall astronaut leaps to his feet and runs to the bars. "We've already told you everything we know," he says. "Leave him alone!"

"You've told me nothing!" the prince snarls. "Nothing I didn't already know." He turns to me. "They started a riot, these four. A portion of the CA lift station is disabled. My station administrator is missing. I can't get a straight answer from the security team." He scowls. "They babble on about bots attacked them. One even talks about rogue debuggers." He lurches toward the cage of the darker-skinned astronaut and jabs the stick in. More screams.

The prince's face is flushed and sweat is beading on his brow.

The stunstick scares me. He could go after anyone with that thing. Anyone.

"On top of all that," the prince says, "our biggest investment has disappeared!" He waves the stick at the cages. "And the only ones who know how to operate it are standing right there." He purposely spits, then with the stick behind his back, prowls the length of the cages. "Where is my ship? Where is DarkTrench!"

DarkTrench? What is a DarkTrench?

The prince addresses the guard. "I think we'll start with the old one. Then when we're finished with him, the tall one."

The guard opens the older astronaut's cage. The man is on his back, still wheezing from his encounter with the stunstick. He looks fragile, brittle, like he's constructed of silicon. He offers no resistance as he's pulled to his feet and then out. The guard drags him toward the central cage entrance.

The prince looks at the remaining astronauts, and smiles. "Please direct your attention to our combat arena. You're about to have a demonstration of an ancient sport. I think you'll find it enlightening. A learning experience." He waves at me then points toward the seats we used for the earlier *match*.

The non-astronaut prisoners were quiet, but they now begin to hoot and yell—jeering at the prince. He seems to relish the attention, smiling and yelling back. This only enrages the prisoners more. Finally, they get loud enough that he has the nano muting partially enabled. The noise drops to about half its previous volume. Present, but not overbearing.

The prisoners gather near the inner portions of their cages, astronauts included. The tall one must recognize what is about to happen, because he rattles his cage all the harder. "Take me!" he says. "Let me go first."

The prince smiles and holds up a hand. "All quiet but that one," he says, pointing at the astronaut.

The room goes silent save a single voice. The astronaut repeats his request, then rattles his cage.

"Ah," the prince says. "Nothing like a little swagger from a fearless explorer. How noble. How very brave."

"What difference does our order make?" the tall one asks.

The prince shrugs. "Honestly, not much. I like our current order of events, though. More learning potential."

"Grackle isn't made for this," the tall one says. "Let me go first. You want a show, right? I'll give you a show."

The prince brings a finger to his mouth, looking thoughtful. "I do like to be entertained..." He glances at me, then scans the entire room. Finally, he shrugs. "Why not?" He claps his hand above his head. "Zargar!"

The guard, now halfway around the central cage, looks our way.

"Switch them," the prince says. "Put the tall one in instead."

The exchange is made then the prince and I find our seats. The table between us has a dark brown beverage for him and water for me. There is also a fried, green snack along with the prince's bot controller.

The tall astronaut is standing in one corner of the combat arena. The bot is in the opposite corner, looking as formidable as ever. Its armor plating seems shinier than before too, freshly polished. The prince's symbol—a yellow ellipsis with a blue star—is apparent on the bot's chest and head.

The prince smiles at me. "Now...how should we begin?

I DON'T WANT TO START AT ALL. Images and experiences swirl in my mind. Seemingly unrelated events begin to connect. Start to finally make sense. The prince and Jahm's association with the space program. The object the missing debuggers were building. Was it that ship? The Dark Trench? And if it was, where are the debuggers now? The prince mentioned debuggers going rogue. Was it them? DRs like 157, 291, and 178? And if so, how? Did they fight their stops somehow? Like Sandfly?

If the man in the combat cage and his friends are astronauts, then they have answers. They might solve the mysteries for me. They might solve a lot for me.

Regardless, I don't want to be a part of the prince's latest *party*. It isn't my job. It isn't what I was made for. I'm a lowlevel who is barely adequate to fix heavies and servs. I'm nobody. And I'm definitely not a torturer.

The prince picks up his controller. Smiling, he seems to relish its presence in his hand. He squeezes it and studies it. "You know, debugger, I love pleasure. I love to taste and to smell and to feel nice things. I've had more pleasurable sensations than most men dream.

"But this, this small little bit of power, it simply..." He looks at the ceiling as if searching for the proper word. "Delights me. Yes, that is it. It *delights* me." He raises the controller and rubs a thumb over the top portion. The bot in the cage jolts awake, imbued with energy. "Let's get started, shall we?"

He touches the controller and the bot leaps forward. The prince's favorite move! The astronaut dives out of the way, throwing himself to the ground. This time, instead of striking again, the prince halts the bot's motion and starts its bouncing footwork. Then it begins to jab too. Bouncing and jabbing, slowly moving toward its opponent. The prince laughs. "Fooled you, space man."

The astronaut regains his feet.

The footwork continues. The bot moves one way, then the other, gradually closing the distance between it and the man, while discouraging escape.

The astronaut mimics the bot's stance and bounce. He brings both hands up and looks focused. Giving the prince his show, apparently. He is being backed into a corner, though. Soon the bot is within striking distance. There is a flurry of jabs followed by a straight punch with its left hand. The last one connects, as the astronaut's head flicks back, slightly. It wasn't a hard blow. The bot could easily use more force, should the prince decide to.

"I've been doing more research," the prince says. "There are four basic styles of boxers, did you know?"

I shake my head. "I wasn't aware, Master. No."

"I know more than a debugger," he says, smiling. "Imagine that. But yes, there are four types. The out-fighter, the slugger, the swarmer, and the boxer-puncher. All have advantages and disadvantages." He nods toward the cages. "Since we have four new prisoners, I hope to try them all."

He points with his free hand. "I like the idea of the out-fighter best. That one fights from a distance with longer and faster punches. In and then back out again. A dancer's move. Fun to watch and less chance of injury."

He grins and nods. "When I fight my father again, that's the technique I'll use." He points at the cage. "It's what I've been using so far today. Watch, I'll illustrate again." He causes the bot to jab. Bouncing and jabbing. Quickly and evenly. "The jab becomes a controlling mechanism, you see. It keeps the opponent right where I want him." The jabs continue—one, two, three, four—then he sends another straight punch.

The astronaut avoids the punch, but barely.

The prince frowns. "Well, I missed there. But you see what I mean? Staying out, but then in for the strike." He rests the controller on his knee and brings his drink to his lips. He takes a long draught, sighs loudly, then starts mashing the controller again. "The swarmer is the exact opposite of the out-fighter. He fights close and fast." He glances at me. "I'm not as familiar with the other two. While you watch, you could read up on them. I'll need guidance later."

I nod, and begin a stream search. My implant fills with boxing moves and stylistic differences. It is fascinating and overwhelming. I view images of fighters in action. People being battered and bruised. I even find variations where the fighter's feet are in play. I'm sure the prince would be interested in that, but I won't share. Not unless I'm asked.

The out-fighter strategy continues in the ring. The astronaut has been hit numerous times. The impacts were light by bot standards, but the areas around his eyes are red, and there are bruises on his arms.

"I've been softening him up," the prince says. "Eventually he will no longer be able to lift his arms. Then the fun will begin."

The astronaut yells, ducks the bot's arms, and rushes straight toward it. He gets close and wraps himself around the bot's legs like a sheet. The bot's head turns down, feeding its optic stream, and its lateral motion slows. Otherwise, it seems unaffected.

I frown and shake my head. There are no vulnerabilities in the legs. Even if the astronaut could break through at the joint somehow, it would be difficult to do anything useful from there. The design is resilient. Not as impenetrable as a heavy, maybe, but almost.

I feel for the astronaut. Whether he started a riot or not, he is completely outmatched here. I wish I could help him somehow. I imagine myself being brave and different. Sandfly-like. I seek out the combat bot's specs on the stream. I find them and pull them in. I start to play over them, searching for hope.

I don't see any.

The prince shakes his head. "Look at him! Trying to ride its legs like a child. Enough of this!" He works the controller again. The bot's left hand comes down, and with a smooth motion, clears the man from its legs. The astronaut falls to the floor.

"Ah, and now this," the prince says. The bot strikes the man again. He is thrown three meters and bounces off the side of the cage.

I wince, almost feeling the impact myself.

The man groans and slowly rolls over. The cage hurt him. A lot.

The prince chuckles. "Now he's softening up. Is he broken yet? What do you think?"

The man gets to his knees, crawls, and begins to get to his feet.

"Oh wait, no, no, he's getting up again," the prince says. "Excellent." The bot resumes its jabbing and bobbing.

This lasts only a few moments before the astronaut ducks and slips past the bot's right arm. He turns sideways and slides along the cage wall, then manages to dodge the right arm and get behind the bot. Using the far wall as leverage, he scrambles onto its back. He then throws an arm around its head and clasps both legs around its midsection.

The prince snorts and shakes his head. "Again with this hanging on." He frowns. "This isn't real boxing. It wouldn't be allowed." He takes a drink, then grips the controller again. "Fine. Watch this!"

The bot's torso shifts one way and then the other. It next begins to shake violently, bucking and twisting, to a degree that is difficult to follow.

The astronaut keeps his hold. Somehow.

The prince brings the bot's arms back behind its head to paw at the man. Its hands don't seem to be able to manage that, though.

I check the specs again: This version wasn't designed for complex grasping. Punching, yes, but it doesn't have the dexterity in its fingers to grip the man and wrench him free.

There, that's a weakness. And I didn't see it. Good job, freehead.

There are ways around the flaw. I doubt the prince will find them, though.

The prince swipes and pushes on the controller and the bot slaps at the man. Occasionally the bot is connecting, but again, it isn't the sort of movement it was made for—behind the head swatting. Plus, the astronaut is fairly good at ducking out of the way. The man can't really accomplish anything from there, though. There's no weakness in the shell near the neck. Even at the seams.

The prince is frustrated now. Beads of sweat are on his brow, and his face is red. "Why can't I get him off?" he says. "Do you know?"

"The hands," I say. "They aren't designed—"

The prince springs to his feet, still grasping the controller. The motion is so sudden and so violent that the table between us upends, spilling our drinks in a semi-circle around us. This only deepens his scowl. He starts to work the controller with both hands, mashing, pushing and swiping. He finally swears and throws the controller to the ground. He circles it, kicks it a meter away, then runs to where it lays and stomps on it.

The bot's movements are epileptic. It is twisting and jumping—arms and legs going all directions. It's like a swarm of bees has been released within its frame.

Still the astronaut hangs on. I have to give him credit. For a free-head, I admire him. He's a survivor.

The same can't be said for the bot controller. Its shell is fractured in multiple places, and the insides, the delicate nanocircuitry, is oozing out onto the floor. I hear screams from the nanos as they encounter the prince's drink there. Can't say I blame them. I felt the same way when I tried the stuff.

The prince is pacing like a hungry lion. He's breathing hard, his face is flushed, and flecks of spittle flee his mouth as he swears. The air is heavy with rage. I'm guessing this is how all the bots got broken. Crazy cubed.

I don't know what a crazy-cubed prince party will bring next, though. I try to remain still and look as detached as possible. But is that the right thing? Do I watch him? Do I retrieve the oozing controller? Focus on the antics of the bot? It is all very confusing.

Part of me wants to laugh. With the controller broken, the match really can't continue. I can maybe return to my job. Work some of the more mundane chores for a few hours. Maybe try to contact Bull-Hammer again? Or search for news about Damali?

I get a tickle of warmth at that last, along with some pain. Her hold on me persists. I shouldn't have any attachment. She won't survive the prince's wrath. The controller didn't. I don't think anything will.

"The cursed thing!" the prince screams. "Useless controller and godless astronauts." He looks at me. "You can fix this, debugger." He points at the cage. "Reach it. Make it work again."

I look between him and the cage. Then at the broken controller. I reach down for my bag, just for the security of it. "The controller will need refusing," I say. "And its fluid levels, the nanos—"

He kicks the controller again, producing another slime trail of nanos. "Not that. We can't use that."

He walks closer. "But you can control the machine. Like when we fought my father. Yes, you can finish him off."

Day 44, 7:41:45 p.m.

I FEEL A KNOT of pain in my chest. I can't do what he asks. I'm not made for torture. That isn't my specialty. I don't *want* to be a part of it.

Yet the thought of disobeying brings me a slight stop. The foreshadowing of pain. "You want me to..." I look at the cage and the bot. It is still in motion, but less now than before. Stepping with an occasional shimmy. Almost like it is mastering a new dance move. One that should be banned. "A debugger is for fixing mechanicals, Master."

The prince smiles, then walks over and takes the seat next to me. "Yes, yes, this is perfect. You know all the moves. It would be as much fun watching you as doing it myself. Do whatever you have to to free the bot. Then finish the heretic."

I shake my head. "Master, I don't—"

But don't I? I've stood by, ignoring everything that happens around me my whole life. I ignored the prince's every move. Isn't that almost the same as participating? I let art be destroyed. I fixed a heavy right before it ran over—

My pulse is rapid. My arms and legs feel light. Tingly.

I'm not a torturer. But I'm not a hero either.

He leans closer. "If you want, you can think of him as that harlot. The one Jahm was asking you about." His voice softens. "I'll let you in on something even the tall one doesn't know...

I feel strange potentials building. Conflicts between the things I desire and the things I've been taught. I always believed that my morality was written in my head. That it was flawless in its design. But is it? Is there a truth that supersedes it? Something that true law should be based on?

How do I know what desires are good, and what are bad?

And what does it mean to be significant?

"That harlot," he says. "That wretched woman...she's his sister."

The stirring in my head stops. All neurons focus on a single idea for a moment. "Damali?"

He snickers. "Yes, that's the one. Years ago I saw her with him and knew I had to have her." He raises an eyebrow. "I am a persuasive man."

I can smell the prince's drink everywhere—on his breath and on the floor. It only adds to my disgust, my turmoil. I look at the central cage again. The circus act it has become. A dancing robot and an astronaut fearlessly bareback riding. I check the nearest prisoner cages. All of them are fixed on the spectacle too. Most are quietly watching. Some are smiling, but it isn't a smile of mockery or of being entertained. It is one of hope.

I lower my head. I stare at the floor and the pattern of the spilled drink. Small tendrils are running out in all directions. Curious.

"Are you connecting now?" the prince asks. "The bot is still a mess. Still moving all around. Fix it, debugger."

Pain fills my brain. Not heavy pain, not yet. But a warning. I need to obey. I'm afraid to even connect with the bot. It is a step down a path. The prince's path. His insanity.

The stop comes again. I push against it slightly. It is like trying to rub the corner off a brick. I sigh. I want to be something. I want to be strong.

I find myself praying. But to the God of which Noah? The one that abandoned his wife and child to the flood. Or the other? Damali's version.

I try to hope, but I feel nothing.

I revert to form. I dip into the stream, reaching out for the dancing bot. It is a giant blob in the stream. A large, bright source. Easy to touch. I find its tap and connect. My head fills with its senses. More confusion to augment my own. Bright colors and sharp angles. There's an object on its back. *Its back!* There are also lots of commands in its queue—the cumulative randomness of a crazed prince and a dying controller. Stupid prince.

I feel another spike of pain. I can't help but wince.

"You're inside it now, aren't you? Is that face because of its condition?" the prince asks. "Can you fix it?"

I want him to be silent. To simply leave me alone. I find the interface for the bot's command queue. I mark the end and the beginning and select everything in between. I tell it to empty, to simply clear it all away. I watch as the commands trickle into oblivion. It is almost like a weight has lifted. The bot relaxes. Its motions cease.

"Ah ha ha!" he says. "You've done it. You've got it now. Very good, ThreadBare. Now get him off."

There's no straightforward way to do that. No way to grab or push. I could smash the bot's back into the cage, crush the rider until he faints or gives up. But that will...not be pretty. Though it would certainly make the prince happy.

I have another move. One a freehead could never coordinate using a controller. There is a chance it will injure the man, but the risks are tiny compared to the alternative. I connect with the bot's spinal column. I build potential in the lower portion, then quickly flash it all the way up the spine. Concurrently, I duck the bot's head and roll its shoulders. That produces a whiplash effect that breaks the man's grip and hurls him over the bot, completely free.

Through the bot's optics I see the man sitting on the cage floor in front of me. He looks tired and shaken. His eyes are wide and he's breathing hard. His face has cuts and welts on it. The bruises on his arms look darker now. Wider.

The prince cackles loudly. "Astounding!" he says, clapping his hands. "Absolutely brilliant." I open my eyes as he gets out of his seat again. He prances toward the cage, waving his hands in the air. "I would've never thought of that move. You will have to show it to me later. After I get a new controller." He walks toward me. "It is not a boxing move, of course. I've only studied those."

He raises a finger. "And I will study more for next time. But now...please, finish what I started. Crush him and we'll move on to the next one."

I digest the bot's visual stream for a moment. The man slowly climbs to his feet and raises his arms for protection. They stop about midway up. They aren't defending his face and head. They aren't defending anything, really.

There are many ways to go from here, combat-wise. Thousands of combinations, played out through a half dozen specific boxing moves. I could contrive many scenarios, or even reenact a pivotal move from a historical bout. A bolo punch. A haymaker. A hook or an uppercut.

What I can't derive, though, is a good reason to. A motivation that doesn't include blind obedience. I'm beginning to think that *obedience* and *meaning* aren't always friends. Sometimes they're enemies.

A stop begins, rolling through my brainpan like a heavy bot, weapons locked and ready. I shake my head, and wince.

"What is it?" the prince says. "Why do you do that? Why don't you continue?"

I try to meet his eyes, but I find myself squinting, barely able to see. I take a breath and wait. Finally, there's a small reduction in the pain level. A period where the current is flowing back out to sea. Gathering for another crash. "I can't...Master."

He grimaces. "What do you mean, you can't? I just saw you move it. It was remarkable." He waves a hand at the cage. "There should be no difference in the interface of this bot and the one you controlled before."

The pain is building again. I shut my eyes and shake my head. "There isn't a difference," I hiss. "I *can* control it."

I have to do what he wants. I have to. I'm nobody...and the pain...it is too much.

He walks closer to me. "Then what are you doing? You got him off its back. He is right there! Hit him!"

I think about Damali. About how she makes me feel. There is something wonderful there. Something mysterious—forbidden, and yet possibly good. It is a feeling that makes me want to laugh. That is her brother there! *Her brother!*

I feel a slap across my face. I pry my eyes open. The prince's nose is seven centimeters from mine. He looks really angry. His face is red. His breath is repulsive.

"Finish him," he says. "Make the bot move! Crush him now!"

Another wave of pain, so hard I can't speak. I can hardly breathe. It dwarfs the sting from his slap. Overshadows and blends with it. Everything burns.

"Debugger! I am ordering you." I hear footsteps. "Guard! Get me Jahm. There is something broken here. Something wrong. Why do I get all the defects! I'm the prince! I'm royalty!"

Another slap on my face. "Come out of it! What is wrong?"

"I don't want to," I whisper. "I want to be brave. I won't do this. For her. For them." The wave comes heavy this time. I can feel the back of my eyeballs. See every vein in them. I focus on Damali. On her...friendship. That glow. The pain puddles up. Starts to break.

I feel so weak, though. The prince grabs my shoulders and begins to shake me. I can offer no resistance. I'm like jelly. Like an unrolled sheet. I'm nano ooze.

He grunts and paces. More footsteps. Then fire everywhere. The stunstick! My body arcs with lightning. Thunder rolls over me. The flood begins. Parts! Explosions. And popping sounds. Lots of popping.

I hear the door clank and begin to open. The fire stops.

"Ah finally! This must be Jahm!" There are more footsteps, followed by: "Why have you come? Where is—?"

I pry open my eyes.

Another guard is speaking with the prince. The prince is listening intently. Nodding his head. "Those fools!" he says. "Very well, I will go now. Prepare the green heli. No! The blue one!"

I feel terrible. My body aches, and while muted, the pressure is still there to do what the prince ordered. In the cage, both astronaut and bot are staring at me. I think everyone is staring at me.

"Lock the debugger up!" the prince screams. "I want Jahm to check him."

The guard, Zargar approaches, places a hand on my right arm, and lifts me out of my seat. He leads me to the right, toward one of the empty cages.

The prince is pacing near the other guard. They are still talking. He looks nervous. He then glances our direction. "No. Not in here! Bind him and put him in his room for now." He returns to his discussion, then walks toward the door. We slowly follow. I look back at the cages, at the prisoners and the bots hanging in varying positions. Could I control one?

No, not to do my will. Not now. It would be too hard. Refusing to act was hard. But performing an action? Impossible. Not with the stops. Not after what I've been through.

We exit the room and the door shuts.

I am done.

• • •

My hands and feet are bound and I'm placed on the couch in my room. Then the guard leaves and the door is shut.

I stream for the door. It still recognizes my indent, which means the access code hasn't been changed. Not sure what difference that makes. I'm still stuck on the couch. I wish he'd placed me in my chute. In my private ark. I could at least escape for a while. Get some rest. I'm very tired.

I lift my feet, struggle to reposition myself, then finally stretch out. It is a little uncomfortable lying on my hands, but nothing compared to what I just went through. I make it work. There isn't too much pain.

I see Noah overhead. Old, lonely Noah who left his wife and son behind.

Should I message someone? One of the other debuggers? FrontLot or BerryMast or someone? If I did, what would I tell them? So much of what has happened is master business. I'd be risking lots of stops. I can't do stops right now.

I can't look at Noah any longer either. Not this wrong version of Noah with his scary animals.

The couch feels warm and my brain is a fog. I shut my eyes.

And sleep.

I'M AWAKENED BY THE door opening. My internal chrono-meter says it is evening yet. I've slept for less than an hour. I still feel worn.

Also, I'm a little sad. I see no way out of this. A debugger that won't do what he's told? Returned to Bamboo, for certain. But with how he feels about me, I'd doubtless lose my implant. End up serving lamb brains and frog legs at a public refectory somewhere. Or worse.

With a grunt, I force myself to a sitting position. My arms are par-tially numb, and my head—rails, it hurts.

Jahm enters the room alone. He's dressed in tan and brown, nicely pressed. He holds the controller in one hand. I'm sure he plans to use it.

He finds a chair and positions it in front of the couch with my cinder chute a meter or two behind it. He sits, crosses his legs, folds his hands and rests them, holding the controller, at his knees. He studies me for a long time. Then he frowns. "I hoped we could avoid this," he says. "Debuggers are valuable commodities, you know. Even for a prince, they require many credits and agreements. Therefore, flawless performance is expected." He smiles. "Another thing we can thank Bamboo for."

"Am I to be returned to him?" I ask.

Jahm sighs and slowly shakes his head. "Unfortunately, no. The work of royalty is preeminent. There is a special no-return clause in every debugger contract. You are ours to keep, regardless of what happens."

"But the implant—"

He raises his fingers while keeping his hands stationary. "Is a valuable thing too, I know. A priceless treasure. It can be cleaned and re-used indefinitely. I'm very familiar with how it all works." He coughs, thumps his chest once, then frowns. "We aren't like other masters, ThreadBare. We get special allowances.

"Even then, your Bamboo is protective. Caring about each and every one of his creations. It is like he birthed you. You are his children." He flashes a smile. "So we are careful. We try not to waste." His eyes search the ceiling. "Which in this house is a bit of feat. Things often get broken...."

He shakes his head. "Ah, ThreadBare, you've disappointed the prince. A pity. I hoped, with your record, you would work hard enough to keep him happy, but not so hard as to draw special attention. A balancing act, but an important one."

"My predecessor—"

"Was beaten to death." He looks up again. "Another pity, because I rather liked him." He smiles toothlessly. "I rather like you too. You are quite talented in your own right. Quite unique." He glances at the door. "Thankfully, the prince was called away before..." He takes a long breath. "Well now, something different needs to be done."

He lifts the controller and looks at it. "These are extraordinary devices. A presumed redundancy, given the stops that are already built in. At least, they should be." He frowns. "How did you do it, by the way? It must have hurt. How did you manage to disobey?"

I shrug. "I don't know, Submaster. Perhaps I'm defective."

He frowns. "Yes, perhaps you are..." He raises an eyebrow. "Did it have something to do with that girl? The runaway?"

I look at the floor, then at the edge of the rug that the chute, and Jahm's chair, are placed on. A corner is flipped up near the chute. How did that happen? The servants, again? Another leprosy scare?

"I...I have no excuse," I say. "Ideas struggle in my mind. Paths are difficult to find. Difficult to follow." I look at Jahm. "I could run a diagnostic on my implant, if you like."

He shakes his head. "That won't be necessary. I'm simply curious. Regardless of the reason, your behavior is dangerous. It will need to be remedied." He looks at the controller again. "This device is unique. Another perk of our contract. Special options." He turns it so I can see and points to the top left corner. To a small, black button. "That, my friend, is a reset."

"A reset?"

"Yes, for your implant. It will wipe it of all residual memories. Return it to the state it was in when first installed."

Is such a thing possible? I've never heard of an implant reset...though now that I think about it, such a thing *could* exist. Makes sense that it wouldn't be common knowledge. Debuggers cherish the data they've accumulated almost as much as their biological memories. Maybe more.

Only the forgotten can truly forget, apparently. "But my functions, the possible side effects..."

"There will be some loss to personal memories too, of course. Especially along the implant interface points." He shrugs. "It cannot be helped. The implant is tightly linked at this point in your development." He leans closer. "Nor do you have a choice, DR. We'll try this and hope that it restores your compliance. If it doesn't...well...more permanent measures might be needed."

I'm uncomfortable. Rails nervous. I would hate to lose all I've experienced. The good stuff, anyway. Especially to a reset procedure I've never heard of.

But maybe I'd be fine. Less tortured! I'd lose all the mixes I've taken in, but again, that could be a good thing.

Would I lose my...new feelings? The Damali effect? The touch of freedom. That hint of recklessness and rebellion. I like that part. But it is also taxing. Tiring. A distraction that got me hurt. Questioning everything.

I remember GrimJack, Sandfly's mentor. He lost his implant. Was that fate better or worse than this? Probably worse.

I glance at the folded corner of the rug. Flips me, that corner. I want to fix it.

Finally, I nod my head. "If you think it's best, Submaster."

"I do." Jahm raises the controller. "Now...are you ready?"

I readjust myself. My arms tingle. My head still hurts. And my chest feels constricted. "I'm afraid, Submaster."

"I understand," he says. "But this is your only path. It is necessary."

I feel like nothing now more than ever. Goodbye to what I am. Hello to...who knows? I take a deep breath. "Very well. I—"

The lid of my chute swings upwards. Inside is someone dressed completely in black. Not an assassin, though. A woman. She brings a finger to her lips.

Damali?

It is difficult to hide my astonishment. I'm not sure whether to say something, or to look down, or what. The implant starts to tweak me, so I end up shaking my head.

"You refuse now?" Jahm says.

Damali raises a black cylinder and brings it down on Jahm's head. He slumps to the floor.

Damali pulls the scarf from her face. "That worked well." She places the cylinder in the chute and climbs out.

"Was that my sajada storage tube?" I ask.

She nods once. "Yes, it is very solid. Easy to swing."

I have questions. Lots of questions. I try to focus on those to keep the stops away. My head fills with eddies. Swirls of emotion and restraint. "Why did you do that?" I ask.

She looks surprised. "To save you from..." She circles a hand around her head. "All the whatever he was about to do. You don't want your head erased, do you?"

"I don't know what I want," I say. "I want things to be normal. I want to do my—"

She raises a hand. "You don't want that," she says. "Whatever he was about to do, you don't want it. He's a monster's servant."

"Yes, but..." I look at Jahm. His face is pressed into the rug. It will doubtless leave a striped pattern on his forehead.

I look at Damali again. "You never left."

She shakes her head. "No, I made it look like I did."

"But you were hidden..." I point at the chute. "Here?"

"Not the whole time, no. For a while I hid in your tree. Guards walked right beneath me three times. Never saw me." She touches her robe. "Especially in this. I blended with the shadows better than you did." She looks at Jahm. "We should tie him up. Do you have anything we can use?"

"To tie..."

She waves a hand. "Never mind. I'll find something." She goes to my storage closet and opens the door. "Ooh, lots of things that will work in here." She rustles around, then returns holding a strand of medium gauge nanopath. She stoops and rolls Jahm flat on his back. She ties his feet and hands, then stands for a moment appraising her work. "I think that should work..."

"It won't help at all," I say. "He'll wake up—" I feel the surge of a stop. "I should report this."

"No, you shouldn't," she says. "Oh wait. You're still tied up too! What am I thinking?" She runs to the closet again. "You have something to cut with here, right? A razor or something?"

"There's a lazburner in my bag." I scan the floor. "Not sure where that is, exactly. But if you can find it..."

She returns to the couch and within a few moments finds the bag behind it. She locates the lazburner as I describe it, and operates it per my instructions. A few minutes later, I'm free.

"Now, let's go," she says.

"Where?" Then I remember something important. I expect a stop at the thought of revealing a master's secret, but it doesn't come. Since everyone involved is on the premises, maybe it doesn't matter. We'll never leave. "Your brother is here."

Her eyes go wide. "Here? In the palace?"

I nod. "Beneath us. There is a torture facility down there. Nasty machines. Lots of cages. Lots of smells."

She shakes her head. "How? How did he get here?"

I give her all the details I can. It is a struggle. I often sound inebriated, but I manage.

"We need to rescue him!"

"The prince's guards—" I feel another stop. They are almost random now. I squint and massage my temples. "It will be difficult." My implant tweaks me again, but this time I realize it isn't a stop at all. It is a reminder. It's the time of evening prayer. I pause, and look at the door.

"What is it?" she asks.

"It is the time of Isha. I should be praying."

She takes my hand. "No. This is an answer to prayer. We should go now and find him. Now, ThreadBare!"

It makes sense. The members of the staff, guards included, will be performing the ritual. And the prince was called away from the palace. At least, I think he was.

My emotions swirl. I'm stuck in place.

"You're a debugger," she says. "You don't need the ritual. Your destiny is secure." She gives my hand a squeeze. "And if it isn't secure, it should be."

The contact, the feeling, is indescribable. I want this connection. I need it. It's leading me toward something important. That something may be my death. I don't know. But it's significant. I shoulder my bag and we're on our way.

WE REACH THE ELEVATOR without incident.

We travel in the shadows as best we can, with her following me at a distance. We don't encounter anyone the entire way. Part of that is Isha, certainly, but the other part? I'm surprised. The prince's palace has never been that devout. Or this empty.

The elevator still operates for me, thankfully. I experience no stops either. I focus only on the work I could do below. The many machines that still need repair or adjustment. It's a hard string to walk. Thin enough that a downrider couldn't travel it, yet I somehow manage. Damali's hand is in mine too, which helps.

At the bottom I lead her past the examination rooms. She's curious, but I explain only in generalities. Some of the things that are done here should only be spoken of in such a way. They are unmentionable. Things no human should have to stand.

We reach the combat room and I stream open the door. I'm not overwhelmed by the smell this time; I'm embarrassed by it. I want to shield her from its meaning. Her eyes are wide as she takes it all in—the cages, the hanging bots, the combat arena.

The nanoshields must be in place, because the room is nearly soundless. Only the clicking movements of the hanging bots as they position themselves on the cages. Many of the prisoners are standing, and some appear to be talking. Otherwise, we're alone here. No guards, no prince.

Her eyes show moisture now. She sniffs and wipes at her nose. "This is awful." She looks at me. "How often were you here?"

I'm struck with guilt. Unsure how to answer.

She's still looking at me. "How often?" She touches her eyes again. "I know you can't control everything...but this..." She scans the room. "They're like animals."

I nod slowly. "I am a debugger. I'm not..." I glance at the floor. "I'm sorry. I am limited." I disengage her hand and take a couple steps forward. "Your brother is over here."

My head is a mess. So much I want to scream. But my problems hardly seem important. I must help her somehow. Even if it hurts. Even if it rips my synapses apart.

I lead her to the far side of the room and the cages holding the astronauts. Damali gasps when she sees her brother, then hurries to his cage. He stands and walks to the shielded bars. The welts on his face have grown and darkened. I'm not sure how she recognized him. The familial connection?

The astronaut speaks, but no sound is heard.

Damali looks at me questioningly.

"There's a shield," I say. "To mute them." A climbing bot is on the third row of cages above us. I stream to it, instructing it to drop the shields. It obeys and there is a rush of human voices—shouts and curses and sobbing.

"We need to get them out," she says. "All of them."

"I don't know how to," I say.

She glares at me. "You talked to the bot. Just have it open the cages. Let them out."

I feel another stop. A big one. "I can't," I say. "Stops won't let me."

"So you still have them," her brother says. "We wondered."

I walk closer to his cage. "Why would you wonder that?"

The older astronaut stands now too. "We met one of your kind on the station. A Sandfly? He appears to have lost his."

"Lost his stops?" I shake my head. "Sandfly? How do you know him?"

The shorter astronaut approaches. "He was on the station with us. Saved us, really. He's a good one, that Sandfly. Him and his lady friend. HardCandy."

"HardCandy too? They were with you," I say, "in space?"

Three heads nod. The other, fourth, astronaut stands and joins us. "On the CA station," he says. "Not on the ship."

"And they went rogue?"

The tall one chuckles. "Not rogue. But uncontrolled. Sandfly was unstopped."

I shake my head again. "That's impossible. The implant is built around stops. They are omnipresent. Everywhere."

"Not to him."

I snort. "I don't believe it."

"You were able to overcome yours, weren't you? Refusing the prince's order."

"Yeah, we all saw that," the short one says. "Mighty brave stuff."

Damali touches my arm. "So can't you do that again? Fight it?"

I don't feel any fight. Even now, the stops are cooking me. Tweaking me something awful. I can barely keep my thoughts straight enough to speak. Yet I find myself saying: "I'll try."

Damali draws closer, hugs me. "Thank you."

I close my eyes. I dip into the stream, but it feels like a tempest now. Hard moving with lots of waves. I try to push through it anyway. To reconnect to the nearest bot. I find its emanations in the stream. Try to sing to it.

I get struck by head lightning. I seize up, feel the muscles in my back clench. "Ahh—"

Damali takes my hand in hers. I focus on that, try to think about that. About how I counteracted the stops before using her presence. The way she made me feel. The tempest subsides enough that I can connect to the bot. It answers me. Recognizes me. Now to quickly send the order to—

"Please hurry, ThreadBare," Damali says. "Someone could come. The guards."

It's so hard now. I almost lose the connection to the bot completely. This is such a simple thing. But again, the maelstrom. The struggle to hold on. "I don't think I can." But I'm still trying. I have to try.

"Can I do anything?" she asks. "Can *anyone* help?"

I shake my head...then stop. Can anyone help? Not Damali or the astronauts. But someone else?

I sift through my datamixes. There was something important in one of them. Which one, which one? It was a while ago I viewed it.

When? Before the missile attack? Back when I was in my old, smelly garage?

Sandfly. The one with Sandfly. He and GrimJack. They cooperated. That might work.

But I don't have another debugger here. It is only me. Could I message someone? Maybe FI them and share the load? Would that work?

Maybe. It's crazy. But maybe.

My first instinct is to message FrontLot. He would help, right? He's rightminded. Fast thinking.

Except there's the problem with what I'm trying to do. No way he'll understand. No way will he see it.

I see the answer, clear as day. It kicks me in the gut. Makes me almost convulse. I hold onto the bot's connection. Almost with my teeth I hang on. Then I message BullHammer.

And hope.

• • •

I message Bull in every way possible—Easy Impact, Extended Easy, you name it. It is all I can do. I can't focus on being concise or cordial. I simply blast him with all I can. Reach out to him. Keep my connection to the bot, and focus on reaching him.

Seconds go by. Many, many seconds. Finally, I make contact.

"Bull!" I stream-shout. "Bull, thank A you answered."

I can see only his face. It is like he's filling my head with bitter smug. I can see every imperfection. Every scar, every oversized pore. "What do you want?" he says. "I'm busy here."

I try to send emotions, but he won't let them through. I want him to feel what I'm up against, my desperation, but there is a wall. "I need...your...help..."

"*My* help?" he says, then laughs. "Why would you need my help? You're the big winner. The stream master."

"Bull," I say. "Seriously. I was only doing—"

"And I should help you?" he says "After what you did? Humiliated me in front of the—"

"*Need* your help because...because you know how it is. How bad they really are."

"Hey, it's your master that's bad," he says. "That's not my deal. Mine's different, they—"

"You know."

He pauses. His image stares at me, looking thoughtful. "Yeah, okay, I know something."

"So help me," I say. "I'm trying to issue a bot a rudimentary command. I want it to unlock something. That's all I need it to do. But I can't do it alone. My stops are too big."

"Stops!" His eyebrows shoot up. "What are you fighting stops for? What are you trying to do?"

"I can't tell you," I say. "If I do, it might not work. I just need you to send the command through a connection point. That's it."

He shakes his head, then leans in to study my image. "You don't look so good, Thread. I'm curious, but I don't think I want Full Impact from you. Looks like it might hurt."

"It will hurt. I guarantee."

He grows silent again, still thinking. "Which means *my* stops will strike me too. I'm getting a ripple of them now just talking with you." He scowls. "You aren't planning to kill someone are you?"

"No!" I scream, then relent. Try to calm myself. "Sorry, but I'm slipping here. Are you going to help or not?"

He looks doubtful. "Will this even work? Never done something like this before. Teaming a stop storm?"

I think even my image's eyes are closed now, and probably looking at the floor. "I've seen it done. It will be hard..." I shake my head. "I'll share the mix later!"

He thinks longer, then shrugs. "Eh, I like to try new things." His eyes shut. "Show me what you've got—"

I push the connection at him. I can't contain all the fire, though. The major, major pain.

"Dali and da vinci!" he says. "What have you gotten me into?"

"Bull..."

"Hey, I'm getting stops now, Bare." He makes a growling noise. "Glad I'm not out on a string somewhere." Another grunt. "This better be something good. Something epic. Sneaking into a leg show or something."

The connection seems to stretch in my mind. Growing tenser.

More liable to snap. In addition, the local stream has a burst of bulletins. All sections and all departments. It is like a stream-wide wail. I push that down and away. I don't need another distraction now.

"Okay, are you still...?" Bull winces now. "Is it all ready?"

"Yes," I say. "Do it."

Damali—someone—wraps their arms around me. I hear voices, but I can't focus on them. All I can center on is moving Bull's command down the pipe, and into the bot's command structure. It is like trying to push a boulder through a strainer. I scream, Bull screams. There is a burst of pain.

Then release. Followed by a series of clicks.

I wilt.

MY MIND SWIRLS AND everything feels weak. I fall, but arms and voices catch me, gently lowering me to the ground. There are still bursts of pain, small tweaks, but I think I'm all right. Still sane. Hopefully it will all clear up eventually. Maybe.

I try to start a sanity check on the implant, but simply thinking of a rainbow is hard. Even worse doing whatever else I have to do with it. Shift colors or something? No reverse it, I think. I try that, but nothing happens. I'm really drained out. Really flatbrained.

"ThreadBare?"

I open my eyes and find Damali hovering over me. She looks worried.

That's nice. Nice to be thought of. There are lots of other people standing nearby too. Hairy, smelly people. The new ones stick out, though. The space people. They are grouped around her. Out of their cages. Good. They're free. That's what we wanted.

I smile at Damali. "You need to go," I say. "All of you. Quickly. Something else is happening."

I hear the door to the room open and glance that direction. The other prisoners are already escaping. Crowds of men—some running, some limping and others being helped—are leaving through the door. I smile at that too. Nod.

"Can you stand?" Damali asks. "Let us help you up."

I nod again, and with her help, struggle to an upright position. It is still hard to focus. A little achy. But I think I can manage...until...whatever comes next.

The tall astronaut moves closer and lightly touches my shoulder.

"I'm called TallSpot, by the way." He motions toward the other as-tronauts, first the shorter one, then the older, and then the darker-skinned one. "And this is Handler, Grackle, and BlueTrain. We need to talk with you."

I shake my head. "No, you shouldn't. You can't. I know enough. That you're astronauts and you met Sandfly and HardCandy. That you've been on a ship. DarkTrench, right? I wonder if there were other debuggers around. The ones that are missing?" I close my eyes, shake my head again. "But you shouldn't share anything with me that you can't afford to have known. I'm not reliable. I'm not safe."

TallSpot looks puzzled, but slowly nods.

"You're coming with us, right?" Damali asks. "We need to get away from here. The prince, Jahm...we all need to leave."

We start to walk toward the door. I can leave the secret area. I can at least do that. But otherwise? "I can't really go," I say. "There is no hiding me. They will find me. I'm infested in my head, remember?" I slow my pace. "No, before they locate me, I'll turn myself in. I can't fight stops indefinitely. It is too hard."

Damali tugs on me, gets me moving again. "You have to try. They'll kill you."

"And if you're with me, they'll kill you," I say. "I don't want that. You're nice." I get a flash of a memory. A piece of one of the data-mixes followed by something FrontLot said. A good idea forms. "You should go see GrimJack. He doesn't have an implant anymore. He might help you. He might be reliable. I know he was nice once. He did a very good thing."

"We've heard of GrimJack," TallSpot says. "Sandfly mentioned him. Told us to check on him."

We reach the door. The prisoner group has pooled up in the hall outside. The hall with the observation windows into the torture rooms. Rooms with awful, nasty machines.

"What are we waiting for?" Damali asks.

"The thing that goes up and down." I look at her. "What is it called? Square up and down."

"Oh my..."

"There appears to be an aftereffect of his having freed us," Grackle says. "He may need medical attention."

I giggle. "I'm fine, old man. Just fine. Downriding in air."

I look at the observation windows. "Hey, you know, there are probably people in those rooms. Someone should free them. Not me, though. I'm all out of free today."

A few minutes later we reach the elevator. We fit in as many as we can. Damali is right next to me. She smells wonderful. I like this, the closeness. If only there weren't a dozen smelly men with us too. I don't like that closeness much, really. The smelly closeness.

We reach the top floor. I hear shouts and lots of running. One thing I don't hear, though, is gunfire. Not even the blast of a nano-pounder. The prince has lots of guards. Armed guards. Where are they?

The prisoners are spreading out in all directions. We take a left and move in the direction of the front doors. We pass lots of pretty things. Paintings and sculptures. Bright colors. We also meet some of the servants. They look worried. Frightened. Some of them are crying. Why is that? This is a free day. What could be wrong?

We reach the front entrance. There are black-suited guards here, but they appear to be as shocked and frightened as the servants inside. They aren't doing anything to restrain the flood of prisoners. There's a sampling of the prince's land vehicles parked here that the former prisoners are getting into. Some are already driving off.

I shake my head. Something is wrong. What is happening?

"I need to sit down," I say, then walk to the side, away from the flow. I find a spot at the end of one of the large entrance steps. I watch as the vehicles circle the drive, then follow the bridge over the moat.

Damali and the astronauts stay near me, watching.

"I expected more of a fight," TallSpot says. "Something."

"You need to go quickly," I say. "Before they wake up. Before the prince returns."

Damali looks at me angrily. "We can't leave you."

"You have to. My head makes me a slave. That can't be helped. Not without a surgeon." I feel pain as I say it. I want to stay with them. But I can't. I'm not a freehead. I'm not sure what I am now, but I'm not that. Nothing is free for me.

"It doesn't feel good," Handler says. "Leaving you."

"Perhaps he's right," BlueTrain says. "We are wanted men. We need to leave."

"I *am* right," I say. "Now go." I force a smile, looking at Damali. "If I need to find you, I can. I know things. Lots of things."

"No." She shakes her head. "Not like this."

"We are different," I say. "You and I. To answer your question, though. Yes, I could like you, I think. I could like you very much." I look at TallSpot. "Get out of here. What happens to me is meant to happen. A's will. I have seen a lot of bad. Bad I couldn't stop."

Another vehicle arrives at the front steps. A red and fancy one. It is already partially full of prisoners. BlueTrain runs up to the door and holds it open. "Come on, everyone."

TallSpot doesn't look convinced, but he's gripping his sister's elbow. Handler nods at me and grabs her other elbow. Grackle is in the vehicle already. Damali is tugging on them, shaking her head. There are tears in her eyes. They are climbing in now, though. That makes me happy.

TallSpot is the last one to enter. He pauses at the door, looks at me, glances inside again, then takes a few quick steps my direction.

"No," I say. "I *have* to stay."

He raises a hand and stoops next to me. "You mentioned other debuggers," he says. "They weren't on the station, but their implants were. Those of the DarkTrench designers."

"Implants? So they're dead then..." I shake my head. "No. Don't tell me."

"I have a theory," he says. "That there might be danger for all of you. That they're up to something. Trying to replace you somehow."

"TallSpot!" BlueTrain says.

"You have to go," I say.

TallSpot still looks unsettled, but I point at the vehicle. "I know enough. Thanks."

He nods, then runs to the door. A second later they drive away.

I think of the prince's version of Noah now. How the same thing is happening here. The unbelievers left behind.

Or are they? What do I believe in now? Not sure.

Peace. I want some peace.

I wait for a few minutes until their vehicle is over the moat and safely away. I stand and drift away from the crowd. Back toward the house. I could really use some sleep. Some good old chute sleep. There's only one of those here and I know just where to find it.

But Jahm is still in my room.

Well, rails. Now what?

I WANDER MY WAY to the arboretum again.

I get a little sad feeling when I pass the small pool where I first encountered Damali. There's a poolbot in the center of it, just spinning in a circle. It tells me one of its motivators is busted. It figures.

I find my favorite tree, climb to my branch, and straddle it. The seat feels warm to me, as if someone had just been sitting here. I doubt that's true. I know it is probably all in my mind. But I like to think that some of her warmth lingers here. Something lingers.

The tweaks are gone now. I'm not sure I'm all right. But I'm better. Plus, I don't feel like nobody now. For a few moments, I was somebody important. Irreplaceable.

I should take a look at those local bulletins. I should also probably fix that pool bot while I'm here too. Hard not to think about what TallSpot said, though. Danger? Debuggers replaced?

I get a FI message, marked urgent. From Bamboo of all people.

What could this be?

I accept the message and shut my eyes to focus. Bamboo is sitting in one of the debugger training rooms. He's dressed in a white jumpsuit. The lighting is dim. There are young debuggers behind him. All with shaved heads and dressed in blue. All with eyes closed. Concentrating.

"I need you to come in, ThreadBare," he says.

"Come in?"

"Yes, you will be reassigned."

"Reassigned?" Reassignments almost never happen. Especially

for the forgotten. It took a missile strike for my last one. Of course, I've exhibited some bad behavior lately. For that I was expecting something a little more severe than reassignment.

"Yes," he says. "Haven't you heard? Certainly you know."

"Know what?"

"The prince has been assassinated. Your master is dead."

But I saw him only three hours ago! "What?" I say. "Who would kill—?"

A voice echoes through my mind. Something a prisoner said: He thinks he's untouchable. But there are those who see. People who will kill him.

"They are blaming antitex for his death," Bamboo says, "but the investigation is ongoing. He had few friends."

I pause, filling with the enormity of Bamboo's words. The prince, dead? And antitex the killers? Maybe. Or maybe someone else. One of the many that he abused, cheated, or otherwise wronged. "Few friends" is an understatement. "But Submaster Jahm—"

Bamboo's eyes harden. "Is irrelevant now. I've sent a ground vehicle to take you to the nearest downrider pylon. From there you know what to do to reach me."

"The Imam...?"

Bamboo glances at the children behind him. "The royal house is in mourning," he says. "The prince's assets will be divided and reassigned. You were one of his assets."

I reposition myself on the branch. It still feels warm. "But where will I go?"

"First, you will report to me for analysis. Your ultimate destination is in the Imam's hands, of course, but until then I have countless chores for you to perform." He indicates the children. "I might even have you help with these lowlevels." He smiles toothlessly.

I feel better than I have all day. Like Noah after the storm passed. I bow my image's head. "I understand, teacher. Thank you."

He sniffs. "There's no need to thank me. This is as it is. A's will."

I nod again as the transmission ends. I give the tree branch a pat. Land vehicle to downer, downer to Bamboo. Then what?

I could go into the city again! Visit a clang and click like Zim-it's. Or Grims!

I straighten. Damali? Could I see her? I look out at the moat. Maybe.

Rails!

THERE ARE MORE ADVENTURES OUT THERE...

That's all of ThreadBare's story for now, but there are more fun books to read!

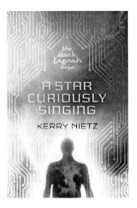

If you haven't read the previous trilogy written in the world of Dark-Trench, then there's no better time. The first book, *A Star Curiously Singing*, is free for a limited time.

You can find *A Star Curiously Singing* at www.nietz.com/ASCS.htm.

Or if you're interested in a non-fiction account of what a programmer's life is like, why not check out *FoxTales: Behind the Scenes at Fox Software*? I may not have had Sandfly's implant or his environment, but I understand the pressure of his job.

Grab *FoxTales* at www.nietz.com/FoxTales.htm to find out why!

Or for something really different, why not try the *Peril in Plain Space* series? The first book, *Amish Vampires in Space*, started as a joke, but ended up being a straight up science fiction story with a generous helping of Amish society and the taste of a creature feature.

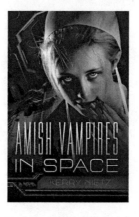

You can find *Amish Vampires in Space* at www.nietz.com/AViS.htm.

YOU CAN MAKE A DIFFERENCE!

Word-of-mouth marketing is the best kind. Not only does it ensure that good books get noticed, it also helps bring the right books to the people who will enjoy them most.

If this book met or exceeded your expectations in any way, please consider telling your friends and/or posting a short review.

Your help is greatly appreciated!

ABOUT THE AUTHOR

Kerry Nietz is a refugee of the software industry. He spent more than a decade of his life flipping bits, first as one of the principal developers of the database product FoxPro for the now mythical Fox Software, and then as one of Bill Gates's minions at Microsoft. He is a husband, a father, a technophile and a movie buff.

Kerry has one non-fiction book, a memoir entitled *FoxTales: Behind the Scenes at Fox Software*. *Amish Vampires in Space* is his fifth novel and is doubtless his most talked about. Following a close second is his cyberpunk tale, *A Star Curiously Singing*.

If you'd like to get an e-mail alert whenever Kerry has a new book out or has a special on one of his already-released books, sign up at nietz.com/EmailList.htm.

ABOUT FRAYED

This book began as flash fiction. What is that, you ask? Flash fiction is an extremely brief story, typically of a thousand words or less. It is written for those who like to read, who often don't have time to. The sort of story you could read in a single bathroom break. (Maybe it should be called flush fiction?)

Shortly after *Amish Vampires in Space* was released, the Editor-in-Chief of Splickety magazine, Ben Wolf, encouraged me to write a story for his speculative fiction magazine, Havok. He stipulated that the story had to be a thousand words or less.

The challenge intrigued me. I hadn't written a short story in quite a while, but I was a little stumped with how to start. A thousand words wasn't a lot of canvas to work with. It certainly didn't lend itself to another Amish story. Every time I go into that universe a ton of characters come out, bringing wagonloads of words with them. I can't go low tech and not use a lot of words. Strange, but true.

So where would my flash fiction story come from?

The only thing that felt right was to craft something in the world of my first novel—*A Star Curiously Singing* (ASCS). Written in first-person-present tense, and centering around a single character, those books tended to be smaller. Plus, since much of that trilogy was set in space, there was still a good deal of its future Earth left unexplored. There had to be a million short stories there.

I didn't want to use the characters from that series of books, though. The story of Sandfly, HardCandy and DarkTrench felt complete in my mind. Well enough, and best left alone.

So who should the story be about?

The debuggers of the DarkTrench Saga are, to me, the most interesting part. Techno-slaves fully connected to their information stream and to each other through an implant in their head. They're introspective, sarcastic, and able to fix nearly anything. Fantastic and fun.

I needed another debugger. Someone equally intriguing, and with an equally cool name.

I read through the first chapter of ASCS and discovered this young, troubled debugger named ThreadBare. Perfect! Then I got to thinking about what Thread did when he wasn't out in a storm with the rest of the debuggers. I saw this dim, smelly garage on the edge of a dusty battlefield. Then I realized Thread worked on battlefield equipment (heavies) and wished for a better life. I had the makings of a story. I started to write.

Twelve hundred words later I was done. I figured it was close enough to a thousand. Shouldn't matter in a magazine, right? They can squish it all in somehow. Use a smaller font.

Nope. The editor of Havok, Avily Jerome, told me the story had to be under a thousand words or they couldn't use it. Being the sensitive writer that I am, I threw my hands up in disgust, and went back to work on another Amish book. Who needs that sort of pressure! All my words are important!

Months went by.

Finally, I finished the second Amish story (*Amish Zombies from Space*...because, why not?) and had a chance to look at ThreadBare again. I started trimming—a couple descriptive words, a backstory sentence there—and slowly marched my way to 1012 words. And the story still made sense!

Wasn't quite short enough yet. Argh.

I went over it again and again. I'd already cut nearly two hundred words. Everything that remained seemed essential to the story. Then I found a sentence that referenced HardCandy and Sandfly. I liked that sentence because it showed that Thread wasn't alone. That there were other debuggers in his world with him. But for the purpose of the Havok story, it didn't add much. I selected it in my word processor to get a word count. It amounted to 14 words.

Cut!

I sent my flash-sized story off to Avily and it was published in Havok a few months later.

I couldn't leave ThreadBare like that, though. All alone on the edge of Delusion? I had to know what happened to him. What was his life really like? He started in a garage and went...where?

A few years back, I read a book entitled I was Saddam's Son. It is the memoire of Latif Yahia, an Iraqi soldier who became the body double for Saddam Hussain's son Uday. It gives a unique glimpse into that brutal and dictatorial regime. It is fascinating reading, but also unsettling—like the story of any tyrant. It stuck with me, and in many ways its portrayal of Uday inspired the prince in Thread's story. (Uday would eat Aadam for lunch, however.)

Frayed was also inspired by a fan question. A person once asked me if I ever intended to tell the story of the "remnant" that survived on Earth following ASCS. Many significant events had to happen, and while later books touched on some of those, there was still plenty of details to fill in.

This book is my attempt to start doing that. I hope you found it enjoyable.

CPSIA information can be obtained
at www.ICGtesting.com
Printed in the USA
LVOW07s1616120917
548429LV00001B/210/P